Fiona Kidman was born in 1940. She has worked as a librarian, creative writing teacher, radio producer and critic, but primarily as a writer. To date, she has published 19 other books, including novels, poetry, short story collections, non-fiction and a play. She has been the recipient of numerous awards and fellowships, and was created a Dame (DNZM) in 1998 in recognition of her contribution to literature.

A Needle in the Heart

FIONA KIDMAN

VINTAGE

National Library of New Zealand Cataloguing-in-Publication Data

Kidman, Fiona, 1940-

A needle in the heart / Fiona Kidman.

ISBN 1-86941-523-X

1. Rural women—Fiction. I. Title.

NZ823.2—dc 21

A VINTAGE BOOK
published by
Random House New Zealand
18 Poland Road, Glenfield, Auckland, New Zealand
www.randomhouse.co.nz

First published 2002

© 2002 Fiona Kidman

The moral rights of the author have been asserted

ISBN 1 86941 523 X

Design: Elin Termannsen
Cover design: Sophie Klerk
Author photograph: Robert Cross
Printed by Griffin Press Ltd, Australia

CONTENTS

A Needle in the Heart 9

Silver-Tongued 69

Families Like Ours 96

Mister Blue Satin 141

All the Way to Summer 161

Soup 188

ACKNOWLEDGEMENTS

I wish to thank Ian Kidman for the many stories he's shared with me; Dr Rob McIlroy for advice on the possible trajectory of a needle through the human body; James Young of Gillespie Young Watson for legal advice for the story 'Families Like Ours'; Jennifer Shennan for her irrepressible insights and knowledge of the world; Alwin Verbeek for his research and Alison Morgan for her constant practical support. As ever, I thank Harriet Allan and Anna Rogers for their patient and skilful editing.

A writing grant from Creative New Zealand is gratefully acknowledged.

The author acknowledges permission from the copyright holder J.C. Baxter to quote from 'The Glass Lamp' by James K. Baxter.

Also grateful acknowledgement is made for the following song extracts:
'Don't Hang Up' — Kevin Godley/Lol Creme © St Annes Music Limited. Used by permission of EMI Music Publishing Australia Pty Limited. All rights reserved.
'Smoke Gets In Your Eyes' (Harbach/Kern) © Universal Music Publishing. Reproduced by kind permission of Universal Music Publishing.
'Look For The Silver Lining' (Kern/De Sylva) © Universal Music Publishing. Reproduced by kind permission of Universal Music Publishing.

*For Witi, with love,
a constant friend in a writing life*

A NEEDLE IN THE HEART

The weather was overcast the day Queenie McDavitt took off her bodice at the races. Queenie's real name was Awhina but her husband had long before renamed her so that people, white people that is, would remember her name more easily. Her husband was known as Stick, because he was a tall beanpole of a man, but it was also an alias for his given name, Robert. He had gone off to place a bet on Sparkling Heels for the next race. There was a queue and, because the day was heavy and languid, the punters idled around, catching up on news from down the line. Stick wasn't concerned about his wife being on her own at the races, she was a woman who could look after herself. Besides, she had half a dozen of their children and grandchildren in tow. She wouldn't be going far.

This was 1925. Times were hard but things could only get better, people said. Of course, what they didn't imagine was that things would only get worse and worse.

'I reckon if we got a lucky break and paid the bills, we'd get ahead a bit,' Stick said.

'Perhaps if we just went without for a bit, and saved a some money,' Queenie said, 'well maybe we wouldn't be so darn hard up.'

'So what have we got to save anyway?' Stick demanded. They never had anything over, and besides there had been an unexpected doctor's bill this year. The couple lived with several of their children in a steep-roofed three-roomed cottage with a number of flat lean-tos added at the back, not far from the Main Trunk Line that ran through Taumarunui. Stick got work on the maintenance gangs now and then, when his back wasn't playing up.

They ended up going to the races anyway, which Queenie knew they would from the moment he first suggested it. She dressed herself in her best dark skirt and a white blouse with a ruffle running lengthwise from the collar to the waist, and over that a maroon coat, a trifle tight under the arms, but the only one that came near fitting her when the Salvation Army came round with their bin. She tied a green and black plaid shawl round her shoulders, pinning it with the special brooch that had been handed on to her by her father after her mother died. Her father was a white man from pioneering stock. When he gave her the brooch, he told her, with a good many tears, that it should be hers, even though he and her mother had never found a preacher that would marry them (he said this with perplexity, so that Queenie always believed that he must have tried and been hard done by that he was refused).

Then he vanished. She heard he had gone to a sheep station down south. The brooch was oval in shape, made of fine filigree gold with an amethyst set in the centre. The back opened up to reveal a tiny shadowy picture of her mother, a woman with long lustrous hair and strong bright eyes that burned through the faded image. To finish her outfit Queenie added a wide-brimmed hat trimmed with green cabbage roses.

'You'll be too hot,' Stick said.

'You want me to come or not?'

There was no question about that. She'd been up making bacon and egg pies and sandwiches half the night before.

She watched Stick pushing his way through the crowds and sighed. He had a pound burning a hole in his pocket.

'Give us a quid, old girl,' he'd said.

'I've run out,' she said, although she had one left which she'd hidden in her shoe. Her son Joe tickled her ankle. I know what's making you hobble, Ma. The devil, that boy, although she supposed he wasn't a boy any more. He was her oldest, a married man with children. Hard to believe that it was thirty years since she'd started on babies. Other of her children were more sober, more industrious than Joe; perhaps she'd spoiled him. He'd been a handsome child, though given to sulking. He followed his father to place the bet. She wouldn't have bet on Sparkling Heels herself. She'd have gone for Fox Fire, but then who listened to her when it came to horses.

On the blanket beside her, Pearl began to cry. Queenie glanced round, looking for Esme, who was supposed to be in charge of the baby. Her daughter was nowhere to be seen. Queenie pulled a face — she couldn't trust Esme not to wander off for five minutes. She took in the scene as far as she could. The girl could be anywhere among the crowd, although the race track, if that was what you could call it, wasn't very big. The ground had been flattened out of a moonscape of felled trees after the railway went through. Bits of rope and chain divided the track off from the crowd, and tents had been put up for the refreshment counters.

Queenie's eyes finally rested on Esme, sitting in the shade of one of the tents making a daisy chain. Like a little kid.

'You tell that Esme to get over here real quick,' she told Lucy, who was ten and one of Mary's children. Mary was second in the family after Joe. 'Tell her I'll give her a clip if she doesn't hurry up.'

'You're supposed to be looking after Pearl,' Queenie said, when Esme came dawdling over. By now she was holding the baby over her shoulder, the practised palm of her hand gently rubbing the baby's back to bring up her wind, but Pearl kept on crying.

'Oh, give her here to me,' Esme, said. She took the baby and held her chest against hers. Pearl stopped crying almost straight away, and Queenie thought, it's not wind, it's the way some babies need to be held against a beating heart, any old heart will do, so long as the rhythm is there. They get so lost and lonely out in the world, after they've spent so long inside, listening to that steady calming sound, like rain on an iron roof at night.

'I'll take her now,' Queenie said. 'Just don't go running off and leaving her.'

'You were there,' Esme said. She had rippling wavy hair that reminded Queenie of her mother's and her eyes were black like hers. Freckles dusted her nose. Esme and Joe, the best looking of the bunch.

'I don't want you hanging around where there's fellas,' said Queenie. 'You keep yourself to yourself. Anyway, I told you to look after Pearl, and that's your job for the day. D'you know anything can happen to a baby when its lying on the ground? I know a baby having a bit of a kick on the grass, and next thing his mother hears him yelling. Well, this kid yells and yells until he's dead, and after he's died a big centipede comes walking out of his ear. You just don't know how quick one of those centipedes can go walking up inside a baby's ear and chew its brains all out.'

'That's horrible,' Esme said. Her eyes filled with quick tears.

Over at the track, the punters were shouting themselves hoarse and the beating of hooves was shaking the ground where they sat. 'Oh my God,' said a man's voice, 'there's Fox Fire — she's down,' and then the cry went up that Sparkling Heels was out by a nose, and, would you believe it, that pony had won.

'That'll be the last we see of your father,' Queenie said gloomily, 'now he's got money in his pocket.' Already she could see his cloth cap in the queue of felt-brimmed hats, getting ready for the next race. Esme had put the baby down in her lap where she lay grizzling, wanting more attention. Queenie took her back. 'I don't know what's the matter with you,' she said. 'You don't seem able to do the simplest thing.'

It made Queenie unhappy, the way Esme was. She was such a beautiful girl but you couldn't say anything without her taking offence. Esme stretched out, face down on the ground beside her mother and Pearl, so that her breasts were squashed beneath her. She put her hands over her head as if to ward off the sun. Joe came back and said he'd lost ten bob on Fox Fire but the old man had made five pounds. He'd heard some man had lost a tenner each way on the fallen horse.

'Did your father send back the quid I gave him?'

'He reckons he can turn it into twenty-five.'

'Spare me the trouble. You go and tell him I want two pounds back at very least, right now, before he gets to that counter. Go on, do as you're told.'

Joe hesitated, but seeing the look in his mother's eyes, decided to pursue his father. A shot rang out as Fox Fire was put down and when that excitement was over a huddle of people began drifting their way, men who were skint like Joe.

'You get some food into you,' Queenie said to Esme, holding out a tomato sandwich with her free hand. 'Come on, you got to eat something.' Esme pulled her hair right down round the sides of her face so that it spread in one dark pool on the blanket. Queenie sighed and touched the living silk of it. The sun was beginning to emerge; soon they would have to shift. Earlier, Queenie had taken off her shawl, carefully pocketing her brooch, and now she wriggled out of her coat. Lucy held Pearl while she took it off.

A man called Dave Murphy stopped beside the family's picnic, a big man with his stomach tumbling over his belt and a large moustache. He wore a yellow checked suit and his shoes glittered in the dull sun struggling from behind the clouds. He owned one of the new timber mills in the district. From the mean look on his face and the amount of money he usually jingled in his pockets, Queenie guessed he might be the man who'd lost a tenner either way.

'You're a bit old for that sort of caper,' he said.

When Queenie didn't answer, he said, 'I'd have thought you were a bit old for babies. Old Stick still sticking it to you, eh? Still making babies in an old lady?' He laughed loudly at his own wit, at the same time nudging Esme on the ground with his foot.

Queenie said, 'That's enough. This little Pearl is my miracle baby.' The baby had gone to sleep in her arms, and she touched her pale cheek with the back of her finger. They could have as easily called her Lily, but Pearl was what they chose, because her paleness and her prettiness had a sheen that made her glow. She'd never held a baby this fair in her arms before. Pearl's eyebrows were like silvery smudges, her eyes milky blue, the fine down round her fontanelle white like kitten's fur.

Esme sat up when she felt herself poked in the ribs. She sat staring down between her knees while Dave Murphy looked them all over. Queenie guessed he knew Stick had made a few quid. Dave smelled like he'd had a few whiskies. He had a way of getting round the liquor ban that was in force in the King Country in those days. Some said he had his own whisky still out in the hills; others said it was amazing what fell off the back of a goods train wagon, if you struck the right moment at the railway station. Queenie made her voice slow and reasonable, not wanting to aggravate him.

'This little girl is an old woman's magic baby,' she said. 'You remember Magic Man came to town, the one who came here about a year back and set up in the hall and did his tricks?'

'I heard about him, can't say I saw him.'

'Yes you did. I saw you there, Mister Dave Murphy.'

'Oh, maybe. A busy man like me can't remember everything. Now you mention it, I went down there to get one of my men who hadn't turned up to work. We had to get some timber wagons ready for the night train. Maybe I was there a half hour.'

'And more. Remember, he did all those handkerchief tricks? Made the handkerchief stretch, and tied it up in knots without letting go of the ends. That was pretty clever. And he cut the lady in half. You saw that, didn't you?'

'They do all that stuff with mirrors.'

'There weren't any mirrors there, I walked up and had a look myself. There were no mirrors.'

'Mum, stop it,' said Esme.

'Then, remember, at the end Magic Man puts the curtain down, and you think the show's all over. Then it comes up again and he's standing there without a head. His head is sitting on the table beside him. That was a miracle.'

'Hmm. Yes, remarkable. Now that you mention it.'

'I tell you, it was a miracle. So at the end, I went up to him and said, 'Mister Magic Man, I want a new baby, because all my babies are pretty well grown up now.'

'Oh, so it was Magic Man who put it there?'

'Now, I think you better talk to Stick about that. Nobody puts anything near me except Stick, I tell you. No, I just said to Magic Man, put a spell over me so I can have another baby, and that's what he did. I got what I asked for, my own little jewel.'

'I don't believe a word of it.' Dave stared around angrily, not liking to be taken for a fool. 'What do you make of it, young lady?' he said to Esme.

'I don't know anything about it,' she muttered, the flood of her hair washing over her face.

'Your mother here's a dried up old lady, wouldn't you say?'

'Nothing dried up about me,' Queenie said.

'Let me see your titties then.'

'You want to see my titties now?' Queenie gave Pearl back over to Esme to hold, even though she tried not to take her. Esme held her as if she was a ticking bomb. 'Don't, Mum,' she pleaded. Her mother's hands were at the throat of her blouse. She freed one button after another until they were all undone. Dave Murphy stared at the mountain of brown flesh being revealed, his mouth open. The tops of her breasts rippled above the corset that held them in place, hummocks of round honey-gold flesh. Later, when Esme was herself growing old, she would think how amazing it was that a woman's face grew lined and seamed so much earlier than the body itself, which stayed not much different from when it was a girl's for years and years (and then the sudden devastating collapse of everything).

A group of men was collecting round Dave Murphy. They nudged each other, with sharply in drawn breaths. You could tell they were astonished at their own nerve, standing here and watching, and already wondering what the consequences might be. But it was like a spell was cast over them, their eyes riveted on Queenie's cleavage. She slid the blouse off her shoulders and her hands moved to the hooks holding the corset in place.

'No,' shrieked Esme. 'No, no, no.' Mary's girl had gone to fetch Stick and Joe but Esme was mesmerised and screaming, unable to do anything except sit there with Pearl.

The first hook popped undone, the second one.

'Magic,' said Queenie. 'That's what it was.'

Then Joe leapt through a gap between the men, scattering them in all directions, his arms flailing, and Stick, following behind, threw his coat over Queenie just as her sleek breasts tumbled free, covering her long purple nipples an instant before they were seen by the men.

Joe smacked Esme on the side of her face with his open hand. 'You never oughter have let her do that,' he said.

'It wasn't her fault,' said Queenie. 'Here, get up.' She tried to yank her daughter to her feet, seeing the blue bruise already forming on her face.

Stick was more interested in getting Queenie out of it. Making sure his coat was well wrapped around her, he began pulling her towards one of the tents to get dressed.

'What about that quid I lent you?' Queenie said, making out she didn't care about all the agitation.

'Forget it,' Stick said. 'Just forget it.'

Joe went to get the horses hitched up to their wagon. 'You get that baby out of here,' he said to Esme.

When Esme McDavitt grew up, nobody asked her to marry them for a long time. She was made various offers of one kind or another but she knew none of them would do her any good. Some nights, under the tin roof of the cottage, she ached, wanting things she couldn't have.

Her father and brothers thought she should go up north, try Auckland, and see if there was anyone on offer up there. This was a time when marriage had fallen off. A lot of couples couldn't afford to set up house together. Men were afraid they would make their wives pregnant straight away and it wasn't worth the risk of more mouths to feed. Queenie said not to worry about it, a girl's place was at home. She set her to some tasks that would occupy her time, skills of her own that she had learnt in the native school when she was a child. Esme surprised her. She sewed the straightest seam you ever saw. She could run up a dress in a day and a half, complete with cloth buttons and cuffs.

'People would pay good money for that,' Queenie told Stick.

'Well, get them paying,' he said. This was what Esme did. She charged modest prices because that was all women could pay, those who could afford anything at all. A dress cost four shillings, two shillings and sixpence for straight skirts, three shillings for blouses. Sometimes, people put it across her, but only once. She found she liked the business side of things and learned how to say no to people who underpaid her. There was the school-teacher's wife, for instance, who thanked Esme for the dress she had made, and given her a tin of shortcake to take home.

Esme got on her bicycle without a word, and rode towards home, the wind whipping her hair which she still wore long and untamed. When she reached the railway line, she was still rehearsing in her head what she would say to the school-teacher's wife the next time she came looking for a bargain. She got off the bike to wheel it over the tracks. Some girls were giggling wildly on the platform. A group of gangers were sitting smoking on an idling railway jigger pulled in on a loop. The girls called out, shouting their names after them. Esme pretended not to see any of this carry on, flicking her hair back from her face, her foot poised on a pedal, while a train from the south thundered through.

Jim Moffit was riding in the guard van that day, on his way to a job.

Esme never forgot the thrill of it, being singled out by Jim. Perhaps that's what it was, the excitement of being chosen, when so often she had been passed over. He'd seen her standing there on the railway station at Taumarunui among the group of girls. Like them, but different. She didn't know he'd seen her and wanted her for himself. 'Who's that girl?' he asked the men in the van. He told her this later on.

'And what did they say?'

'Just your name. That's Esme McDavitt, that's what they said.'

'Was that all?'

'Well, it was enough, wasn't it?'

'Nothing else?'

'Not that I can think of. I said, "Does she live there? Will a letter find her?"'

Jim Moffit wrote:

Dear Mr McDavitt

You do not know me although I have met some of your sons in the course of my work on the railways. I have something to ask you, but first I should tell you one or two things about myself. I am an Englishman who has been in this fair country of yours for some three years now. Times are very hard back home, in Birmingham, even worse than they are here. My mother, God rest her soul, was very keen for me to come to New Zealand to see whether I could make a better life for myself. I have been fortunate in finding work. I have a responsible job, I think because I was considered to have a quick brain as a child and got a reasonable education. I am one of the signallers who operate the train tablets. So my job is steady, more than most can say, even in these troubled times. I have an offer of a railway house if I should marry.

Which brings me to the point of this letter. I am very desirous of making a closer acquaintance with your daughter Esme, with a view to marriage. I do promise you, sir, that my intentions towards her are entirely honourable.

I am thirty-four years old but I do not see a dozen years making a great deal of difference as I am very healthy of body and mind. It's a lonely life for a chap out here, despite the advantages, and I promise I would make her an excellent husband.

Yours very truly
James Moffit

His wild girl, snatched up from the side of the railway, his clever English head turned in an instant. A bachelor, reformed into a husband, all, it seemed, in the twinkling of a flashing eye.

Esme made herself a dusky pink wool dress for her wedding. It had a collar, and long sleeves, puffed at the top, and a bodice that was pointed at the waist. Before they walked over to the church, her mother pinned her gold filigree brooch on her shoulder. 'Just for today,' she said. 'One day I'll give it to Pearl.'

'I thought you might give it to Mary,' Esme said, surprised that her mother would overlook her oldest daughter.

'Well, you know how it is,' her mother said. 'You know Pearl's my special baby.'

At the last moment, Esme didn't want to go with Jim after all. She hung on to Pearl, and cried, trying not to let Jim see her tears. 'You be a good girl for your Ma,' she said, and climbed on to the train.

Jim took her to a hotel in Auckland for her honeymoon. None of her family had ever had real honeymoons, and none of them had stayed in a hotel. Already, married life was conferring an unexpected grandness.

'Make the most of it,' Jim had said, laughing at her wonder. 'It'll be down to real life once we get home.' Home would be at Ohakune Junction, down south of Taumarunui beneath the volcanic mountain. In a way she would have liked to go straight there to see the house they had been allocated in Railway Row, the street by the line, but Jim said plenty of time for that.

They travelled on the night train. It was running late, so they had to sit on the platform in the cool darkness for a long time, waiting for it to come. The waiting room had closed. Esme had told the family to go to bed: there was no point in everyone being worn out. There didn't seem a lot for her and Jim to say, as they huddled there in their coats. She realised how little she knew him.

On the way north, he opened up, talking about his job, and describing the train tablet system. He worked out of a hut, one of a series along the Main Trunk railway line. He travelled there on goods trains, and at the end of his shift he got picked up and taken home. The tablets were part of the spacing system that set the course of the trains and ensured that there were never two on the same stretch of line at once. The numbered tablets were picked up and carried from one section of the line to the other, and only when the tablet, or the 'biscuit' as the men called it, was safely under lock and key at the other end of the section was it safe for the train to proceed. That was when the green light beamed its semaphore message down the line, giving the all clear. With express trains and timber trains and other goods trains rattling backwards and forwards there was no time for a lapse in attention, no failure of detail that could be admitted.

'I see it's a very important job,' Esme said soberly. They were rushing through another small town. Dawn light was breaking. A deep wide river flowed past them on their left. Stained and grimy miners were gathered near a station, as if their day was ending as others began. Esme felt like them.

'I hold life in these hands,' Jim said, holding out his splayed palms for her to look at. She shivered, wondering if she was up to the task of supporting Jim in his work. He seemed to read the way she felt. 'Don't worry, we'll be a team. It's going to make a big difference to me, having a wife and comfortable home to come back to at the end of my shift.'

'I'll do my best, Jim.'

'Think of it like a performance. Like Shakespeare,' he said. 'Pretend I'm a great actor who needs someone to change his cloak for him between scenes.' He said this with a bit of a laugh, as if it was something he didn't quite expect her to understand. There were a lot of things about his life that she wouldn't know about. When she sat quite motionless, in the seat opposite from him, he said, 'I can teach you things.'

'What sort of things?' she asked faintly. The train wheels beneath her said click *click tschick click click tschik.*

'Wait and see.'

'I left school when I was thirteen. Didn't my father tell you that?'

'It's got nothing to do with how clever you are.'

'I wasn't very clever,' she said, not looking at him.

'Don't worry about all of that right now,' he said. 'It's just you I want.' They still had to get to Auckland, to make love for the first time, to discover who each other really was. She thought that they were both talking a great lot of nonsense, or he was anyway, and she was becoming frightened of him. Then she thought it was just because they were both exhausted and it was taking each of them in funny ways. She wondered if they would go straight to bed when they got to the hotel.

But that wasn't the plan. After they checked their bags into the hotel, and collected the key to their room, Jim had organised a day of sight-seeing for her. She remembered walking round looking at lions and polar bears and monkeys, and then, later, in a daze, admiring the talking parrot in Farmers' tearooms.

When she sat at breakfast the next morning, she felt strangely untouched, recalling more of the clean white cotton sheets that had covered her than his body. She had turned to him first thing when she woke. Some mornings at home, Pearl climbed into bed beside her. They would go back to sleep; in cold weather Pearl warmed her feet on the backs of Esme's legs. So it was Pearl she looked for, when she felt someone in the bed with her, but it was Jim. He looked as if hadn't slept well, but he leaned over and kissed her forehead. 'Good morning, Mrs McDavitt,' he said. She thought then that this was what her whole life would be, and she had felt a weightless sensation, as if she was not really there. Soon after, the housemaid had knocked on their door and delivered cups of tea.

'Milk and sugar everyone?' she'd called.

'Jim, do you take sugar?' Esme said.

'Hush,' he said, when they were on their own again. 'She'll know we're just married.'

While they were waiting for their breakfast to be served, he pointed out the cutlery on the table. 'Do you see how they set the knives and forks out?' he said. This was how he liked things, everything exactly in place, the knife and fork straight beside the table mats and the bread and butter plates square on the right-hand side of the knife with the small knife pointed straight ahead. A quick learner like her would have no trouble at all.

2

In the morning, after Jim had gone, Esme walked to the window and looked at the mountain, or the place where the mountain should be if the rain was not falling so heavily and turning to sleet. Behind her a thin fire spluttered, spitting sap from wet bark, emitting a smell like incense. It reminded her of the magician she had met up Taumarunui way when she was still a girl, of the strange soft scent in the air that somehow proclaimed that nothing is real, nothing you ever knew exists. There is only illusion. The whistle of a train sounded through the mist, a long exhalation, a breath, another one. There he goes, she thought, there goes Jim, up the line, the fate of travellers in his hands.

The house in Railway Row was one of twenty-four, twelve on either side of the straight street that ran exactly parallel to the railway lines, just a few feet away. The houses stood face to face, one row with its back to the mountain, one looking towards the railway lines and the station itself, glimmering still with dim lights. Esme and Jim's house was one of these. Although there were one or two larger ones, most of the houses were exactly the same: a porch, a kitchen, a square front room, a passage, two bedrooms and a bathroom you could just turn around in. Rough bush covered the slope above, while flax and toetoe bushes like soft calico flags shivered in the wind alongside the tracks.

Esme gathered up dishes from the table with a snap and a rattle. His irritation with her had started before breakfast. She had got it all wrong and she knew she wasn't functioning properly. Her limbs wouldn't work. Everything about her felt heavy and tired. It wasn't as if she hadn't slept; in fact, she'd slept so deeply that when the alarm clock went off she hadn't known where she was.

'Hurry up, will you,' he'd said, razor in his hand as he came into the bedroom bare-chested, with his braces hanging in loops over his thighs. He still had soap on his face. He hadn't parted and oiled his hair yet, so that it stuck up in spiky bristles. 'Can't you see I'll have to go without my breakfast if you don't get moving.'

She wanted to say to him, how about you get your own breakfast for once, but she knew that wouldn't do. It wasn't as if she didn't work too. On a good week she could earn almost as much as Jim, not that she mentioned this because it made him angry in a way she couldn't understand. Her dressmaking skills had followed her to Ohakune Junction.

When he did sit down to eat, breakfast didn't please him. He liked his eggs on the right side of the plate, bacon to the left, and it just looked like a mess, something that had been thrown at him, and the bacon was only half cooked. He looked as if he was going to cry.

'I'm sorry,' she said, pleating the edges of the tablecloth between her finger and thumb. 'I don't know what's come over me.'

'Perhaps you're doing too much,' he said.

'I need something to fill the days,' she said, surprised to hear herself answering back.

'Yes, I suppose you do.' He sighed and folded his napkin, leaving half his food on the plate. 'You should get Pearl to help you more.'

'Pearl? She's only a little kid.' Pearl was asleep in the spare room that was hers when she came for the holidays. It was the room put aside for babies.

'She's ten. Lots of girls her age have to do a bit around the house. Her mother spoils that girl and you're just as bad.'

'She's going back in a couple of days.'

'Oh well. I suppose we can manage for that long.'

She smiled at him, then, put her face up for him to kiss and he seemed restored to good humour, pinching her cheek and looking down fondly at her for a moment, before picking up his coat. He glanced out the window at the ugly weather.

'The truth is I could do with a day in bed myself.'

'That it'd be a good 'un. What would your boss have to say about that?'

'He'd probably say what a lucky devil I was, spending the day under the blankets with a fine looking woman like you.'

'Jim. He wouldn't.' She felt herself reddening.

'You're the most beautiful girl in the world,' he said.

Now that he was out of it, she considered cutting a pattern right away instead of washing the dishes. Routine, Jim said, and she could feel him looking over her shoulder. It put her back in a bad mood, so that she clattered around the kitchen, banging dishes about. You couldn't tell how things were going to turn out. She liked this house. In the front room there were crocheted lace curtains that had taken her months to make. Her mother had taught her how to crochet. The curtains were difficult, getting the tension right for such a big piece of work, so that they fell the right way. The room was furnished with three wooden-framed armchairs, with red slip covers on the cushions, and a stand-up gramophone. All the floors were covered in green linoleum with a mottled yellow and brown pattern, that Jim had let Esme choose for herself. But now, just when everything was finished, Jim was talking about going for promotion, trying to get a job closer to a city. She didn't know how she would fit into a big place.

'What's the matter?' Pearl stood in the doorway in her nightgown.

'Oh, it's you. Go and tell your mother she wants you.' She was surprised at the sharpness of her voice.

'Is it breakfast time? Have I missed?'

'I've kept you some.'

'I thought you were mad, all the noise you were making.'

'I'm tired,' Esme heard herself say. 'I wouldn't mind if you got dressed and washed the dishes for once.'

'It's just like home,' Pearl muttered.

'Well, you'd better get used to it. The holidays are nearly over.'

'I could go to school here.'

'No, you can't.'

A Needle in the Heart

'You are mad, aren't you?'

Suddenly Esme wanted to cry. She hated Pearl going back to Queenie. She told herself that it was just that she liked having a kid around the place, one of the family. There were times when she missed everyone back at home, in spite of the nice life she had here, and the little business. But this morning she wanted to cut out her pattern by herself, in peace, with just the sound of the rain coming down.

No, she didn't even want that. What she wanted was to sit and work out what was happening. There was something going on that she couldn't figure out.

Pearl picked up a dishcloth and swiped it backwards and forwards as if she didn't know what to do with it. Esme bit back a rebuke. Pearl was a sweet kid. My little sister, she said proudly, when she introduced her to folk at the Junction. She still had creamy skin and fair hair. Her teeth were prominent with one tooth much whiter than the others, giving her the appearance of a slightly lopsided rabbit when she smiled. Her talent was singing. She knew all the hymns and at Christmas she sang a verse of 'Silent Night' on her own at the church:

Round yon Virgin, Mother and Child,
Holy infant so tender and mild . . .

You could hear a ripple round the congregation: her high notes would make crystal shiver. Her singing was the one thing about Pearl that pleased Jim. He'd been brought up in the Church of England.

When everything was finally cleared away, and the tablecloth folded, Esme laid out the material for the dress she was about to begin, pink linen for the postmistress's wife. Esme would have liked to tell Norma that the colour wouldn't go with her red hair, but Norma was a woman who fancied her own taste. All the same, they got on well enough. Norma paid her promptly and liked a chat. Esme put the pattern on the oilskin cloth that permanently covered the table and considered it. She could see the sleeves were going to be troublesome; she might have to improvise a bit.

Her sewing machine was a treadle, which meant she could keep both hands free to guide the material, while her feet pumped backwards and forwards down below, going really fast.

'Look,' said Pearl, 'there's a whole lot of men running down to the station.'

'For goodness sake,' said Esme, and it was at that minute, when emergency sirens were beginning to wail all over the town, that she ran her hand under the speeding needle; it snapped in two, the top shaft entering her thumb as it jerked free of the spindle that held it.

'Oh,' cried Esme, 'oh, oh.' Her hand was covered in a froth of bright blood.

Pearl was at the window, peering out. 'There's been an accident.'

'Well, there's nothing we can do about it.' All the same, she went to the door and opened it, with dread in the pit of her stomach. Men in heavy coats were dashing towards a jigger. 'What is it?' she called, but nobody heard her, and in a minute they had disappeared down the line.

'Shut the door and come inside,' she said at last. Her hand still ached where it had been struck by the needle. She was sure it had gone in, but as there was no sign of it she began to think she'd imagined it. The sharp end of the needle was lying on the floor where it had landed. Perhaps the other half had flown across the room, and landed in the wood box.

She set to work installing and threading a new needle. The pain in her hand persisted but when she pressed her thumb, and then her whole hand, she couldn't locate the source of the pain. It occurred to her that the needle might have floated away in her veins.

'Perhaps I should see the doctor,' she said to Pearl.

'Does it hurt?'

'It's better now.' Funny, but as soon as she thought about going to the doctor it stopped. She and Jim kept a guinea in a jar on the top shelf in the kitchen in case they needed the doctor, because that was what it cost, money up front, and you didn't want to get caught short for emergencies. There might be other needs, more urgent than a stray sewing machine needle that she couldn't see or find.

And now, some new knowledge entered her, a mysterious unravelling of something so obvious, so already known that she didn't see how she hadn't worked it out already.

'How would you like to be an auntie?' she said to Pearl.

Pearl screwed up her pale short little nose. 'I am an auntie. I'm a great-auntie.' Which was true. The children from both Joe's and Mary's families had already started on children of their own.

'Well, you're going to be one again.'

'Are you and Jim having a baby?'

'Yes, that's right, we are too.'

'I thought you couldn't have babies.'

'Who said that?'

'My Mum told her friend. She said maybe Esme and Jim won't have any kids.'

'Well, you can tell her she's doesn't know much.'

'Is Jim pleased?'

'He doesn't know yet.'

'You mean you've told me first?'

'Yes, it looks like it. Don't tell him I told you.'

Pearl seemed more pleased about being an aunt then. She said she'd come down in the holidays and help Esme bath the baby and change its clothes.

'I reckon you'll be good at that,' Esme said. 'I'd like it if you did that.'

When they had had lunch, or rather Pearl had some sardines on toast, because Esme suddenly found she couldn't eat a thing, they thought they would go over to the station and see if they could get some news of what was happening along the line. It would be just the worst thing if Jim had had an accident, the very day she'd found out about the baby, but she didn't think this was a serious possibility. A tablet controller's job was safe compared with most. Besides, someone would surely have come by now and told her if anything had happened to Jim.

The rain was clearing and the hooded mountain began to reveal itself, pointing its ice fingers through the clouds. Just looking at its snow-clad slopes made her shiver. A big knot of people was gathered on the platform, the women emptied out of the houses, waiting. Esme felt guilty that she hadn't come over sooner.

The stationmaster, Alec Grimes, said yes, there'd been a collision on the line, a couple of goods trains. A man had been killed. The Daylight Limited pulled in and wasn't allowed to go any further north, so that now passengers joined with locals, looking helpless and shaken, while the steam engines panted and hissed on the track.

That evening, very late, Jim came in, white round the mouth. There was a new man in the control hut, a man who was supposed to have finished his training. He hadn't read the tablet right, taken out the wrong one. He was a Maori chap. Probably couldn't read, if you wanted to get to the truth of it. 'It wasn't my fault,' Jim said, 'even if I was in charge. You can't have eyes in the back of your head. They shouldn't have let that Maori loose. He should never have been allowed the key to the tablets.'

Afterwards, he said he shouldn't have said that.

She could see how he might have said it and not meant it. Or how he could have meant it and wished that he didn't.

Jim didn't lose his job, although the managers said it was touch and go. He was known as a good worker; perhaps the whole mistake couldn't be laid at his feet. But his chances of promotion had gone for the time being. What irked him most was that the other man didn't lose his job either.

When Esme and Jim's son Neil was two years old, she saw Conrad Larsen and fell in love, for the first and only time in her life. All the rest were things, things that just happened, accommodations good and bad, but not love. He was leaning out of a locomotive window as it came into the station, his red cheeks alight from the glow of the firebox he'd been stoking, his navy blue cap pushed back on his head. Later she discovered the bald dome beneath the cap, saw the way his head shone in sunlight. His big gleaming teeth sparkled against the soot where he'd wiped his hand across his mouth.

It happened on a day when she'd had what amounted to a quarrel with her friend Norma. Since Neil was born, she and Norma had gone past a business relationship and visited each other in their homes, although mostly Esme visited Norma, in her big house with

A Needle in the Heart

its verandah and trim, on the other side of the railway tracks. Neil was just at that stage when he was into things and opening cupboards. She had to watch out for him, because Norma had cream and green Irish Belleek china that you could almost see through, and fancy figurines in her cabinet. Norma had blue eyes and reddish hair that she wore in tight curls, and a way of flicking her head back over her shoulder when she spoke, as if there was somebody behind her. At first Esme thought that Norma was afraid someone was following her but then she decided that it was a nervous tic, something she couldn't help. Norma seemed like a lonely woman. Her daughters had already left home. She liked looking after Neil, and it suited Esme. Jim wasn't sure she should leave him with someone else, even for a little while, but what harm could it do, while she walked down to the shops for their meat and a few groceries. She didn't tell him about the times when she just went for walks along the paths that led towards the mountain or along the banks of the stream that led to the waterfall. Some days she wondered whether she was cut out for motherhood.

It was high summer and the mountain was stripped of all but its crown of snow and surrounded by a blue haze, the day Esme fell out with Norma. The heat inside the houses had been building since the sun came up.

When they'd had a cup of tea, Norma said not to go, that she felt like company. She stood at her bench mincing leftovers from the night before's roast to make into rissoles. Her eyes were on Neil, seated at the table eating a biscuit. He was a quiet child with a narrow face and slender curved eyebrows. 'If you like, you could go down and see your mother for the day. Take the morning train down and back on the night train. We'd like that, wouldn't we, little man?'

'I couldn't do that, he'd miss his feed.'

Norma stopped what she was doing. 'You haven't still got that kid on the tit, have you?'

'Just a couple of times a day.'

'That's disgusting,' Norma said, dusting flour off her hands. 'A big boy like that. What does your husband think of that?'

'We'll go and meet your dad,' Esme said, lifting Neil down from the chair, not looking at Norma. 'It'll do us both good, a breath of fresh air.'

'Not that it's any of my business.'

'No,' said Esme, 'not really.' She fled from the house, gathering up Neil and his toys, as if she had been caught out. Her breasts felt heavy and ripe and shameful. The image of her mother's exposed flesh flashed before her.

'You'll be back,' Norma said, as she paused to open the door. Esme knew, then, that Norma saw into her, understood that Esme was not really happy in her life, yearned for some kind of freedom that, in a small measure, she offered her.

It was too early for Jim to come home but she and Neil waited on the platform all the same. Esme heard a train's warning whistle and, as it arrived, the sound she loved — the steam belching up while the brakes of the massive machines ground to a halt, the big engine straining like a horse in its stall.

Jim wasn't on the train, but Conrad was.

When she remembers, she thinks how unlikely it was that he would look at her twice. Already she had adopted the ways of an older woman: wore her hair up in a bun, and had taken to cheap glasses because she couldn't thread a needle without them.

Still, it was she who saw him first. One of the things she liked was that this time she chose him. When he looked down she had already said yes.

'Could you look after Neil for an hour?' she asked Norma the next day. She knew what time his train came in. She knew that if she waited on the station he would follow her.

Just like that.

Not, is this all right? Are you sure about this? Nothing of that. Just the two of them on her and Jim's bed. Her hair falling down around her face, her glasses left behind on the kitchen bench, him carrying her through the house holding her legs around his waist until he could put her down and they could do their business. He had a sweet oily smell on his skin that she wore on her all that day.

His hands reached up for her cone-shaped breasts when she swung them above him.

'Steady on,' he said, 'I can't pull out like this.'

'I'm still feeding the baby. I can't get pregnant while I'm breast-feeding.'

His mouth then, everywhere.

His chest and arms bulged with muscles. On the river ascents when the trains climbed from Waiouru to Tangiwai, through the Junction and on towards Raurimu and the great central plateau of the island, from Taumarunui up to Frankton Junction, he threw three, perhaps four tons of coal through the firehole, placing the fuel from corner to corner along the near end of the grate. His wrists were swivelling steel. The sinewy arms that held her were like a high fence around her body.

She thought, fleetingly, of the needle that wandered around in her body. Somewhere, drifting among her blood, the thick red soup of herself, the needle had moved, perhaps entered her heart.

Norma said she'd have Neil at the same time the day after that, but Esme could see she looked at her oddly. She thought, I look different already.

All through the summer, the geraniums were in a red hot heat around the house, and he kept coming to see her. After the first few days she stopped asking Norma to mind Neil. She put him to bed in his cot and hoped he wouldn't wake up. In moments when she tried to behave like a normal person — a person who wasn't frantic with love, a person who mashed potatoes and made gravy and said here you are, here's your tea, dear, and hung out the washing and snapped the napkins when they were dry — she thought that her son would wake and know what she did.

She stopped going to the post office, didn't see Norma any more.

Queenie sent word that Pearl was coming to stay. She'd seen Jim at the Taumarunui station when he'd gone relieving on a job down there, and told him to pass the message on to Esme.

'She can't come now,' Esme cried.

'I thought you liked having her.'

'It's not that I don't want her to come, of course,' Esme said carefully. 'It's just that, well, you know, I'm busy with Neil.'

'One baby's not that much work.'

'Oh, what do you know about housework?' This was what love did to her, it made her bold and reckless in the way she spoke.

'There's no need for that,' Jim said. For an instant, she expected to be hit. And yet, she thought, he couldn't do that, not Jim from Birmingham with his good manners and his kindness. Because, even though he wasn't always happy in himself, and he complained about little things, he never did her any harm. Something about his look silenced her. She thought he must be able to sense the permanent swollen ache between her legs that he only made worse when he touched her.

'I guess Pearl could come for a few days.'

'It wouldn't hurt,' he said.

The day before Pearl arrived, she wrapped her legs tightly round Conrad's waist. 'I love you,' she said, running her tongue in the inside of his ear.

'I know,' he said. 'I know that all right.' He didn't say I love you back to her but he pulled her in closer to him so that she didn't know where he began and she left off.

Pearl was nearly thirteen. She had grown bosoms and a head taller since Esme last saw her. She was rounded and plump and her fair hair had spun into ringlets that she wore down round her face. She'd sung in the end of the year concert at school.

'Would you like me to sing my solo?' she asked on the first afternoon of her visit.

'Yes, please,' said Esme fervently. It was twelve thirty. The train was due in at one.

A Needle in the Heart

Pearl sang
Early one morning,
just as the sun was rising,
I heard a maid sing in the valley below,
oh don't deceive me,
oh never leave me ...

At any other time such pure clarity would have wrung Esme's heart but before Pearl had finished singing, she said, absently, 'Could you mind Neil for me, d'you think? Just for half an hour.'

'You weren't listening,' Pearl cried.

'Yes, yes I was. Did you get that song off the radio?'

'I hate you. It's true what they say about you, isn't it?'

Esme snatched her wrist and held on to it. 'What do they say about me? What? You just tell me who says what about me. You hear me.'

'Nothing,' said Pearl in a sullen voice. Esme let her arm drop. There was an angry mark where she had twisted Pearl's delicate flesh. 'All right then, I'll look after your rotten baby.'

'Thank you,' Esme said, and walked out, shutting the door behind her. She shivered as she hurried to the railway station, wishing she had brought her cardigan. It was autumn now and all week there had been a hint of frost in the morning. In the blue shadow of the mountain, the cold started early. She stood at the station, as she had that first time, only now she felt that people on the platform looked sideways at her, wondering what to expect next. She thought she was like Norma, flicking her head back and forth.

In fact, nothing much happened. The train came and Conrad wasn't on it, and as soon as she saw that, she understood what she'd known all along: that he wouldn't be there. She would never see him again. There was no real way of knowing this, just the feeling that things had gone too far and something had to change. She glimpsed her reflection in the murky painted window of the station waiting room, dishevelled and clutching her arms around herself.

Blindly, she turned and walked away from the station and through the town. Past the butcher's shop where she should be going to buy some liver and bacon for Jim's tea, and perhaps a sausage for Pearl who wouldn't eat liver. On past the greengrocer's shop where a patient quiet Chinese woman put apples and oranges and spinach in the front window. On beyond the tobacconist's shop where a group of men looked at her in silence as she hurried on by.

Nobody greeted her. So it was true then. They knew about her, knew why she stood so brazenly, in full sight of everyone, waiting for him.

She set off at a run, along the track beside the Mangawhero, where she used to walk before all this madness began. Further along the stream bed there was a rocky incline that dropped to a pool. She wanted to lie down in the water and let it freeze her, until she dropped like a stone to the bottom. Would Jim think to look for her there? He might, but she hoped that if he did he would simply leave her there. As winter closed in perhaps she would float to the surface and be rolled by boulders and glacial ice further down, out to sea or to one of the great lakes in the centre of the North Island, wherever it was the river went. She didn't really care.

Nothing like that's ever going to happen again, she said to herself, and it felt as if she had had an amputation of some kind. She found herself looking at her body as if she could see something missing. But it was all there, all of it. She thought about Neil, home alone with Pearl, and how, after a while, the boy would cry for her. Her breasts were leaking milk; she touched herself where her dress was wet and saw herself alone in the bush, a crazy woman with streaming hair, falling blindly across tree stumps and the dry grass of summer that was dying away as the cold weather set in. The river bubbled over the stones, shining where the water and the falling light touched them. She saw clouds, and bodies and floating, waving arms and the star faces of babies in them. Perhaps Pearl could look after her baby; she would soon get into the way of keeping house, the way Esme had. Then she thought that if that happened, Pearl would be with Jim, and that wouldn't be right.

She turned and walked back towards the town. The sun had dropped away, blood red, followed by the amber light that strikes just before dusk under the mountain; darkness started to settle. She began to be afraid of what she would find, and how she would have to face up to Jim's anger if he discovered she'd left Neil with Pearl. I went for a walk and I got lost, was the first story that sprang to mind. If he wasn't home already, might she not gather up Pearl and Neil and take them to the station to catch the train home? To Taumarunui. Only the train wasn't due for hours and he would find them there on the station. Perhaps they could hide somewhere.

Then she told herself she had imagined everything. That nobody knew. Conrad had had a day off sick, or his roster had been changed. He'd be on the train the next day. By the time she got to the house, she found herself believing this.

Inside, the kerosene lamp had been lit. Pearl was stoking the fire under Norma's instructions. Norma sat at the table with Neil in her lap, trying to get him to eat some food she'd mashed up for him. There was no sign of Jim.

'I'm sorry,' she said to both of them.

'I didn't know where you were,' Pearl said sullenly.

'The girl came and got me,' said Norma. 'Thank goodness. She's got more brains than I'd have given her credit for.'

'Has Jim been in?' Esme asked.

'Wouldn't be surprised if he was having a drink or two with his mates.'

' Jim doesn't go drinking.' Which was true. Jim wasn't a drinking man: it was one of those things that had recommended him to Queenie.

'Happen he might be now,' Norma said. She stood up patting the creases in her skirt. 'You know, Esme, it doesn't pay to get your meat where you get your bread.'

'I don't know what you mean.'

'There was a letter came for you this morning. Seeing you hadn't been in for the mail I brought it over when Pearl called me. My husband said take it to her, it might be urgent.'

'Thank you,' said Esme again, glancing at the envelope. She didn't recognise the big block letters that spelled her name on the envelope, but she saw the soft glue that held the flap of the envelope in place. She guessed it had been opened.

'Aren't you going to open it?' Norma asked.

Esme crumpled the letter in her hand as if it wasn't important. 'Probably a bill. That's all the mail that ever comes, isn't it?' She opened the door and held it ajar, so that Norma had to walk through.

The letter said:

Dear Esme

You don't know who I am but I think you ought to know that a certain man has been told he will be killed soon unless he takes some action to stop it happening to him he might have an engine run over him it will look like an accident I can promise you but it will happen he has said he will do what he must or rather what he must not. yours a wellwisher.

When Esme's next boy was born she nearly died. The doctor and nurses at the cottage hospital gave her so much chloroform that if the baby hadn't killed her coming out sideways, the dose almost did.

Norma came to visit and took a long look at Philip. 'He might pass,' she said, in a doubtful voice. Philip had been born with jet black curls and olive skin, nothing like his brother at all.

'Pass for what?' asked Esme.

Norma hesitated. 'A white boy.'

Esme held Philip close to her, remembering the way her mother had taught her to soothe a baby. Already she could tell he was not a placid boy, but every limb seemed so perfect and unblemished she thought he couldn't be real.

'What would you like to call him?' Jim asked.

'What about Philip?' she said, tentatively. This was the name of Jim's father, although of course she had never met him. Jim's parents had both died that year, the announcement of their deaths coming weeks later by sea mail, in letters edged with black.

'Yes,' Jim said, 'that's a nice idea. You go ahead and call him that.' He stroked the baby's cheek with his forefinger. 'He's a throwback this one,' he said. 'A right little darkie.'

A Needle in the Heart

'One for Mum,' Esme said.

Jim smiled and tickled the baby. It wasn't like Norma said. He'd never come home drunk. He'd never had a word to say about anything that happened. If anything, he seemed more calm, and less willing to find fault with her than he had before.

The year the world went to war, Jim Moffit said I wish I could go (only he couldn't because he was too old and he was needed for essential services anyway), and Ned, the fifth child of Awhina and Robert McDavitt's eight children, said I'm going, and learned to sing the Maori Battalion song, and Lawrence Tyree, the film projectionist, said I'm glad I can stay here.

Lawrence had had a hernia operation, which he reckoned would keep him out of the war. He had blond hair and very smooth skin, so much like velvet you would think he had no beard except for a stain of mottled shadow that appeared at the end of the day. He'd come up to the Junction to live just before the war started and ran the picture theatre on Wednesday and Saturday nights.

'You a shirker?' asked Ned, on his visit to say goodbye before he left for the war. It was half time at the pictures on Saturday night.

'I'll show you my operation scar, if you like.'

'All right,' said Ned. 'I'll put two bob on it, there's no scar.'

Everyone squeezed into the foyer to buy lemonade, stood watching as Lawrence began to undo his belt. Someone in the crowd reminded them that there were women and children present.

'Don't bother,' said Ned, 'we don't really want to see it, mate.'

Lawrence shrugged and laughed, as if it was their loss, and caught the florin Ned threw him. After that, there wasn't any more trouble.

'I wish he had shown us,' Pearl said to Esme afterwards.

'You don't want to talk like that,' Esme said sharply. 'People should keep their private parts to themselves.'

So then Pearl asked her, was it true that their mum had shown people her boobs at the races.

'You don't want to listen to gossip,' Esme said. 'There's some people have evil tongues and if Jim ever heard you say a thing like that he'd make you wash your mouth out with carbolic soap and water.'

'Jim couldn't make me do a thing like that,' Pearl said, laughing at her. She laughed a lot these days, her lips a big oval round the pushed-up teeth, her tongue darting in the pink cavern of her mouth.

Pearl often stayed at the Junction now. The afternoon Esme had gone away and left her to look after Neil seemed to be forgotten. Neil was due to start school the following year. Philip was a more challenging child, constantly on the go, a child who said No! when he was told to go to bed, and Why? when asked to pick up his toys: a wooden truck Queenie had given him for Christmas, and two guns from his father. Bang bang you're dead, said Philip, especially to Neil. Esme had her hands full and she was pleased to have Pearl around. At fifteen, Pearl had become helpful and willing. She was seeing a boy called Raymond who was a guard on the railways. He had deep-set eyes and eyelashes like a girl's. His mother was an Italian from Island Bay, in Wellington.

'She's too young to be seeing a boy of eighteen,' Esme said. She had electricity and the telephone installed now. People rang through with sewing orders, although Queenie had to ring from the post office in Taumarunui to talk to her.

Queenie just sighed on the other end of the line. 'What the heck, he'll be called up any day. Reckon you can take better care of her than your dad and me, at our age.'

'I wish she was still in school,' Esme said.

'Oh school. The authorities are rounding up everyone and making them stay in school these days. What's the point of it? Look at you — it didn't hurt you, did it? You've done pretty well, Esme.'

In the evenings Esme did Pearl's fine fair hair up in rags for her. She liked running it through her fingers, her time to relax. She was busier than ever. She'd never had so many sewing orders coming in. All the girls were getting married before their sweethearts went away. She wished she felt happier, but at least it was easier to pretend life was normal.

It gave her a shock one night when Jim said, 'I wish I could take you back to the Old Dart.'

'What d'you mean?'

'Home. To England. I could show you my place, where I come from.' They were lying in bed, Jim smoking, with an empty tobacco tin perched on his stomach for an ashtray.

'For a holiday? Jim, there's a war on.'

'Well, I know that. But some day I'd like us to go back and live there. Things would be better.'

'What things?' She had thought that he was settled, even though the promotion he hoped for never came. It flashed through her mind that Conrad might be back, that he might be planning to try and see her, and Jim knew about it.

'Just everything.'

'Don't be silly, Jim. We've got our home here.'

'Oh, I don't suppose you'd want to leave,' he said with what sounded like a trace of bitterness.

For a day or two she found herself afraid and hopeful all over again about Conrad. There was no way of asking anyone, and no sign of him. On days off, Jim went around in his braces, with grey stubble on his chin. So that was it, England was the pay-off, the price of Philip, and she wasn't going to give him that.

One morning, she met Lawrence at the butcher's shop on the corner of Thames Street, when she was choosing calf brains. She had the children with her, because Pearl had left again. First Pearl had gone home to see Queenie, who said she could go down to Wellington to be near Raymond while he was in training at Trentham, and now she'd gone south. Esme was so angry that Queenie had agreed to this, that for the first time in her life, she and her mother were not speaking to each other.

'I'm going to run the next movie through this afternoon,' Lawrence said. 'It's called *A Star is Born*. Why don't you come over for a preview?'

Esme laughed. 'You'd soon get sick of my kids.'

'I'll take them for you if you like,' the butcher's wife said. 'I'll have finished my accounts by lunchtime.' Joan Stott was a tiny lively woman who used a cigarette holder. She was considered a snappy dresser, one of Esme's best customers. Esme had whipped up some dresses for Joan at short notice, when she was going on holiday.

'Well, if you're sure.'

'You could do with a break,' said Joan. 'Your eyes are falling out of your head.'

The movie starred Janet Gaynor; it was about a girl called Esther Blodgett who arrived in Hollywood from the sticks, and learned different ways of walking and talking and making herself up, and got a new name and became a star. A big title came up that showed her destination as being 'the beckoning El Dorado, Metropolis of Make-believe in the California Hills.' Esme didn't know why but it made her think of Pearl and she wanted to cry.

The theatre was empty, except for her and Lawrence who came and sat with her once the film was running through the projection machine. He had to duck back to change the reels, but the rest of the time he sat leaning slightly towards her so that their shoulders touched.

'You like that?' Lawrence said when it was over. They still sat in the dark.

'I loved it,' she sighed.

He leaned closer, breathing against her neck, like a hot gust of wind. When he ran his finger lightly up and down her bare arm, she didn't stop him.

'What's this then?' said Lawrence, his finger stopping at a point beneath her elbow.

'What's what?'

He rubbed his thumb and finger together. 'It's something hard.'

'It's my needle,' she said.

'Your *needle*?'

She told him then about the way the needle had broken off and how it was still floating about inside her, how it didn't really hurt, that mostly she'd forgotten all about it, even when she was in the hospital having Philip and should have mentioned it to the doctor. Just sometimes it surfaced in funny places. Perhaps she'd have it taken out if it ever caused any trouble.

A Needle in the Heart

'You could be dead by then,' Lawrence said.

'Yes, well, thanks very much.'

'I could show you my scar if you like.'

'No doubt you will, whether I like it or not,' she said. She reached out and touched the raised red mark on his flat milky-white stomach. It reminded her of her children's stomachs.

When he guided her hand further down, beyond the scar, to his busy entertaining penis, she thought, why not? Well, why not? She liked being able to give something to someone. She'd had a nice afternoon.

At home, she looked in the mirror at her smudged face. 'You fool,' she said, and couldn't help laughing, the ridiculous position she'd put herself in, the awkwardness of seats in movie theatres, the way they sprang up behind you when you shifted.

I should leave, she told herself. It's time to get out of here.

But not yet.

Her new baby slipped into the world with hardly a murmur, just a stretch and a wriggle when Esme was standing at the back door saying goodbye to Joan Stott who'd been visiting, as if birth was a frivolous occasion, a good story to be told. Esme hardly had time to lie down on the sofa in the front room. Joan cut the umbilical cord with Esme's pinking shears.

The new baby didn't look like anybody in particular. She had wide eyes which, when she was older, would assume a slightly staring gaze that alarmed people, as if she was looking too closely at them. Jim seemed pleased to have a daughter.

'I think I'd like to call her Janet,' she told Jim, before he had a chance to ask. She'd thought about Esther, but it sounded too like her own name, so she settled for Janet.

Dear Esme wrote Pearl

I'm having a great time here in Wellington. There's Americans everywhere and their so good to us girls who are entertaining them. I just love the Marines. You should have seen me down Manners

Street the other nite wearing one of their caps. Laugh. Me and my friends laughed and laughed. I sing in a club. You see all that singing and stuff in the choir paid off. Give your baby Janet a kiss from me, the one I never saw and tell those little brothers of hers to be good boys and do their homework just like their auntie did (ha ha).

Love from your sister, Pearl

For all her easy delivery, Janet cried a lot. Jim walked her up and down and stayed home some days to help look after the children. He had warnings from management at the railways, and they took him off the tablets and gave him a clerical job at the railway station. His pay was down so Esme took in still more work, although it was wrecking her eyes. She always seemed to have her knuckles in the corners, rubbing her lids raw. Someone had threatened to burn the picture theatre down and Lawrence had taken himself off because some of the servicemen home on leave were throwing rocks on his roof. Norma and her husband moved on, back up to Auckland, which was a relief to Esme. People shifted from this place all the time.

'I'm sorry we didn't get to move away from here,' she said to Jim one evening when she was serving him mince on toast. She was holding her daughter on her hip with one hand while she put his plate on the table with the other. 'I expect we should have gone anyway.' She didn't say 'after the accident' although that's what she was thinking. Any number of accidents, if it came to that. It was hard to fathom how their lives had become so pulled apart. She didn't feel exactly responsible. Something had started a long way back, before she could in any way decide for herself how things should have been. Back when she was young. Somewhere in the deep sleep of her early life, in a place she didn't recognise.

'I don't want to leave here,' Jim said, in a mild, alarmed voice. 'This is where I live.'

Things had shifted between them. Before, she had been the one afraid to leave. Before the Depression was over, before the war started, before the movies. Now she wanted to go, but she couldn't see how.

A Needle in the Heart

'I thought you'd settle down, now that you've got children.'

No more babies, she resolved. She'd take herself more seriously. Another letter had come. It said, like the song, I Wonder Who's Kissing Her Now. She screwed it up and put it in the fire, but her cheeks burned at the memory of it.

That night, she had a dream. She was in the middle of a bush clearing and, all around her, pointing towards her, were giant engines, heaving and grunting. They were driven by men with coal black faces, and they were laughing, their mouths stretched like heads on a coconut shy. She couldn't recognise any of them but she pleaded with them to let her go. She promised that if they would let her escape she would never mess things up again. Then suddenly the trains and the men were gone and she was alone in the clearing. This abandonment was worse than when the engines were there, because now there was only silence, and the trees, and she couldn't see what was behind them. Cobwebs caught her clothes when she tried to pass between the trees. When she woke up, she lay in bed panting, trying to brush the threads away from her face.

Later in the war, Esme got a phone call from a woman who ran a boarding house in Hawker Street in Wellington. It was about her sister Pearl who'd been living there. The woman said she thought she should let her know that Pearl was in the hospital in Newtown and she was really sick and it would be as well if Esme could come and see her, because the doctors weren't that hopeful. Bad pneumonia, the woman said, in a sombre way.

'I'd better get the train down tonight,' Esme told Jim.

'I should go,' Jim said. 'You don't know anything about cities.'

'I've been to Auckland. Anyway, I'll manage. She's my sister.'

What she would remember were the flags down Cuba Street, like clothes on a washing line, outside the People's Palace where she stayed. And all the cars. She counted twenty-five in the street at one time. She looked in the Union Clothing Company for things to take home for Jim and the boys but decided she could make them just as well herself. This was while she still thought she was going back. The men in uniforms who whistled when she passed. The tram that took her out to Newtown to the big red brick hospital with the endless corridors painted yellow-cream and the unrelenting yards of brown linoleum that squeaked when she walked over it.

And collecting Pearl's things from the hospital — not much, because she'd been taken there by ambulance in the night: just a nightdress and a gold-plated watch that looked new. Signing her name so that Pearl could be released for burial. She glimpsed Pearl at the undertaker's and said yes, that was her. So she had to believe it was Pearl in the coffin. It is her, she told herself, it's Pearl, it's Pearl, that's Pearl in there. At the boarding house, clothes to pack, dresses with skirts that would have been billowy in Wellington's wind, and hair combs and make-up, and some bits of jewellery. Esme remembered the brooch then, the one her mother planned to give Pearl, and wondered what would happen to it now. Some packets of cigarettes that she gave to an American who came to the door looking for Pearl because he didn't know she was dead. A few photographs, one of Queenie and Stick, and a couple of Pearl and Raymond taken at the Junction. There was one of them at a dance together, Pearl wearing a dress made of green and black dappled satin of which Esme knew every seam. She remembered how impatient Pearl had been for her to finish it, and that there was a gusset in the bodice where she'd made it too small because Pearl wouldn't let her fit it on her properly, just kept jigging around and singing little bubbles of some song or another. The next day, Queenie and Stick arriving at Wellington Railway Station. Stick with vacant watery eyes, Queenie hobbling on a cane by this time, older and fatter and tired. Just a touch of gout, she said, nothing she wouldn't get over when she was back in her own home again.

Later in the day Joe and his wife drove down in their big black Hudson from Taihape where they were sharemilking on a dairy farm. Joe had a shock of grey hair already. So there was family there at the cemetery in Karori. Joe stood close to her and she found herself moving away from him. He'd never been too well disposed towards

A Needle in the Heart

Pearl. Her mother said, 'Now stop it, you two.'

The minister who the woman from the boarding house had found said, 'The Lord gave, and the Lord hath taken away; blessed be the name of the Lord.'

'I'm so sorry, Esme,' said Queenie. 'It shouldn't have happened.'

'It's all right, Mum,' said Esme, who'd done with crying the night before they all arrived. 'It just wasn't meant to be.'

'She was just too good for this world,' said Queenie. 'Our magic girl.'

'Yes,' said Esme, 'Magic.' Perhaps Pearl really had been a trick of the light.

'You've got to get on with things,' Joe said. As brothers went, she supposed he was all right. A bit rough and ready, that was all. 'It was probably for the best.' For a moment Esme hated him.

The service was said and done in the space of half an hour; they went to James Smith's afterwards and had a cup of tea and some sandwiches and a cake apiece.

'I don't get the connection,' one of Esme's daughters-in-law said to her once. 'Is that why you left? Because Pearl died?'

'I suppose so,' said Esme. 'Well, she had something to do with it.'

'But you left the children.'

'I sent for Janet.'

'What about the boys, though? You left the boys.'

She was going to remind her daughter-in-law that the boys had their father, what a good father he was, but she could see that wouldn't add up. Jim had died before they'd grown up and, after all, the boys did end up first with Queenie and Stick and then with Joe and his second wife Bunty who he married after the first one died of a thrombosis, then, after that, with Mary's family because Bunty couldn't manage another family. Backwards and forwards, no regular place to call home.

Why people leave. There are as many answers as there are people who go, dividing and uncoiling their lives from one another. Esme thought you could drive yourself crazy, thinking about things like this. She did feel things, though. Whatever people thought.

'Yes, it was to do with Pearl,' she told her daughter-in-law. 'It's hard to explain.'

3

Philip loved the way Petra looked, the strong eyes, the big tender mobile mouth. If he took her features apart one by one, he couldn't have described any of them as gorgeous, except perhaps for that mouth. She wore her hair in a straight brown bob, her breasts were so small she looked flat-chested some ways she stood, but she had a vitality about her that made him feel at home with her, as if he was in the presence of someone he had always known. Every time he saw her he experienced a swoop of joy, one that never went away, even when they were older, and things turned to shit, as they did, for a long time, when the children were growing up, and they were busy making their marks in the world, and not paying a lot of attention to each other. He swore the joy would never go away, never leave them.

Right from the beginning, the way she dressed made him proud of her when they were out. They were students when they met. She wore straight plaid skirts with dark sweaters, black stockings and flat-heeled lace-up shoes. When she came towards him on the street she would have pulled a beret over her hair, pouched towards the back, and a long scarf would be trailing behind her. The year that he became engaged to her, Petra was rehearsing *As You Like It* with the university. She was Rosalind. Of course. He was helping to build sets in his spare time, not that he had much of that, but he made it anyway.

'My parents will drive you crazy,' she told him when they had chosen the ring at Stewart Dawson's, the big jeweller's shop on the corner of Lambton Quay and Willis Street. 'This is a very tasteful ring,' the attendant had murmured, as she showed them the diamond on a bed of velvet.

He had been surprised by her insistence that they do things

A Needle in the Heart

properly. This was a time when young women like Petra were throwing convention out the window. She was a banner waver like him, a ranter and a raver, hurling herself into causes like ban the bomb and trade unions, and the polemics of poetry; she believed it was all right for her to tell him when she was hot for him. All that stuff. She'd read *The Second Sex*.

'They're rich. We'll have to have a big wedding. D'you mind?' (I do really love them, she said, as a little parenthesis she used from time to time when she spoke about her parents. Like an apology. She was their only child.)

'Just as long as you're there,' he'd said. Trying to sound resolute.

'They'll want your guest list before you can blow the fire out,' she said.

'I won't have one. It's simple.'

'What d'you mean, you won't have one?'

'Well, just that. Your friends and mine. The rest's up to you.'

'Don't be silly, darling. Your family and all that.'

'No,' he said. 'I don't have any family to ask.'

The Blue Rose China shop was in a long elegant room with timber panelling. Margaret Ellis and her husband Nicholas, who was a dentist, owned the whole building. Nicholas had his rooms upstairs and her shop was on the lower level facing one of the main avenues in Tauranga. It got good afternoon sun which made the glass and silverware sparkle. She kept a set of rapier fire irons and the Peerage brass plaques down the front to give extra brightness in the winter.

Each day Margaret and Nicholas had their lunch together in the stockroom at the back of the shop. They considered themselves a convivial mix of commerce and the professions, or that's what Margaret said. Margaret, or Mrs Ellis as she preferred to be called by her customers, was a trim woman, invariably dressed in smooth straight black dresses when she was in the shop, her blonde French roll immaculate and lacquered into place, never a speck on her dark upright shoulders.

One lunch hour, their conversation concerned their daughter

Petra who had just become engaged. Striking the right tone for the newspaper notice was giving both her and Nicholas long pause for thought. 'What on earth are we going to put about Philip's parents?' she said in a strained voice.

Even Nicholas, who was used to pain and blood and people looking their most unattractive, or shouting for mercy, pointed his scrubbed pink-nailed fingers together and hesitated. 'Perhaps son of the late Mr and Mrs Moffit.'

'But I understand that Mrs Moffit is still alive.'

'But she's not Mrs Moffit any more, is she?'

'So I believe, but we can't just kill her off.' She knew her husband was trying to be reasonable, in a humorous kind of way, but she felt a surge of panic overtaking her. If only she hadn't arranged for the couple's photograph to be taken for the fortnightly *Photo News* as well.

'Son of the late Mr Moffit then. Just because she exists doesn't mean to say she has to be in the notice.'

'Everyone will know there's something fishy if we say he's the late and there's no mention of her.'

Nicholas looked as if he had just come across a particularly unpleasant mouthful of decay. He was a tall man with beautiful iron-grey hair. Because of his height he suffered back pain in his profession which often made him look slightly tight-lipped. She had to remember this insidious discomfort when he looked like this. 'What is the mother's name then?'

'I don't know. Well, Petra muttered something about her being a Mrs Pudney.'

'Well then, son of the late Mr Moffit and Mrs Pudney. We'll just have to accept that.'

'Petra says Philip won't hear of it. He hasn't spoken to his mother in years.'

'He didn't mention this when he spoke to me about Petra. I thought, a budding young lawyer. I wish you'd told me earlier, Margaret. We've given our word.'

'She'll marry him whatever we say. We should never have let her

A Needle in the Heart

get into the theatre.' Margaret Ellis groped for breath. 'She's so radical.'

'Oh no,' said her husband. 'Not that.'

In the end, the notice that went in the paper said: 'Mr and Mrs Nicholas Ellis are delighted to announce the forthcoming marriage of their daughter Petra Jean to Philip Moffit of Wellington.'

Margaret remembered this conversation one afternoon not long afterwards. She was on the phone ordering in a meat platter for a special customer, a superior sort of person who demanded attention. Not someone she could hurry. She spotted a woman turning the Denby Chevron mugs over and pursing her lips at the prices. An older woman, a bit rough round the edges. Hair crimped in a fraying ginger perm and bulging bunions. She had a way of flicking her head backwards as if to see whether someone was watching.

'Can I help you?' Margaret enquired, replacing the phone in its cradle at last. 'Something for yourself, or a gift? A wedding in the offing, perhaps?'

'No,' said the woman, putting a mug down harder than was necessary. 'But I hear you've got one coming up, Mrs Ellis.'

'Yes,' said Margaret, letting the distance in her voice lengthen. 'I imagine you've been reading the newspapers.'

The woman introduced herself. She was a widow. Her husband used to be in the post office but he'd passed on a few years back. They'd had hard times in the old days but she'd learnt to count her blessings. She had daughters and they'd married well enough. She went to stay with both of them for two weeks each year so that helped pass the time. Her conversation was more of a continuous monologue than an exchange. She paused when Margaret glanced at her wristwatch. 'You reckon that boy Moffit's from Wellington?'

Margaret steadied herself on the edge of the counter as if she'd been caught off balance. 'Our daughter's fiancé?'

'I reckon I know that face. Or one pretty like it. Family came from Ohakune way, didn't they?'

'Philip hasn't mentioned that. We haven't spent a lot of time with him yet. The two young people are studying, you see. Philip's nearly finished his law degree.'

'The law. Young Philip's in the law. Well, my oh my. There's a few things I could tell you about that young man's family that I'll bet you don't know.'

'I'd love to have let her have her say,' Margaret told Nicholas that evening. 'Perhaps I should have.'

'It was probably lies.'

'She said she was the postmaster's wife. It sounded pretty convincing.'

'It's too late now,' he said with real regret. They looked at each other, knowing it wouldn't have done for Margaret to let the woman go any further. As if hearing it would make it true. Whatever it was.

'She said he was a surly looking young bugger. That's what she said. From his picture.'

'He looks serious,' said her husband.

'She said, "I suppose he's had plenty to be sorry for himself over. Tell you about his dad, did he? Whoever he was." I asked her to leave then. I told her I was shutting while I went down to the bank. So she left.'

'You did the right thing.'

'You don't think,' Margaret said carefully, 'that there's a touch of, well, darkness there? If you know what I mean?'

'Spanish, I think,' Nicholas said vaguely. There couldn't be any going back with this marriage. You knew when the horse had bolted. As it were.

'Oh, that's all right then.' She still sounded doubtful. Her husband knew how hard all of this must have been for her.

He said, 'I think you have to put this behind you.'

'Darling,' Petra said, one evening, soon after this. She and Philip were walking up the hill towards Kelburn where they shared a flat with four other students. 'Darling, what about the invitation list?'

'We've been through that. You ask who you like.' He'd explained to her already how his mother had gone off with a man called Kevin Pudney and left him and his brother with his father. How none of it had worked out, not for him anyway, and how he'd left all of that behind. The going off with Kevin Pudney part was an elaboration, not exactly true, but Kevin had been there when his mother next surfaced in his life.

'They just can't seem to get it through their heads that you're not going to ask anyone from your family to the wedding. Couldn't you put up with your mother just for a day?'

'No,' he said. 'No, I couldn't. My mother was a destructive bitch. My father went to pieces after she left.'

'There might have been two sides to it.'

'Don't you believe it. My father was a saint. It killed him, I reckon. Her leaving him.'

'You said he had cancer.'

'Well, she gave it to him.'

'Oh don't be silly, Philip,' she said. 'People don't catch cancer. It's something that grows inside them.'

He walked out of the café then, knowing she would follow him. They would say they were sorry to each other, her, then him, in that order.

4

The day of her son's wedding, in the spring of 1964, Esme Pudney got dressed in the small boarding house near the bus station where she was staying in Tauranga. The air was fragrant, scented with citrus blossoms; the gardens were full of daffodils and forget-me-nots. She put on a blue silk dress with a hint of pale silver flowers in the weave, liking the way it fell in a soft swathe of colour from the pleats at her hips. She dabbed lavender water between her breasts, powdered her sun freckles. She and Kevin took long summer holidays in caravans, staying in camping grounds or just on the edge of the wilderness, near lakes and streams. This was after Kevin retired from contract fencing. He was older than her by twelve years, but then she had often settled for older men. Their children were grown-up, the two they called their children: Esme's daughter Janet, and his girl Marlene, who were pretty much of an age. Marlene had been his youngest, as Janet was hers. He'd been left with Marlene after his wife died. They didn't have a fortune but, when they were chatting over a beer to the new friends they made along the way, they liked to say they had enough to get by on. Enough for a bit of fun. A beer and a few laughs and the wide open spaces. Now wasn't that what life was all about.

The day before, she'd prepared a casserole that would last for two days and put it in the fridge for Kevin. She left a note for him to say she'd be back on the bus on Sunday evening. It wasn't as if she was afraid of him, it was just that he would have thought her a fool. He couldn't see why she bothered with those sons of hers, especially the second one. He'd given him the rounds of the kitchen more than once. It wasn't that Philip didn't deserve it, impudent kid that he was, but she did wish Kevin had tried to talk things over with the boy before he let fly. But that was Kevin, a man of action. Like Philip's father, perhaps, although when she remembered Conrad now, there wasn't much she could tell you about him. Where he came from. Who he really was. Not even how old he was. She hadn't asked. If she was honest, it was Jim she really admired. His goodness and the way that he'd stuck to the boys for as long as he could. The way he'd gone on till the end without asking her to say she was sorry though, Lord knows, she was.

A crowd of well-wishers had gathered outside the Church of the Holy Trinity, the way people did in those days when a wedding was the best show in town on a Saturday afternoon. Especially a wedding like this.

Esme stood at the back of the crowd, but slightly to one side so she could still get a good view. She'd learnt about the wedding from Joe's second wife Bunty, who'd seen the engagement the year before in the local paper. She and Joe were sharemilking on another farm out near Katikati; it would be their last. Esme got on with Bunty, who Joe had insisted on bringing to visit with her and Kevin. She turned out to be an interesting woman who belonged to a library and read books, and kept up with the news. She called Joe the old bugger, and didn't let him get away with much. Privately, Esme thought she was wasted on Joe. When Joe heard about the wedding, he told his wife to let it go, Philip had moved on from the family long ago. He said this with a sense of injury in his voice. But of course Bunty couldn't do that. She felt a bit guilty about Philip, the way she'd sent him off to Mary's to live, but he'd been such a handful, that kid. It was the least she could do to let his mother know about the impending marriage. She promised to let Esme know if she heard when the wedding was, and sure enough a friend of hers heard the banns being read in church, and told her.

Esme glanced round, anxious in case Bunty had decided to come, but there was no sign of anyone she knew. It would have been too far to travel at this time of year when the farm was busy; besides Bunty wouldn't have thought of Esme doing a crazy thing like this, coming on her own. If she'd seen her, Esme expected Bunty would pity her, and that would be worse than Kevin being wild with her.

The wedding cars appeared, decorated with ribbons, and when they had stopped, the bridesmaids, dressed in pale cinnamon-coloured gowns, alighted. When the bride stepped out of the third car, astonishment rippled around the onlookers. She wore a sunflower yellow satin dress and wide-brimmed matching hat with a crushed stitched crown. She carried three lilies, casually, as if they had just been picked from a garden.

Esme felt enchanted, at once. A performer, a woman of daring.

As she came close to the church, Esme was able to see Petra clearly. The sculptured features, shadowed by the hat, were composed in an amused, almost mocking expression. As she recognised faces, she lifted an ungloved hand.

Her father offered her his arm and she took it. Just at the church door, he paused for a moment, and spoke close to her ear. Petra hesitated longer than she needed to, as if a moment of indecision had overtaken her, while a bridesmaid straightened the back of the gown. She looked sideways, then turned her head to look straight at Esme.

Esme could see the way her eyes were looking for some sign that she might know her, so she smiled and lifted her hand, as if she were a friend. The young woman gave a half smile and turned back to her father.

Inside the church the organ started to play 'Here Comes the Bride'. The wedding party moved on into the dark church, with its stained glass windows, and the cream freesia favours that lined the pews, on and up towards the altar, and the huge vasefuls of flowers.

Esme slid into a pew at the back, not that there was much room for the uninvited. She knew Philip wouldn't look past the radiant woman in yellow as she moved up the aisle. There was just time enough for her to see him look towards Petra, his curly hair crisply cut, a flower in his buttonhole, his face creased with a wondering smile. Then he turned his back to the congregation and took Petra's hand. Even at the back of the church she could hear his responses, his voice, cracking a little with emotion as he said, 'I, Philip, take you, Petra Jean, to be my lawful wedded wife.' She and Jim never did get round to giving him a second name.

She wondered for a moment how Philip would manage. Was he up to this, a true golden girl?

Then he said, 'With this ring I thee wed, with my body I thee worship', according to the exact old order of service. When he said these words, about worshipping Petra with his body, she felt herself bowled over, so that she had to press her hands tightly together on top of the shelf holding the hymn books. She didn't want strangers to see her crying.

Jim had been playing with the children when she came back from Pearl's funeral. It was raining outside, a solid sleety rain that stung her face. He'd pulled blankets off the beds and draped them over the backs of the kitchen chairs so that they made tents. Neil and Janet were inside the tent with a dish of chopped apple between them. Only Philip stood apart, biting the knuckles of one hand, his eyes like saucers. His black hair sprouted in curls that no amount of brushing could subdue. His eyes, when he looked up and saw her, were huge and incredulous with joy, as if he had never expected to see her again.

'Mummy's back, Mummy's back,' he cried.

This was the moment when she might have lost her resolve. She looked at Jim and his expression was cool and unfriendly.

'We're having an inside picnic,' Neil said. 'It's good fun playing with Dad.'

Jim said, 'I won't stop you taking the girl. I can see that she needs to be with her mother. But you're not taking my boys.'

Patient enduring Jim. With his names on all the children's birth certificates.

'You're not taking my boys.'

'Philip,' she began, and stopped, seeing the expression in Jim's eyes.

'They're my boys,' he said.

That was pretty much the last thing of any consequence that he said to her. His head wreathed in steam from the train's engine as he walked back up the platform, a little bent over now, one of the boys' hands in each of his own. Only the little boy, Philip, looking back and crying, and wanting her to come back.

Esme had been on her own for six years when Queenie died. Stick had already gone. It was at Queenie's funeral that Esme met Kevin Pudney.

The way she lived, she took Janet to different farms where she did housekeeping work in return for room and board. Janet, after a patchy tearful start, was a child who accepted whatever was asked of her. She stayed obediently in farmhouse kitchens, drawing and playing with plasticine and her dolls while her mother worked. After she started school, things got easier all round. Esme had a couple of jobs in the King Country which meant she got to see her mother and Neil and Philip now and then. She couldn't take the boys because the accommodation she got offered on the farms was always too small, although at one place she did rent some shearers' quarters but the boys ran wild and got into some guns and ammunition belonging to the farmer and caused no end of trouble. When Queenie needed a rest, their Uncle Joe took them in, or they went up north to stay with Mary, Esme's oldest sister.

Since she left Jim, Esme had gone on a self-improvement course, because now she chose to, and not because he said that she must. She read magazines about how to improve her dress sense, make stuffed toys, decorate cakes and arrange flowers. The people she worked for liked the way she left little unexpected gifts for them. A woman with a generous heart, one of employers wrote in a reference. She met some men but, usually, if you dug around a bit, you found there was a woman somewhere in the background. These years were also taken up with the divorce papers that Jim had served on her, although his death spared her the day in court. It was like a final gift. There were some things she'd rather not have had to talk about if she was cross examined. She wasn't keen on the idea of it all being in *Truth* which reported on divorces, the messier the better.

The morning of Queenie's funeral, Esme saw her mother for the last time. The family had taken turns sitting beside her at the undertaker's. Not all of the family were there. Ned McDavitt had been killed in the war and later on the youngest McDavitt boy, Hunter, died at the very end, just days before it was all over. One of the sisters lived in Australia. Mary had left Neil and Philip up north with her husband who couldn't take the time off work to come down for the funeral. It was still a big crowd.

At the very last moment some strangers turned up. They were Maori and although they said that they knew Queenie had lived as a white woman most of her life, they were related to her and weren't going to let her go without saying goodbye. Kevin, who was their boss, could see that he wasn't going to get them to work for him that day, so he said he'd drive them over. They were doing a bit of fencing on a hill farm near Taumarunui.

Esme slipped back into the viewing room one more time, after the unexpected visitors had left to join the mourners heading for the church. She felt shaken by this visit, as if some corner of her life had been turned over for inspection. There was something she wanted to say to her mother that she couldn't seem to tell her while the others were there. By that time Queenie had been dead for four days and her skin had taken on that blue-ish waxen tinge that means it really is time to close things down and say goodbye. Her face felt like ice when Esme touched it. She was going to kiss her once more but she couldn't bring herself to do that, the flesh so shrunken and pulled in that the bones were showing. What she had come to say had dried up in her throat. Instead, she let her fingers trail over her mother's cheek. As she was taking her hand away, she felt it touch something hard at the base of Queenie's throat. Leaning over, she looked into the coffin. She saw what she hadn't seen before: the gold brooch with the amethyst glowing in its heart. Perhaps Joe, or Mary, or someone in the family had decided that that was where it belonged.

'That was Pearl's,' she said, voicing her indignation in the empty room.

A busy persistent blowfly circled the room.

She reached in and unpinned the brooch and slipped it into her handbag. It felt like the right thing to do.

The wake went on into the evening. The men had had a few drinks by then. Joe, swaggering drunk, kept following her around, wanting to talk to her, as if she wasn't his sister but some loose woman on her own. In order to get away from him, Esme got talking to Kevin. She explained then how she had these three kids, one of them a teenager already.

He said how hard he found it to believe that. He did know what it was like, getting left with a kiddie to raise, after his wife died.

'I'm a widow myself,' she said. She hadn't thought of herself like this, but it seemed more or less true. She touched the brooch in her pocket. There were some things one simply had to do. Kevin seemed like a gentleman.

Kevin was a great father to Janet. She called him Dad and she and Marlene were like real sisters. He turned out handier with his fists on the boys than Esme would have liked. Neil he could tolerate. A lazy little bastard, but he didn't have ideas above himself. Not like the other boy. In his eyes Philip was a cocky little prick, needed knocking in to shape. Neil got a job farm labouring when he was fifteen and could leave school. Philip went back to Joe's for a while and, when that didn't work out, back up to Mary's. A teacher at the school she sent him to (it was his twelfth school) took a fancy to him and the next thing he was off to boarding school on a scholarship.

'Fancy,' said Esme, 'to think my boy's got brains.'

'They shouldn't give him ideas. He's probably a queer,' Kevin said.

'I wonder where he got them from,' Esme said dreamily, as if she hadn't heard him.

'You ought to know, he's your kid.'

'Yes. Well. So he is.' Her face closed up, shutting him out. They were living in another farmhouse, out the back of beyond. She didn't have to work the way she used to, though she still kept her hand in. There was never any trouble between them, except when the subject of Philip came up. After the boy went off to boarding school she sent ten pounds to Mary to give to him every holidays.

After a bit, Mary wrote and said she'd better send the money straight to the school because Philip was taking his holidays with his new friends. In the long summer holiday he'd gone on a tour of the South Island and walked the Milford Track. In winter, he went skiing with a friend's family. They were staying in a lodge at Ohakune Junction. Esme laughed out loud when she read that. She didn't mention it to Kevin, because he wouldn't have understood about the Junction, and the irony of it all.

He and Esme and the two girls were happy on their own. They moved closer to town so the girls didn't have to travel so far on the bus to school. Both of them did secretarial courses afterwards, and then went off on an overseas trip. They sent cards from Rome and Paris and London. Neil, who had grown into a thin-faced man with quiet ways, got married to a girl called Leonie straight after his twenty-first birthday party; they had a son and a daughter, just eleven months between them, so that, before she knew it, Esme was a grandmother.

These were some of the things Esme Pudney thought about while her son was being married. She understood why she sat anonymously at the back of the church. She wished it wasn't that way, but she didn't see how else things could have worked out. Just as the service was ending, while the triumphant march from the church was forming, she tiptoed past the ushers at the back, out into the spring sunshine.

5

There was a wrap party the night Petra's first movie finished filming. It had been a punishing schedule, up at five each morning, some nights going on until ten. There never seemed enough time to eat and sleep, but all the time in the world to talk. Everyone was someone's best friend, and sometimes their lover. People told each other outrageous things about themselves that they'd never told anyone else. They made dramas out of their own lives which, whether they were true or not, they knew they would believe from then on. Now suddenly they were all having to say goodbye. Not that it would be truly goodbye because there were only so many movie sets and so many jobs to go round in Wellington. And if there wasn't a movie there would be a stage play, or a stretch of radio drama, though that was never more than a week's work at a time. Or a television commercial if you got lucky because that was enough to pay for a few months out of work. Petra had done a couple of those.

Philip, looking across the room at her, could see why they wanted Petra's face. It had a wild vitality that at this moment seemed unbridled. He had only seen her for a few hours here and there over the previous month because a lot of filming had been taking place out of town. He knew she didn't want him to be there and, at the same time, that she did, a kind of affirmation that he was part of her life, that he accepted what she did.

At breakfast, the first they had shared since filming began, she had run it past him. 'D'you think we could get a sitter in?' she asked, her coffee balanced between the fingers of both hands, elbows on the table. She had big shadows under her eyes and a trace of make-up at her hairline.

'We've had sitters in about three times a week for the past month. I've still got a life to lead, you know.'

'Okay.'

She had sat there in silence, blowing the top of her coffee.

'You said ...' she began.

'Yes,' he said. Because he didn't want her to remind him of what he had said, the last time the subject of a wrap party at the theatre had come up. 'Is there any way I can get caught up in your brilliant orbit?' he had asked her, and she'd said, 'Well, come to the fucking party, if that's what you want.' He'd finished up staying home, and she hadn't come back until morning. When things like this happened, he was aware of a queer electricity in the air, something that repelled him and yet attracted him to her, the way it always had. He thought she'd been with other people: it might be a man or a woman. She said on nights when they got drunk together that she wouldn't mind either, not that she'd do it of course.

'You'll come then?'

'The kids are used to Debbie.'

'Don't start on me again.'

'No, I didn't mean it like that,' he said. 'They really like her.' Debbie was the girl who had been sitting for them for the past year. It wasn't as if they were little children any more, twelve and ten, a boy and a girl.

'You work as hard at doing good as I do at acting,' she said then.

'Yes,' he said, because it was true, and he wanted to agree with her and have him back to himself. His life was full of causes. In those days, young lawyers like himself (he still thought of himself as young) jokingly called themselves storefront lawyers. They believed in helping the poor and giving the underdog a chance. A lot of his clients couldn't afford to pay him properly. He organised food parcels for their families when they were in jail and saw to it that their children went to school, even if it meant calling round to their houses and banging on the doors until the mothers got out of bed (it was

A Needle in the Heart

usually the husbands who were in jail) and dressed the kids while he waited. His luxuriant hair was thinning a little but he still wore it round his collar. He wore suits that were rumpled and he didn't care. In the lunch breaks from court he and his friends gathered in a café over a bookshop and exchanged case stories.

'I have to work,' Petra told her friends. 'Philip might be a lawyer, but he doesn't give a damn about money.'

It wasn't true about needing to work, but it was a fact that he took on cases which seemed unwinnable; that he had an affinity with people who were not particularly attractive but might be innocent. You don't have to be good looking to be innocent, he said. He suspected that there was a raffish charm to this that she had still not fathomed; it kept them together when other things failed. As for the money, his father-in-law had paid for the house they lived in. They had looked at it just as a fun thing, and dreamed about how they could scratch a deposit together for it. Of course Petra had told her parents when they were up visiting for one of the wedding rehearsals, and that was their present: the title to the house. The house was full of newly delivered furniture and there was a car in the garage. There were things Philip didn't want, wouldn't have chosen.

'I don't want it,' he said at the time. 'I never asked for any of this.'

'We'll send it back them,' said Petra, 'and you can spend the rest of your life chasing lawsuits for the rich and famous and licking boots. I don't care, it's your life.'

'I thought it was ours,' he'd said.

'I can't change who I am,' Petra said, 'any more than you can. That's my dowry. Anyone who got me would get the same.'

It had taken him some time to get over this, caused a bitterness that he later regretted. One day he'd woken up and thought how unfair he'd been to Petra, how he needed to recover things before it was too late. He had enjoyed the freedom of unexpected wealth. We do our own thing, they told people, we make our own choices. Sometimes it worked and other times it was awful.

He had been nursing a drink for half an hour without speaking to anyone. 'For God's sake, you're not doing your Heathcliff act, are you,' she'd said, the last time she went past him to the bathroom. 'There are heaps of people here for you to talk to.' He edged closer to the group she was in. Someone said, 'I've got this great idea for a movie. It's about a black alien in Harlem being chased by two white aliens. It's a really fantastic idea.'

'That's actually such a gross idea,' said Petra, stabbing the air with her cigarette.

Then an actor called Mel wanted to tell them about the most gross experience of *her* life, which was about going to Indonesia and being felt up by a tame orangutan. 'He knew I was a woman,' she said, 'Honestly, can you imagine having a large shaggy ape with his arms around you getting an erection?'

'Easily,' Petra said and everyone laughed.

'So what's your weird story, Petra?' asked Mel.

'Um.' Petra took a draw on her cigarette and pondered. Somebody had produced a bottle of cognac which was being passed around. A fire had been lit in the grate using Bleu de Bresse tubs for kindling. Philip felt his stomach turning over as he waited.

'Philip's mother has a needle floating around in her body that you can actually feel when it gets into her arm.'

'Oh yuck. How could that be possible? She'd be dead.'

'No,' said Petra, 'apparently it can happen. I checked it out when Philip told me about it. It's like bits of shrapnel that soldiers who've been shot at might carry inside of them. If it's blunt and it doesn't get into a vein a piece of metal can float around in someone's body for their whole life. It usually builds up a bit of fibroid tissue round it over time.'

'Couldn't it go through your heart?'

'It could but it wouldn't necessarily kill you — it might just pass through it. Could stuff up your lung though. You can feel it in her arm, can't you, Philip? You can wriggle it around.'

Philip stood up; he felt his face burning with shame.

'Haven't you actually seen it?' asked Mel.

'No, I've never met the woman.'

A Needle in the Heart

'What? Philip, is this true?'

Petra looked up and saw the space where he'd been standing. 'I'd better go,' she said.

Their bed had a big crocheted quilt over it, made with very fine yarn. It had come in the mail after their wedding. Philip said it was old-fashioned, that it wouldn't fit in with their new furniture and the modern decor. Petra left it in a cupboard for a few years and then brought it out. 'I like it,' she said. 'I want to use it.'

'That was my mother you were talking about last night,' Philip said. They were lying under the quilt, around ten o'clock in the morning. The children had made themselves breakfast and switched on television.

'So what? I mean, Philip, really, so what? I've asked you about her often enough and you just turn your back on it.'

'I told you that. What you said last night. And look at you, making a big drama out of it. A joke.'

'There are some things I don't get,' she said.

'There are some things I don't get either.'

'It's not fair to our kids. Not knowing anything.'

'Fairness doesn't come into it,' he said, drawing her closer to him. 'I never knew anything that was fair until I met you.'

'I'm tired,' she said. 'Philip, I'm tired. Help me.'

'What are you tired of?' he said, ashamed to hear the panic in his voice.

'Of being directed. Being told what to do.'

'I don't tell you what to do.'

'I didn't mean you.'

'Your work? You could stop.'

'But I don't want to. Sometimes I just don't know what you want, that's all.'

'I want you to stay with me,' he said. Simple as that. That was all he wanted.

'Oh,' Petra said. 'That. Well, of course.'

When Uncle Joe died, his son, one of Philip's first cousins, rang to tell him.

'Do you want to come to the funeral with me?' Philip asked Petra.

'You mean you'll go?' There had been other calls like this, over the years, which he had ignored.

'Yes. We can drive up tonight, stay with your folks.' He'd come to like her family well enough, had forgiven them for buying him. It could have been worse, he thought sometimes. Much worse. 'So will you come?'

'Yes,' she said, 'of course.'

'Will she be there?'

'My mother? I don't know. Perhaps.'

'Did you like your Uncle Joe?' she asked on the drive north.

Philip shrugged. 'He was a rough bastard, no worse than the rest of them. I'd rather have stayed with him than Mary, but it didn't work out. Besides, my mother didn't seem to like me staying there. As if she had the right to choose.'

Petra saw her first, at the other side of the cemetery. 'Who is that woman? I know her face.' She was looking at a plump and rolling woman, with pink-framed glasses and tinted hair.

'That's her. That's my mother,' he said.

'She was at our wedding.'

'Don't be silly.'

'Yes, she was. I saw her outside the church.'

Everyone was there. Neil and Leonie; Janet and her husband Darren, a boisterous man who kept shaking hands two or three times whenever he met someone; Marlene, who introduced herself to Petra as her sister-in-law, and her husband, Wayne, and all their children. Philip and Petra had left Jesse and Marigold at home in Wellington with Debbie who was happy to stay over and had asked if her boyfriend could spend the night.

They went back to Joe and Bunty's place for the wake. There were sponge cakes and sandwiches and cups of tea and beer laid out

A Needle in the Heart

for them on the back lawn, under the trees.

'Is it true you're a lawyer?' the cousins kept saying to Philip, in a kind of astonished wonder. 'Well, we'll know where to go next time we land ourselves a speeding ticket.' They laughed awkwardly at their own jokes.

'Aren't you on the telly?' Marlene asked Petra. 'Where are your children? You haven't left them at home, surely to goodness?'

And then there was Esme, who came to the edge of the lawn and stood looking at the gathering and turned away.

'Poor old Mum,' said Marlene. Petra could feel Philip pulling himself away from the woman. 'It's hard for her since Dad's been gone.'

'You mean Kevin's dead?'

Marlene looked at him with loathing. 'My dad. What's it to you?'

'I'm going over to say hullo,' Petra said to Philip. After a moment, he turned and followed her.

'Hullo,' Esme said. 'I was just going.'

'So are we,' said Petra. 'Can we walk with you?'

On the way home, Philip cried, wiping his face with the back of one hand while he drove. 'I don't want to think about her,' he said.

'But you do,' Petra said. 'You never stop. You never have.'

Dear Petra, Esme wrote. *I feel as if I have known you forever. I'm sure lots of people say this to you, because your face is so well known, but although I'm proud that my son is married to a person like you, this is more than about you being on the television. It is something that comes from inside me. It's something that understands why he would have looked towards you for his wife. I was once touched by a magician when I was a girl, and it changed my life forever. There is good magic and bad magic and this man brought some of both kinds to me, but I was never the same afterwards. I know about spells and how they are cast. Some spells can't be broken. I hope I hear from you some time. Yours, with love, Esme.*

'I told you she was a liar,' Philip said. 'That's an old yarn of my grandmother's about the magician, it's not her story at all. Something to do with my Auntie Pearl. The one who died. My grandmother told me she had my auntie after the magician had been to town, even though she was old. A kind of a miracle. You see, she takes everything as if its her own.'

'Yes,' said Petra. 'Yes, I see what you mean.' At the time she was working on another film. Budgets were leaner and filming schedules tighter to save money. As soon as the film was over she had a major role in a television series. She meant to write back to Esme straight away but it took her ages to get round to it. When she did she enclosed pictures of the children. Later, Esme sent her a brooch, a tangled old gold piece of jewellery that needed fixing.

Philip held it in his hand when he saw it, as if weighing it. 'Funny,' he said. 'I never knew she had this. I remember my grandmother wearing it. Well, you are a hit. I'd have thought she'd have given it to Janet.'

'I must write to her.'

'I'll fix it,' he said. 'Leave it to me.'

Esme knew he would come. She knew if she waited long enough, lived long enough, that he would come to her. The girl (for that is how she thought of Petra) had her own life. She didn't begrudge her that at all. She was pleased to get a postcard from her to say thank you for the brooch. I'll always treasure it, Petra wrote. The postcard showed racks of brightly coloured preserved fruit in jars standing at a roadside in front of a farmhouse. It had been sent from Australia where Petra was on tour. Petra was like her, but she'd got lucky: she'd married the right one, at the beginning. She'd make his life hell, but she wouldn't leave him.

Esme's apartment was in the second storey of a block of council flats. She had to climb stairs that were bare and had been pissed on, and she was afraid of some of the young people who hung round there after dark, but the view across rolling country hills was just what she liked to see and she had no great need to go out at night.

A Needle in the Heart

Her name was down on the waiting list for a ground-floor place but she didn't care if it didn't happen. Anyone stepping inside her door quickly forgot the ascent through the graffiti in the stairwell. She had turned it into a magic cave, the chairs covered with peggy square quilts, the shelves laden with bits and pieces of other peoples' lives: a silver vase from a farmhouse in Taranaki, a ruby red glass from another, a blue and white ashet from a house where the wife died, a collection of shells that she and Janet and Marlene had collected one holiday at the Mount, pot plants and photographs galore.

'I can get you somewhere better,' Philip said, when he came to visit. He had turned up unexpectedly with Jesse and Marigold.

'I wish you'd given me some warning,' she said. 'I'd have liked to have food in for them.'

'Don't worry,' he said, 'we've sussed out the fish and chip shop. They're going down the road to get some lunch, aren't you kids?'

'You tell them to be careful,' she said anxiously.

'Oh, there's worse places in Wellington,' he said. 'They'll be okay.'

So that they were alone in the flat together.

'They're beautiful,' she said. 'So handsome and tall for their age. So full of self-confidence.'

'They take after their mother.'

'Perhaps,' she said.

'About another place for you. I can afford it, you know.'

'I don't need another place. I like it here.'

'You can't.' He gestured helplessly.

'What's wrong with this?' She looked around the room and then her eye travelled to the hills beyond the window. It was spring at the time, bare trees in the distance were flushed with sweet unfolding buds. 'Pretty as a picture. I wish you children would stop nagging me.'

'Did you ever care for my father?' he said, his back to her, as if contemplating what she saw outside. She could tell he knew that he sounded banal, even a bit silly. That he couldn't help himself asking this question, and didn't know of a better way of putting it. 'You know, did you love him?'

'Of course,' she said quickly. Too quickly. She steadied herself.

'Yes,' she said. 'I did.'

He passed his hand over his head. His hair was trimmed neatly these days; in the centre of his forehead a triangle of hair grew down to a point, his scalp gleaming on either side.

'About Pearl.'

'Well, that was a long time ago,' she said, holding his gaze. 'A sister.' Not my sister, or your sister. But that old needle, the jostling bit of pain. She wondered if he would understand. About the old days, and the magic that wasn't so mysterious after all, about how Pearl had come into her life when she was still a child herself and nothing had ever healed that — and the way her mother tried to make things all right, but they never could be fixed.

'What about her?' he said. 'You left when she died.'

'Do you remember her?' Not answering him.

'Not really,' he said.

'Never mind. Look, that's her in the photograph with her boyfriend. I think he was killed at the war.'

'She was pretty.'

'Pretty enough. A bit flighty. She could sing. You wouldn't believe how long she could hold a high note.'

'I see.' From the way he said it, she wondered what he knew, what he had already worked out for himself. There was a stamping of feet on the stairs leading up to the apartment as his children returned.

After they had all gone, she lay down on the bed, overtaken by a kind of dizziness. It wasn't new to her. It amazed her that so far she had survived death's steady rhythm, that she had out-lived so many people. She heard a car start below. Somewhere in her old aching bitten heart, she thought, there he is, there he goes, my clever boy.

He would, she believed, have some secrets of his own.

SILVER-TONGUED

A few years ago, I met a young man who, had I been a younger woman, I might have considered to be romantically inclined towards me. As it was, he was looking for someone to listen to his troubles. He chose me because I had told him a dramatic story in a bar in Banff, about a night when I raced across a darkened countryside in a state of blind panic, totally lost in a place I knew well, looking for and continually missing the road that would lead me to the side of a woman I loved, who was dying. Although this happened on the other side of the world from Canada, I think he was struck by the immediacy of the way I told the story.

'You tell this as if it happened quite recently,' he said.

'Well, it's ten days ago now.'

'Ten days.' He looked as if he'd been stung, as if something had brushed past that was too close for comfort — all the intimations of mortality that people entertain when they are in some sort of difficulties of their own. I was with a group of writers who had just swum under the stars at an elegant spa resort where the sudden presence of a noisy uninhibited group was clearly viewed by the other bathers as an intrusion. We were hot and rosy and flushed with steam and the conversations that happen when new friendships are developing. Let's have a drink, we all said to each other, but by the time we found a bar open we'd gone off the idea and drank coffee instead, knowing we would keep ourselves awake, but needing to be alert, because we had so many revelations to make to each other. Much later in the evening, the young man and I walked back to where we were staying, arm in arm in the starlight, peeling away from the others in the group. He was dark with crinkly hair and stealthy fingers that rested on my inner arm. We had been told to watch out for rutting elks which might charge us if they were disturbed. Elks have rights over humans in Banff. They walk down the middle of the streets while motorists wait, and stalk through gardens and backyards.

The previous week, I had been on another tour, back home, in New Zealand. In case this sounds like coincidence, I should say that this is how writers earn much of their keep: they go from one place to another, talking about their work to whoever will listen, while booksellers stand behind a little table and exhort the audience to buy books. It's not as bad as it sounds. Some of the best days of my life have been spent in halls and libraries and rooms set aside in old country pubs, talking to people who love books the way I do. I would go even if it were not a necessity, although, that once, I would rather have just sat with my aunt. I had been sent a message that she was ill and didn't have long to live.

This was no ordinary aunt, if such a person exists. I mean, she wasn't someone else's mother — she had no children of her own — and I've often thought of her as another mother of my own. That's what I would call her when I spoke at her funeral. Of course, I felt the pull of needing to be in two places at once. But I had a new book out and I'd promised my publishers I would go on this tour. And there was a real coincidence, one of those elements of random chance that

Silver-Tongued

seem so significant they are like an omen, an instruction in themselves. The tour was of the Waikato, where Flo had lived for most of her life, and when I, from time to time, had lived too. That green heart of dairy country, full of pastel-coloured cows with contemplative eyes. All the venues, except one at the end, were within driving distance of the cottage hospital where my aunt was being nursed. It had been arranged that I would drive a rented car from one place to another, before flying on to the last town. There was a serendipity about all of this, and the idea of calling off the tour didn't really arise.

I began with a visit to the hospital. As I arrived, I heard Flo's voice, frail and yet fierce, echoing down the corridor. She cried *come and get me, come and get* me in an incessant high drone. Her cloudy eyes didn't recognise me straight away, although there was a hint of their old blackness beneath the cataracts.

When she did, she said, more calmly, 'You've come for me then.'

'I've come to see you.'

'Just to see me?'

'Hush,' I said, 'it'll be all right. I love you.'

She turned her head the other way. 'Love. Don't talk to me about love,' she said.

I thought, then, that I had always just been coming and going in my aunt's life, I was never permanent. Yet for as long as I could remember, she had been waiting for me. But at least I came back, whenever I could. In those last days before she died, she would wake with a start, from bouts of laboured breathing, and I would say 'I'm here.'

'I'm here,' she would mimic, and yet there was something easier about her breathing every time she realised I really was there beside her.

On that first evening, the night nurse said she needed morphine. 'Personally, I think the pain relief that's been offered her is too light,' she said. Every we time we tried to turn Flo, she screamed *please please leave me leave me please leave me*.

'What can we do about it?' I asked the nurse. I liked this young woman; she was very small and neat in her movements, almost as if she was a dancer, which I learned later she had trained to be, until her ankles lost their shape.

'Get a doctor,' she said. 'You're the next of kin, if you say she needs a doctor we can call one.'

'Do it,' I said.

The doctor, a young Indian man, took one look and then drew me outside out into the corridor. 'As much as she needs,' he said, 'as much as it takes. But you must tell her.'

I went in and sat down beside her and said, 'Flo, can you hear me? The doctor says morphine.'

Her eyes widened. 'Morphine?' she breathed, as if being offered a love potion. She must have known its power: she had nursed more than one patient towards their last seductive inhalation.

Only this morphine was neither inhaled nor injected but rather drops placed on her tongue. 'Bitter,' said Flo, 'bitter.' It reminded me of one of her sayings. 'Life's had a few bitter pills,' she would say, 'but you get by.' She slept for a while. When she woke the morphine had begun to wear off and it was time for her to be turned again.

Please. No, not that.

And then I understood: it was at the height of each turn, the moment before her body pivoted down, that she began to scream and her free arm to flap wildly. When I caught it in my own, it was like a cold old fish flipper. 'You're afraid of falling, aren't you?' I said.

And she agreed that yes she was, and if I held her hand, she wouldn't fall. It was much the same as walking over a height: that sense of relinquishing control, fear of abandonment. I suffer from that too.

I said to the nurse, who was called Joy, 'How long do you think this will take? I mean, I don't want to see her go on suffering like this.'

Joy gave me a careful serious scrutiny. 'Do you mean,' she said eventually, 'do people go on with their lives, or keep vigils like our grandmothers did?'

'Yes, something like that,' I said. 'I want to be here for her when she needs me.'

Silver-Tongued

'I think you're doing the best you can,' she said. 'I can't tell you when it will happen exactly. Death's no flash in the pan for the old. It needs a lead-up, a preparation time, that says it's done when it's ready, not when it's convenient.'

'Like baking?'

'I guess that's a way of looking at it.'

'That's Flo,' I said. 'She was a terrific cook. You should have tried her orange loaf.'

I saw Joy look at my aunt in a new less clinical way, as if she could see beyond the helpless creature she had become, to someone younger, more vital — a glimpse perhaps, of the person I still saw.

'You should get some rest and do whatever it is you have to do,' she said.

Early the next morning, as dawn was breaking, I heard Flo again, before I saw her, only this time she was singing *Look for the silver lining, whene'er a cloud appears in the blue. Remember somewhere, the sun is shining And so the right thing to do is make it shine for you.* Her room looked out on a grove of orange trees; I could see rabbits skipping beneath them.

After I had seen Flo, heard her singing, and spoken quietly with her, I drove north to give a lunchtime reading from my work, and when that was over, I drove back again. The colourful Waikato landscape is like a sky banner: it should be trailing itself behind a helicopter. The grass has a green shimmer like Thai silk. On good days, like the ones that followed me through most of that week, the buttercup yellow of the sun shines out of an electric blue sky. Then there's the way gardens grow there like tornadoes of colour. But there's an unpredictability about it, too — the way passing clouds can turn the landscape black, and the night so dark that starlight is not always enough to show the way.

I decided to stay on in the town for as long as I could. I took a room at the edge of the park overlooking the thermal spa resort. I was struck, just a week or so later, by the way the earth is connected, when I found myself in another thermal town on the opposite side of the world. This one, near the hospital, used to be the haunt of fashionable people early in the twentieth century. They had built pavilions and a tea kiosk called Cadman House. I have a white china teapot stand, with a picture of the teahouse drawn in worn gold gilt, which I bought for a dollar in a secondhand shop. In the picture, a woman in a long full skirt is playing tennis on a court in front of the kiosk. This was just what Flo would have loved: it was like the beginning of her own life and my mother's, and their sisters as well.

That afternoon, Flo and I talked for almost the last time. Mostly we spoke about old times, times when I was a child and used to come by bus from up north, and she'd come to meet me; the time I'd lived with her after I left school, the way I'd driven her crazy when I was a teenager, and how things pass.

'Through my journey of life, I've simply liked to help people,' she said. And in a way it was true. There was nothing grudging about what she remembered that afternoon.

'I should be getting along,' she said, as if she was visiting me. 'Theo will be waiting for me.' She began to knead my thumb between her own and her forefinger with a strong clawing intensity.

'I reckon it's time you went to him,' I said. ' Forty years. You've kept him waiting long enough.'

'He'll be there.'

'What will you say to him?'

'What time's the quinella?' she said, and gave a gentle snicker of pleasure.

Towards five in the evening, something altered: she slipped into unconsciousness and her breathing became shallower; at times I thought she had stopped altogether. I didn't call anyone because I believed this was it, the moment she had waited for, when I would be with her, and she would simply let go.

Only she didn't die, she went on living for several more days. In the mornings when I went back, she had begun to shout, wails of grief echoing through the corridors of the small hospital. *Do not go gently into that dark night* I said grimly to myself.

It seemed that it was only the beginning.

Silver-Tongued

What followed for me was a kind of dreamtime, a compulsion to keep going that I still can't explain. Driving, speaking, coming back again in the middle of the night to be with my aunt. What did I say to people I met? So you want to be a writer. Well, you must learn to live with yourself, however difficult that might be at times, because you're on your own in this job; you need to make space in your life, settle on your priorities. A writer's life is not spent in an ivory tower. Learn to accept that real life is full of interruptions. You have children? Yes, of course, many of us do. Write for fifteen minutes a day — it's better than nothing at all. No, I agree, this is not about craft and style, but it's about how to survive, which is the best I can tell you right now. Can I guarantee this recipe for success? No, no of course not. Nothing is certain. Forgive me, I have to leave now.

Not all of my vigils were alone. (What had Joy seen in me that made her so sure I would keep watch, as my grandmother might have done?) I got to know others on the staff — Betty and June I remember in particular. They were both capable women; unlike Joy, they nursed part time and worked at home on their farms. They chatted about their lives and families and asked me about what it was like to be well known, to be in the papers. I said that, when it all came down to it, it was pretty much like other people's lives; certainly, the big important things were, like birth and death. They said, yes, they could see that, and wasn't it strange how everyone was interested in much the same things. She was so proud of you, they said, looking down at Flo's inert body. It's as well she had you.

As well as these nurses, there was my aunt's neighbour, who had lived close by for several years, a middle-aged woman called Pamela with dark hair swept up in frosted peaks, and beautiful country casual clothes. She organised speakers for the Lyceum Club and was on the local National Party branch committee. I could see why my aunt would have got along with her, although the unease between Pamela and me was palpable. I was the sort of woman she could never trust. I saw her eyeing my appearance and comparing it with her own. Mostly I wore a loose-fitting roll-neck grey pullover made of fine Merino wool, black pants and a gay floating blue and yellow scarf, which I didn't change from day to day, because I was travelling light and fast. For my part, there may have been some element of jealousy present, because it was clear that, in some ways, Pamela knew Flo better than I did. She had shopped for her, cut her toenails, intimate things like that. And she'd collected the mail every day for Flo, which meant she knew exactly how often I wrote.

When Flo was conscious, she would stop shouting long enough to look at me with a certain malice.

'And where have you been?' she said, each time, glaring through one half-closed eye.

'I was just out for a while, you knew I'd come.'

'I'm here,' she said in her mimicking piping voice.

'Oooh,' said Pamela on an indrawn breath, on one of these afternoons.

'Don't be upset,' said, Joy, who had arrived with a damp flannel for me to wipe Flo's face. 'This isn't the Flo you know. She's left.' I knew what she meant, but Pamela looked bewildered.

'I think I'll go home for a shower,' she said.

'What a good idea,' I said, trying not to sound too eager.

Joy lingered in the room, looking at objects taken from Flo's house. Pamela had brought them there, some weeks before, as a kind of pathetic reassurance to Flo that living in the hospital room was like being at home. Not that I disapproved — I would have done the same thing myself, had I been around to do it. There were bits of pretty porcelain china with floral motifs and a little silver-rimmed vase with a hand-painted Egyptian scene on it that Flo had been given for her twenty-first birthday. But there could never be enough in that room to explain what Flo was really like, had been like for over ninety years of life. Joy studied Flo and Theo's wedding photograph. 'How pretty she was. What a stylish, vivacious looking woman,' she remarked.

'She reminded me of the queen,' I said.

'Really?'

I couldn't help elaborating. 'I met the queen once,' I said. 'The tips of her gloves stuck out beyond her fingers, so I simply had to wriggle the soft white kid. From the look in her eyes I realised I'd held on longer than I should have. But I wanted to say, you're so like my Aunt Flo. I didn't, of course, because she might have taken it as rudeness, or too personal.'

'She might have taken it as a compliment.'

'I doubt it. Or if she did, she would have said nothing. They say she never acknowledges compliments, simply accepts them as of right. Or she might have said, "Why? Why do you think this?" and I would have had to explain that her skin was of a similar texture and she wore her hats at much the same angle. Although when she was young, Flo wore her hats much more rakishly than the queen. I could have told her that when Flo smiled in unguarded moments, the dour look she often had melted away. Like hers.'

'What did you really do?'

'Oh I smiled nervously, like most people do, and made a funny awkward curtsey, the way we were taught to at school when we won a prize.'

'If I'd gone on to be a dancer, I might have got to meet the queen too,' said Joy.

'You met Flo instead,' I said with a laugh, but when I looked at Joy's face, I saw how thoughtless I had been: she did have a sense of loss which she had hoped I might acknowledge.

To cover the discomfort between us, I set out to describe my aunt's house, the one Theo built for her at the end of the Depression when the building trade was slow and it gave his men work. He could still afford to buy Flo a diamond ring, if not as big as the Ritz, at least the Nottingham Castle Hotel. The house was expansive, flowing out in all directions from the central heart of the kitchen. There were several places where you could be by yourself: the formal sitting-room, used only on Sundays; the closed-in sunporch that was big enough to hold a bed; the small pretty bedroom that I occupied when I was there; Flo and Theo's own bedroom with a dark dresser and a fat mattress on the bed which Flo never changed in the forty years she was a widow; the dining room with a copper coal scuttle gleaming on the hearth, and Theo's miniature spirits collection lining the head-high shelves on the walls. Yet in spite of its generous proportions and spaciousness, it was a dark house. For a start, the walls were all stained timber panelling, and then Flo kept the brown holland blinds three-quarters drawn in every room — all day, every day, until it was time to close them right up again at night.

Theo wasn't young when he married Flo, and she made him wait. She said she'd marry him, and then she changed her mind. For a while, after he'd built the house, his own mother and father lived in it, so she was not its first mistress and I think that may have had something to do with the trouble between her and Theo later on. Certainly, the parents weren't happy either, when she changed her mind for a second time, and said she'd marry him after all.

All this thinking on Flo's part took some years. She was, perhaps, thinking about, and remembering, Wilf Morton.

My mother told me about Wilf Morton and Flo. The family lived on my grandfather's sheep station, one of the big prosperous runs of the 1900s. As well as my mother, the youngest, there was Helena, the beautiful frail daughter, Monica, the clever one, and Flo, the funny laughing girl, at least when she was a child. My mother had been irrepressible and cheeky and was sometimes slapped by her big sisters for bad behaviour. She rewarded them by watching everything they did, especially when they brought young men to stay at the farm. Later, she paid them back in a different way, by giving birth to me while they remained childless. Not that they saw it that way: they envied but never disliked her. I brought my mother status she never anticipated when her sisters shouted and pleaded with her to leave them alone and mind her own business.

Wilf Morton was Flo's fiancé, and he stayed on and off at the farm for years, without showing any sign of setting the day for a wedding. Other young men who stayed at the house lent a hand with the stock, took their turn in the shearing sheds, trying out their hands as fleecos, collecting up the wool as it peeled off the sheep's backs, dragging it away in preparation for storing it in the presses.

Not Wilf.

Wilf was always playing tennis. He stayed around the house

wearing whites, the extravagant cuffs of his trousers turned up so they wouldn't brush the grass. His hair looked as if it was permed; his eyebrows beneath a long white forehead were dark and straight as pencil lead; on the little finger of his left hand he wore a signet ring inset with a grape-coloured garnet. Even if you couldn't see the ring you could tell he was flashy by the way the men in the family looked at him. Beside him, Flo looked a trifle plain, although she wore the most fashionable clothes of any of the sisters, and she was the one with a dimple in her chin. She also got herself engaged to Wilf, although her father didn't approve of the match, said he didn't feel he knew enough about the man and, since she was a girl who liked nice things, would love be enough? But the fact was, when he was around she shone as if lit within, and when he wasn't there, she was withdrawn and miserable, refusing to take part in conversation at dinner. This led my grandmother to say to her one day, when Wilf had been absent for a week or more, and nobody was sure where he was, 'Really, Flo, I'll be pleased when you're married and out of it.' This was an unusually sharp rebuke for her to give Flo, who was her favourite child, apart from her son Martin who was, well, simply a boy.

The next day, all Flo's sulks, as her mother had started calling these black moods, had disappeared. Wilf arrived back at the farm driving a new Model T Ford and bringing with him two men and a boy. The men were very well dressed, the younger man with his hat pushed back on his head so that the brim tilted upwards. He walked around the farm with his arms folded and an inscrutable look on his face, while the other man linked his fingers in front of his chest and made jokes. The boy with them was different from the boys on the farm: he wore his shirt open down his chest and put a hand on one hip and crossed his legs and pointed his foot like a dancer. Wilf tousled his hair and said, 'You're a real little bounder, aren't you?'

As usual, Flo's face glowed at the sight of Wilf. She must have known he was coming because she was dressed up in a pretty flapper dress with a long straight line to the knee and then a band from which fell several straight pleats. She wore white stockings and strapped shoes.

What were these men doing at the farm? They didn't say immediately, although it emerged that one was a stock and station agent and the other a man from the bank. They were planning to foreclose on the farm, but that was a common enough story in the years that followed. What mattered was why Wilf Morton was with them.

'I'm going to spend the summer teaching this young man to play tennis,' he said indicating the boy, whose name was Ralph. Ralph had a nearly grown-up sister called Annabelle who would be home from school for the holidays soon, and their father, the bank manager, was keen that they improve their athletic skills. Wilf had been offered a live-in job coaching them. Wilf smiled round the table when he told the family this.

It was clear that this was the first time Flo had heard about the arrangement. 'Does this mean you'll be going away?' she asked.

Wilf looked sideways at her. 'Well, I guess so. I mean, I can't teach Ralph and Annabelle here, can I?'

'So you're going to live at their place?'

There was a long silence while everyone examined their plates for a last speck of gravy. The rat, my mother said, when she recounted this. He knew my grandfather was going under and he'd found himself a better prospect. Not that she could see it, poor fool. My mother had a strong sisterly affection for Flo, but her later position in the family had given her a kind of second sight about her sisters, as if she had become the wise adult.

'For a while,' Wilf said. 'It's a job.' He sent one of his wide disarming smiles in the bank manager's direction.

Flo put her napkin to her mouth as if she was going to be sick, and stood up.

'Flo,' said her mother. 'Manners.'

'I thought you'd be pleased,' said Wilf.

Anyone looking round that room would have known that the person who was most pleased was my grandfather. His own grief and sense of betrayal would come later, when he learned what the visit was really about, and how the bank manager and his adviser were calculating the number of wool bales left in the shed that he couldn't

Silver-Tongued

pay anyone to take away. Flo walked out of the room without a backward glance and stayed in her room for several hours. She drew the curtains and when Wilf went to the door and called her she didn't come.

'Flo,' he said. 'I'm off now. Aren't you going to say goodbye?'

When she didn't answer, he said, 'All right then. All right.'

The Model T roared into life, and some muted goodbyes were called.

'Just leave her,' my grandmother said. 'Let her alone.'

'It was a queer sort of business,' my mother said.

I went to live with Flo and Theo after I left school, so I could get an office job — good skills for life. I learned to type and write letters for an accounting firm, and gained a working knowledge of how to handle money. I had money of my own to buy clothes and jewellery, which gave me a happily independent feeling.

Theo said, when it was suggested I live there, that it would be a good thing for Flo. 'She's come a bit unstuck,' he told my mother, scratching his thin sandy hair. He didn't say this in front of Flo, of course. My mother had come down to talk over the idea with the pair of them. I think she was worried about my going there, but Flo had written and suggested it, and my parents were at a loss to know what to do with me, an awkward girl, described as 'having brains' who refused to take up any of the standard careers open to girls in those days.

Theo had a strong builder's face, with lips worn thin by the elements, clamped around the twenty or thirty tailor-mades he smoked a day. He recited his Masonic pledges in the bath behind closed doors and visited his mother at her house along the road every other evening. The two houses were at each end of a long street in a town that was rich in memorials, sparse in trees, with three hotels and a railway station straddling its main artery.

I liked it all well enough in the beginning. My aunt was enraptured by my presence, as if now she had me all to myself, and I really lived with her. She planned my meals with care, and made my favourite foods, and worried about who I would marry. Although I was only sixteen, she had her eye on a young man called Tommy Harrison. He was a persistent lugubrious boy who wore a brown hat when he went to town on Fridays, the important day of the week, when farmers attended to their business. His father was a rich farmer, and Flo set her heart on my making a match of it with him, as if I could somehow rescue the family fortunes, however belatedly. He called at the office to bring the farm accounts up to date on a regular basis, and asked me to dances, in a whisper, as he handed over the invoices. I could see his palms sweating. I went once or twice, but found excuses after that.

At the same time my aunt was doting on me, I was learning other things.

I thought Flo was happily married. I thought she had everything a woman could want. But when I went to live with her, rather than just being there on holiday, I found out things were different.

Some of the problem, at least, appeared to revolve around Theo's mother, now a widow, in that house at the end of the street. Theo would say he was just popping in to visit his Ma on the way home, and then he'd stop on until eight o'clock or so, while the dinner Flo cooked him ruined in the oven. Often his mother would feed him the food that Flo had brought her at the weekends. Theo's mother, now widowed, had been moved sideways from her expectations, when Flo took over her house, and she wasn't going to let the matter rest. She was used to laying claim to her son. Theo worshipped her; it was that common male problem of wanting to spend his life divided between two women, only this wasn't about a wife and a mistress. There would be quarrels when Theo came home late, and silences that lasted between them for days, then Flo would relent.

'I suppose I'd better call on the old bid,' she'd say in her most vicious voice. 'Are you coming with me? You'll give me an excuse to get away.' Flo would normally visit her mother-in-law at the weekend, when I couldn't plead work.

We always set off for his mother's house laden with cakes and casseroles that Flo made in preparation for her visits. I can see now that food was Flo's vocabulary for an inner life, a way of saying, at best, that she truly cared for you; at least, that she was making a peace offering.

'She tarts herself up, that girl does,' Theo's mother said to Flo one day when I'd gone on a visit. She usually spoke of me in the third person. I was wearing my latest acquisition, a pair of wheel-shaped clip-on earrings made of blue feathers with diamanté centres.

'Don't speak like that,' said Flo, looking at me. 'She's like a daughter to me.' I felt her edge her chair protectively towards me.

'Well, really. I do beg your pardon,' said the mother-in-law, snorting. She had a lined face like a small old berry, very pale, and dusty with powder.

'I'll put your cakes away,' said Flo. She clattered tins as she got them out of a kitchen cupboard and banged the lids as she shut them. She draped a clean tea towel over the enamel casserole dish she had stood on the bench. From the way her lips were pressed together it was clear Flo wasn't planning any more conversation.

'You're so kind to me,' her mother-in-law said, in an exaggerated way. 'What's in the casserole today?' You could tell the way she really wanted to know: an old greedy expression glanced across her face.

'Chicken.'

'You sure you haven't put liquor in it? I thought I tasted liquor in the last one you brought.'

'I wouldn't waste booze on you.'

'I thought I smelled it. I go to church you know,' she said, turning to me.

I nodded, without speaking. I thought that anything I said would be wrong.

'A pity you don't have a Frigidaire,' Flo snapped. 'This food won't last five minutes in the heat.'

'Oh well, who's a spoilt girl? We know you have the best of everything.'

'Theo'd buy you one in a flash,' said Flo. 'You know you only have to snap your fingers and you can have what you like.'

'I'm too old to be filling up expensive contraptions like that. Tell that girl to help you more.'

'We're getting out of here,' Flo said ominously. She snatched up her bags and pulled her cardigan off the back of her chair. 'Come on.' She indicated the door.

'Feathers and paint, make a little girl just what she ain't,' said the older woman, as we were leaving. 'I guess she's better than nothing.' She slammed the door shut, as if afraid Flo might hit her.

But Flo was staring straight ahead as she marched down the street with me at her heels, and I saw that there were tears glistening in her eyes. 'I've had a few bitter pills in my time,' she said, as if her jaw was aching, 'but that really has to be the limit.'

The barren daughter-in-law. The childless woman. I see now how I was her trophy child, her daughter for the moment.

Of course she had wanted children. Once when I was visiting, we chatted about people I'd known in the town.

'What became of Tommy Harrison?' I asked. My children were playing in the garden where we could watch them. The sun was melting out of the sky and I thought the children should come in and put on more sunblock but Flo said, 'Oh leave them, the sun's good for them,' the way she said, 'Oh leave the young people alone, let them smoke,' though she didn't herself and I think would have hated it if I did.

'Tommy Harrison? Oh, he's around. Full of himself.'

'I could have told you that.'

'Well, never mind. I'm glad you didn't marry him.'

'Why? You were keen enough at the time.'

'He didn't have any children. You might have ended up the same as me.'

'Oh Flo,' I said. I didn't know whether I wanted this conversation to go on, but this was the moment she had chosen to tell me. About the missed periods for a month or two, and the heavy swelling of her breasts, all the hope that followed her round and then the stains in her panties, a day of cramps, and it was over every time. And how this happened, not once, but often — endless farewells in the bathroom.

'Oh well,' she said, 'you know, there've been a few bitter pills. We were too old, me and Theo. I don't know what I was thinking of, that he could give me kids. Don't you think those children of yours should come in out of the sun?'

'Yes,' I said, relieved.

She had a sliver of snot on her lip that she wiped away with the back of her hand.

'Hayfever,' she said.

Not everything in that house was darkness, but when it came, it fell quickly. In their early years together, Flo and Theo loved the races and dressed up whenever there was a weekend race meeting. This went on for years, until suddenly Flo wanted a change, and they stopped. But they'd decorated their lavatory like one of those joke toilets, with pictures of racehorses, dozens of them, especially of the famous Phar Lap, whose heart, it was discovered when he died, weighed a whole fourteen pounds, as well as with cartoons that reflected their enthusiastic support for the right-wing politicians of the day.

And, deep in the house, there was a wide passage with a recess, which was like Flo's throne room. A low seat made of plaited leather on a carved wooden frame sat beside a highly polished mahogany table. On the table stood three objects: a brass box containing photographs of the family, several of me as an infant, and of the farm where she grew up; a swirling cloudy green Crown Devon jug, kept filled with flowers (hydrangeas were her favourite); and the telephone. Flo sat on the low seat and talked on the phone for hours, either to her older sisters, or to her best friend Glad Dean with whom she'd nursed in the tuberculosis sanatorium during the war.

One evening, while I was talking on the phone, I let one of my new silver bracelets rest on the table. When Flo called out, that dinner was ready, I swung around from the table, scraping the bracelet along the surface and leaving a deep gouge behind.

'You stupid cow,' Flo shouted at me. 'Stupid, stupid, stupid.'

And then she didn't speak to me for a week. Theo slunk around the house not speaking either.

As Theo was taking his lunchbox out of Flo's Frigidaire one morning, I said, 'I'm sorry, Uncle Theo.' Flo was taking a bath and the door to the bathroom was firmly closed. Suddenly the big sprawling house seemed too small for the three of us and I had been thinking that if things didn't improve soon I should probably pack up and go back up north to my parents. I felt joyless and as stupid as Flo had accused me of being. I had thought that Theo liked me living with them but now I felt unwelcome. He gazed through me as if I wasn't there.

'About the table. I didn't mean to do it.'

He shook his head as if to clear it. 'What about the table?'

'About the scratch.'

'I don't know what you're talking about.' He was a bulky man, a bit big around the ears, with a small fold of fat between the base of his head and the beginning of his neck. He put his arm around me with an awkward little squeeze. 'C'mon little tart, you're doing all right.'

It was Friday when this happened. In the evening he came home very late.

'Been at our mother's, have we?' Flo said, without looking up from the bench. His dinner was like a mud cake on a plate.

'No, as a matter a fact, I havven been to Ma's.' He walked down the passage towards the bedroom.

I thought she would stay still in the kitchen but she followed him, telling him to speak to her. 'Well, just say something will you,' she shouted.

His voice when he answered her was too low to hear, but I heard hers, full of contempt. 'You're drunk. Think again.'

Then she said something else I didn't hear.

'It's not my fault,' he said.

So any number of things could have been going on in that house and the scratch on the table was beginning to seem like the least of them.

Flo kept up her silence for a week. She spoke to neither Theo nor me, not even pass the butter stuff. Flo would suffer and eat dry bread rather than ask anyone for anything.

Then, as suddenly as all this had started, she was herself again. She resumed the preparation of my favourite foods and was seemingly peaceful, at least with me, until I left at the end of the year to go to another job, further south, which my parents had arranged. In the week before my departure, Flo moved back inside herself, although not in the same furious way that she had before. It was more as if she was resigned to something over which, again, she had no control.

Less than a year after I left, Theo complained one morning of not feeling well. He went to the doctor, and discovered he was dying. He fought a brief battle, which hardly seemed like a fight, with a rapid moving cancer that had started in his prostate.

The day after the funeral, Helena, the beautiful, sickly sister, arrived at Flo's house with all her bags, and said she'd come to stay for a few weeks.

'You don't need to, I can manage,' Flo said.

'I doubt it,' Helena said. She stayed for twenty years, until she, too, died. After Theo's death Flo turned her back on nursing, and took a job in the county office, keeping minutes for all the council meetings. She had talents nobody had ever guessed. In the evenings she went home and cooked Helena's meals, and although Helena talked in a lively fashion whenever I was there, I never heard Flo speak to her directly.

Once Theo had gone — a builder one day, a man dead and buried a month later — Flo discovered him, as if he'd been the love of her life. I think this was a fiction. A reconstruction. People believe what they want, I told my audiences on that tour. You can say what you like about the boundaries between life and art: people decide what they believe and that's that.

Which I have supposed is what Flo did, what kept her going, through the years with Helena, and the years beyond that.

Flo's poor old rotting hulk had a stale smell hovering about it that no amount of bathing and attention would remove. She breathed in shallow puffs beneath an oxygen mask, not appearing to know us or hear us.

I was due to appear on a panel of writers in the town of Cambridge that night, nearly an hour's drive away. I was ready to move on. The driving backwards and forwards to the hospital had taken a toll. I spoke in a kind of dream when I stood up in front of an audience. In my head, I knew Flo must die soon, but how long is soon? I was going abroad, and in a day or so there would be nothing for it: I would have to say goodbye. I was to go to Gisborne the next day, the last stage of my journey, and then home.

'I'll stay with Flo,' Pamela said, when I explained the situation. I could see how reproachfully she looked at me. I had changed into clothes more appropriate for an evening gathering: a long dark skirt with a fuchsia-coloured jacket.

'I might see if I can get a later flight tomorrow,' I said. 'I'll stay over there tonight, and come back first thing in the morning.' Putting it off.

I met the group in Cambridge and checked into the room next to Davina Worth, who is a playwright. She writes monologues for solo voice, some of which she performs herself. She's got clear green eyes and dark hair streaked with grey that falls from a centre parting. She's a great person to be around, a formidable presence on stage. I began to think I need not have worried: she and the poet who had come as well would be enough in themselves. I saw the way Davina looked at me. 'What have you been doing to yourself?'

I tried to explain, told her how I might still have to go back to the hospital that night. I'd rung and spoken to Joy, and she'd been noncommittal when I asked her how Flo was.

'You'd tell me if she got worse, wouldn't you?'
'Yes,' she agreed.
'Promise?'
'I do, yes, I promise.'
'You're driving yourself nuts,' Davina said, when I relayed this

conversation to her. 'You're going to Canada next week. Stop doing this to yourself.'

The booksellers sold fifty-seven copies of our books that evening in Cambridge. 'Well done,' they said and gave us cheques for our appearance fees.

'I should go back to the hospital,' I said.

'You're exhausted,' said Davina. 'You need to come out with us. When did you last eat?'

She and the poet and I ended up in a café, a reckless kind of place, full of celebrating Cambridge horse breeders having a night out, because someone had sold a horse for a million dollars that day. I can't remember what I ate, but I drank two glasses of wine and laughed a lot. Davina told us a story about when she'd done some training in Australia for the theatre (she'd decided that she was better at writing for it than acting), and she'd rehearsed Ophelia. No matter how hard she tried, she couldn't find her way into the character, which didn't surprise me. Davina is too much of an extrovert, too thoroughly optimistic about life. 'I couldn't get it right. I said to the director, this Englishman with his broad Midlands accent, I said, "Barney, what am I going to do?" And Barnie just threw his hands in the air, and said, "I don't *know*, perhaps you should think of yourself as a cross between a piece of jasmine and a booterfly."'

I laughed so hard I cried, that terrible cracking up sort of laughter, that isn't about humour; it's painful and uncontrollable. The others looked at me with concern. When I'd recovered myself, I said abruptly, 'I'll ring the hospital.'

My cellphone wasn't working when I tried to get through. 'I'll phone from the motel when we get back,' I said.

Davina said, 'You needed to do this. What you've been doing is too hard on you. You have to stop.'

The motelier had stayed up for me. 'I've got a message for you,' he said. 'Its about a relative of yours. I'm sorry, it's bad news. She's not expected to live through the night.'

'I'm away,' I said to Davina.

'I'll come with you,' she said.

'No. No, you won't. I'm going to sleep at the hospital.'

'Shall I let the organisers know you're not going to Gisborne tomorrow?'

'I don't know,' I said. 'I'll let tomorrow take care of itself.'

I set out into the dark Waikato night.

Five or six kilometres out of town the emergency petrol light came on. Slowly, and very carefully, I turned and drove back to town. Everything had turned into a terrible slow motion drama.

The first petrol station I came to was self-service only at that hour of the night. The young man behind the steel grilles wouldn't come out for me.

'My aunt is dying,' I said.

'That's what they all say,' he replied. He had a cold lunar face with shadows under his eyes. I couldn't get the bowser to work.

'Please,' I said, crying and shaking the grille. 'Please. Flo's dying.'

'I'm under orders,' he said.' He was eating a steaming pie out of a wrapper.

I said, 'I won't hurt you. I gave a talk here tonight.'

He didn't even answer me.

I drove further up the town, further away, in the opposite direction from Flo, but I found another petrol station and was able to fill the car. An hour had passed since I set out. Then I turned the car into a racing boat of a vehicle, opening her out on the long straight roads as if she was under sail with the wind behind her. Was it the wine? Confusion? Terror at not, in the end, being where I had said I would be? Not being there.

And where have you been?

I'm here, Flo, I'm here, in the middle of a dark road and my eyes are blinded by tears and I cannot see the familiar landmarks.

I had missed a vital turn-off and suddenly I was spinning again in the opposite direction from where I was supposed to be going. I reversed, tried to retrace my route, found I'd gone in a loop and was heading towards the nearby city of Hamilton, down the motorway with no off ramp for several kilometres. I came to a roundabout, slowed, understood at last where I was, and set off again. Two hours.

The car flying — a hundred and twenty on the clock, a hundred and thirty, a hundred and forty. I remembered Flo ringing me one evening years before, after she had driven her ancient Mini Minor into a ditch somewhere round here. It had floated in the water, rocking gently, until someone pulled her back to safety. The car went again when it was dried out but the council office wouldn't give Flo her licence when it came up for renewal at the end of the year. 'You'd think after all those years I worked for them, they'd have had more respect,' she said at the time. 'Young whippersnappers.'

A hundred and sixty. I had never driven this fast before. I started to sing to keep myself awake. During the previous winter I had taught a creative writing class. On the last day, my students had sung a waiata, a song of respect and thanks. I was honoured by them. They sang *te aroha, te whakapono, te rangimarie, tatou tatou e* and that is what I sang. It means, roughly speaking, in love, in peace, in faith, all of us, all of us. I don't think she would have liked the song much but somehow I thought that if I sang and sang it, it would sustain me and take me to where she was, and I would, after all, be *there*. That when she said, 'And where have you been?' I would say, *I'm here*.

And then I was there, and at the front of the little country hospital, in a pool of light, clustered on the verandah, I saw a knot of women standing, and I knew that I was too late, that it had already happened.

Pamela came forward to embrace me, and I pushed her away.

'She went at seven minutes after midnight.' It was twelve fifteen and frost was gathering under the trees outside the hospital.

I walked down the corridor without looking at any of them. I didn't say I was sorry that I hadn't been there.

'I'm here, Flo,' I said. But she was not going to reply, not ever. My poor old wounded starfish, her hands together, fingers pointed towards me, poor old fish, stranded for good.

I shouted at her, 'Why didn't you wait?'

I tore some flowers out of a vase and strewed them all around her. When I came through and joined the others somebody said, 'We'll get you a cup of tea.' They looked frightened of me. Even Joy.

I told them I didn't want any damn tea and walked out of the hospital and got into the car. Nobody tried to stop me, though I think now they probably should. I drove very slowly as if I was a blind person who'd been allowed out on the road. When I got back to the motel I found I'd locked my keys inside my room. I banged on Davina's door but she didn't hear me. It was three o'clock in the morning. I thought I should sleep in the car, but then I thought I was grown-up now, the next in line to die, one of the old people, and I rang the motelier's emergency bell.

I left, headed for Gisborne at six o'clock in the morning, and when I got there, I talked again. About writing. About the imagination. Don't be constrained by the truth, I said.

Some days after that, we sang 'Sheep May Safely Graze' at Flo's funeral, and the next day I flew to Canada.

The Sylvia Hotel at English Bay in Vancouver. It seemed the most perfect hotel in the world. It was covered with ivy; the interiors had dark old beams and rich stained-glass windows. I slept in a bed of such deep comfort in a large airy room that when I woke up late in the afternoon I was happy and felt free. I walked along to a shopping centre and bought face-mask products from a kind of cosmetics supermarket shop, complete with an open cool bin of products that looked as if they should have been in a delicatessen. I bought a face mask made from shitake mushrooms which I was given in a pottle, resting on ice inside another little container. Elsewhere, I bought an umbrella, a Vancouver newspaper. I went back to the Sylvia Hotel and put the mask on my face. It seemed as if flesh was being drawn to the surface. Afterwards, I felt totally cleansed, as if I was making myself over into a new person. I sat and watched the sea and ate mushrooms stuffed with crabmeat followed by a chicken breast served with ginger and grapefruit.

On the flight from Calgary, my plane flew into the eye of the sun, its bright glare leaning through the window. I sat beside the young man I'd met up with in Banff. We had reached that state of intimacy

Silver-Tongued

that insisted (or he did any way) that we sit together on aeroplanes in order to continue, uninterrupted, with the story of our lives. A seemingly endless narrative. I remember the feeling of being dazzled in the sunlight.

Flo flew in an aeroplane only once her life, the only time she left New Zealand. She and a group of her friends from the council decided to go for a holiday to Rarotonga. As she went to the departure lounge her foot caught in the escalator and she fell down and knocked her head. She went on with the journey because she was with her friends, but she didn't like it, didn't have a good time. Give me good old New Zealand any day, was all she said about it. Fear of falling. One way or another.

Once, in the town where my parents and I lived when I was young, my mother ran into Wilf Morton. She was standing in the hardware shop in the village where we lived, and she heard a voice asking for a pound of nails. She knew him straight away, she told me, even though his hair was iron grey, and he was standing with his back to her. It was something about the way he spoke, as if asking for a pound of nails was a favour he was doing the shopkeeper.

I only knew about this meeting at the time because I heard my mother telling my father in a low angry voice that evening. But, later on, I could see it very clearly. I have a photograph of Wilf, which was tucked in an envelope inside one of the recipe books that I salvaged from Flo's house.

'I said to him, "What are you doing here?"'

'And what did he say?' my father asked, with unusual animation. He enjoyed stories in which my mother's family came out worse than he did, not that Wilf Morton had ever been family.

'He lives here,' my mother spat.

'Oh Gawd, that's serious,' my father said.

'On the other side of the inlet.'

'Well, I suppose that's not so bad. You can keep your eyes skinned when you go to town.'

'Why should I have to cross the road to avoid that man?'

'Fair enough,' my father said. 'Did he say what he was up to?'

'He said he was retired.'

'Retired from what?'

'Exactly,' said my mother. 'That's what I said to him — "And what have you retired from, Wilf Morton?" He didn't answer me, just smirked.'

I reminded my mother of this once, when we were talking about family matters, and the interminable question of why Flo was like she was. (This surfaced when Flo had been irascible or silent, especially in the days when Helena lived with her.) I'd heard the bones of the story about Wilf leaving Flo from her once before.

'Oh, that Wilf Morton.' My mother shrugged in the oblique sort of way her family had.

'What made him so dreadful? Apart from leaving her like that.'

'There were some things missing,' she said.

'You mean he stole things?'

'Something like that.' They didn't go into details in that family. A trinket, a farm, a heart — my mother could have meant any of those things. A sense of honour, perhaps; we might think it misplaced nowadays.

I had been asleep. The young man had kindly placed a pillow against me. I looked down on a tapestry of forests and lakes beginning to cloud with ice. Soon we would be in Winnipeg. The young man had quickened my senses, but I was old enough to know that what seems romantic on the outside can be a substitute for grief, and I was grateful to have gone on in the world long enough to understand that. Later, we would send signals to each other from afar, messages through mutual friends, invitations to book launches that were impossible for the other to attend, things like that, not the conspiracies of the heart that letters and emails involved. I've known any number of silver-tongued men, but I think my aunt only knew one.

I sat in the Sylvia Hotel and watched the sea. Some of this story hadn't happened then but in a few days it would. The young man I would meet in Banff, he was as dangerous as an elk. He was going to meet up with his wife later in the tour. He was nursing one of those harsh little secrets that men have, the kind that are common enough, but will tear lives apart. I've made several generalisations about men here: by and large, I think they're not bad, which is one of those sweeping assertions that don't get as much press as the other sort. Let me say here that I thought Theo was as decent and kind a man as it was possible to meet. I knew nothing unpleasant about him, nor have I heard anything since to alter my opinion of him. It was just that he lacked judgment in some aspects of his life, that he was helplessly in love with his wife and that he was undeniably homely.

You could say people bring it on themselves, but I'm not sure it's true; one will be absent from a marriage — there in the flesh, but absent in themselves. And then it's too late. You can tell from looking at some couples, even in photos, that one person's eyes have slid outside the frame. I have a picture of a group of us writers who went on that tour, and the young man from Banff is there with his wife. On that day, he is in the marriage still (although not for much longer), but his eyes are following the exit signs.

I came across a quote written by a young Frenchman in the seventeenth century. I've kept it for so long I don't know where I found it. It's written in my handwriting on a brown scrap of paper, brittle with age:

L'absence est à l'amour ce qu'est au feu la vent.

Absence is to love what wind is to fire.

FAMILIES LIKE OURS

There was that day in the science laboratory which people always talked about at school reunions, even if they hadn't been there when the accident took place, the day Lester Cooper blew off his hand with a pipe bomb. His sister Patricia hadn't started high school at the time but later she was expected to go to science classes in that same room, as if nothing had happened.

As if her brother's flesh and blood hadn't been spread on the walls.

The room had been painted by then, the same drab institutional light cream it had been before. If you didn't know, you wouldn't be able to tell what had gone on. You would simply never know. But when Patricia looked across the room, she saw her brother's freckled boy's hand outstretched in the basin where it landed, among the pipettes and petrie dishes. The nails would still be slightly bitten, a piece of sticking plaster on the little finger where he had nicked himself with a chisel at woodwork class, a small wart on a knuckle, fine downy hair covering the back of his hand.

The accident happened during the lunch hour when the science lab was supposed to be monitored by a prefect, but Clarence Mills got leave to keep a dental appointment in town and forgot to tell someone in charge. Some people would say it was Clarence's fault; others would blame the school for lack of supervision. But it was Lester who had taken the pipe for the bomb to school, Lester who hammered the end out flat, and he who had emptied the powder out of the leftover fireworks from Guy Fawkes the night before. Lester, with his friends watching, screwed the bolt down on the neck of the pipe, the end of an old tap from the farm. Windows were broken in the explosion, and a boy got his glasses cracked, but Lester was the one who left his hand too long on the bomb and joined in the laughing and cheering at the size of the explosion until he saw his hand sitting on the other side of the room.

After he came out of hospital, he spent another year at Ramparts District High School, the hook he wore on his stump mostly concealed in his pocket. He learned to write with his left hand. He answered questions when he was called on in class and passed his university entrance examinations, and then he left town.

'Les, you don't have to go,' his father, Os Cooper, said. This was one night at dinner when the matter of his leaving was first raised. 'We can find some things for you to do here on the farm,' he said. Os was a fair man with broad furry arms and a slight limp which he had brought back from the war. He had been a gunner: he was in the firing line at Tobruk, got hammered by Rommel in the desert, could recite the Battle of Cassino as if it had happened yesterday, and not a quarter of a century earlier.

'Yeah, shear sheep,' Lester said. He raised his hook for his father to see. They were eating roast lamb and minted peas and new potatoes. His mother had cut up his meat for him before she covered it with gravy, as if by concealing what she'd done, he would believe he'd done it for himself.

Os said, 'I bought this farm out of sharemilking. D'you think that was easy? It's meant for you kids.' The farm was mostly dairy but Os ran dry stock, sheep and cattle, on the hills. When people stopped him in town and said how sorry they were about the boy, he'd said, over and again, 'He's not a bad kid, you know.' No one argued with him. Most of the men had played around with gelignite or explosives of one kind or another in their lives.

'The old order changeth,' Lester muttered under his breath, although Patricia who was sitting beside him, heard what he said.

'You can cut out that fancy talk with me, boy,' Os said.

'Yeah, right.'

'Where will you go?' his mother said. Vonnie was a skinny woman with small neat wrists and ankles. Her complexion was scrubbed by too much wind and sun and tobacco smoke. On Thursdays, when she went bowling, she wore a white dress and a hat with green canvas stitched on the underside of the brim. When she was putting out Os's lunch she looked like a grown-up candidate for confirmation. Os said she smoked too many cigarettes but Vonnie said there were plenty who smoked more than forty a day and she had a little way to go to catch them up.

'I'm going to university,' Lester said. 'I've enrolled to do history and English at Auckland.'

Patricia still sees the way her father's face dropped, like a child who has had chocolate snatched away from him, yet knowing at the same time that it had already gone. This is a look she has become familiar with, now that her father is old. At the time, her mother rolled her knife and fork backwards and forwards between the thumb and forefinger of each hand. Patricia thought, then, this is a set-up. Her mother knew about this.

Os threw his dinner at the wall, not something Patricia had ever seen him do before. He had been a genial friendly man when she was small, a person who liked practical jokes. 'Get the hell out of here,' he shouted. 'Why don't you just bugger off right now.'

'Okay, I will.'

'You don't mean that, Os,' his mother said.

'Yes, I do.'

Families Like Ours

Lester stood up then, pushing himself away from the table with his good hand. 'I'll be seeing you all,' he said.

At the end of Patricia's first year in high school she said she would like to transfer out of sciences and take sewing and cooking for her options. She was a blonde girl with bright thick hair and big greeny blue eyes, the colour of clear sea in the shallows. You're a bright enough girl, her teachers said, above average anyway. Don't you think you're throwing away your chances? Plenty of time for home-making.

Patricia had shrugged. 'I'd like to get on with things,' she said. These days she thinks she would have been sent to the guidance teacher for trauma counselling, victim support, something like that. There would be someone trained to make connections about her lack of ambition and drive.

'I don't understand the way you're letting yourself down,' her best friend, Kaye Swanson, said to her. Kaye was a tall girl who could be sharp and imperious with people, even as a child.

'I'll be all right,' Patricia said, surprising herself. 'I know what I want.' She could have said she didn't want to sit in that room where Lester had screamed and screamed, four people holding him down until the ambulance arrived, and where the policeman sent to the scene had thrown up. She didn't say this, because she was a girl who spared the feelings of others.

Besides, Patricia and Kaye have spent more than half their lives apart now and Patricia isn't envious of women with careers. The thing is, she's done exactly what she liked: living on the farm with Dan and their four children, driving her four-wheel drive along familiar roads each afternoon to pick them up from school when they were small, entertaining their friends as they grew up. Not everything in life is perfect, but then show her a life that is. She misses her older children more than she admits to others, now that, with the exception of their 'bonus baby', Benjamin, who came along late, they have all left home. Her father, who is in the local rest home, frustrates her because she can't make herself understood anymore, and there have been some irreconcilable losses in her life, like that of her mother, and her brother Lester whom she hasn't seen since she was a girl. Sometimes when she is working in her garden, and looking in the cool dark places between ledges and under hedges where spring bulbs germinate, she finds herself doing sums in her head about how old she was then, and how old he was, and what age he would be now, and is astonished to think that if he is still out there, he will be nearly fifty. There was a case of a New Zealand man with a shadowy past who had had a hand transplanted on to the stump of his arm, a world first that made international headlines. She remembers how she had studied the television pictures, and searched the newspapers looking for clues. Could it be him? But it was not, there was nothing she could see that remotely relates this man to her brother. On other days, she wonders if her father might have hidden something from them, or simply not recognised some scrap of information that would have led them to Lester. She has left it too late to ask him. He had his own way of keeping things to himself, and now he doesn't know what day it is, and has to be fed because he has forgotten that people need to eat to stay alive.

All the same, she has survived, she tells herself, alive and whole, and still easy to look at, confident and smiling, a woman people turn to in times of crisis.

When Patricia and Kaye were children they believed their friendship would never end, despite the differences in their natures (something neither of them analysed then). They did almost everything together. They were in the same class at school, and both belonged to the Gold Epaulettes Marching Team which Patricia's mother Vonnie coached. Vonnie had been a marching girl too. The girls marched until they were nine and then the club went into recess because the treasurer embezzled the funds and the team couldn't make the annual tournament. Kaye was midget captain the year they won the trophy. Her height was an advantage, but it drove Vonnie mad trying to contain Kaye's hair under her cap, when she was dressing the two little girls; fizzy hair the colour of mouse fur that was pulled tightly into a plait, but still stood out in a strange transparent halo where it escaped from its bondage. Patricia was never as keen on marching as Kaye and was secretly pleased they could just hang around together, but Vonnie felt badly about Kaye's disappointment, especially because, as she said to her friends, the poor kid's mother, Wilma, is always having a bad period. A permanent monthly, if you asked her. She invited Kaye to stay at the farm, and it became a regular thing, the girls spending the weekends and summer holidays together.

Kaye stayed at Patricia's more often than Patricia stayed in town, even though the farmhouse was shabbier and more run down than the Swansons' place, which was full of couches tightly covered with blue velvet and ruche curtains. The Coopers' farmhouse was ramshackle and one part of the roof needed replacing so that when it rained hard they had to put buckets out to catch the drips. Os often promised Vonnie that it would get done in the spring, but spring passed into summer and the leaks went away and Vonnie, whose real interests were the bowling club and having a bit of a knees-up at the weekends with her friends — she called them 'the girls' too — didn't seem to mind. There was a piano in the front room and the girls, leathery looking women like Vonnie herself, and their husbands, came out with a couple of flagons of beer, or a keg. Os enjoyed himself too on nights like this when everyone sang and told raucous jokes. People got quite drunk out there on the farm at the weekends. You could see some of them leaning against the cars when they'd had enough, sometimes throwing up. Os used to go out with a few shovelfuls of dirt on Sunday mornings and chuck them over the evidence.

Nobody took much notice of what Patricia and Kaye did. Before his accident, Lester used to take the girls down some Saturday nights to the river bank where there was a camping ground beyond the outskirts of the farm, on the way out of town, and shine torches on tents, so they could see what people got up to. Not that they ever saw anything interesting, just people getting mad and yelling at them. There was only so far they could go along the bank, because the course of the river changed and abruptly fell away to steep bluffs. At that stage, Lester was a boy who looked as if he would grow into a mirror image of his father, his hair slicked up in a tuft with Brylcreem, the gingery hint of a beard on his chin, although Os said, with real anxiety, now and then, that he was a moody kid and he should get over it. He wasn't like that when he was a boy.

The last summer holidays before Lester's accident, Patricia and Kaye built themselves a house in a honeysuckle hedge. The perfume from the flowers was so sultry and sweet it was like they imagined being drunk, the way Os and Vonnie's guests got at the weekends. It instilled in them a dizziness and a portent of sin, although, when it came to it, Patricia wonders if either of them ever discovered sin. She is vaguely aware of it as something other people do, but she has done little that she can think of. The two of them, she and Kaye, stumbled around like the nursing bees that hovered over the golden flowers. When Patricia poured them each about half a glass of gin from a bottle in the drinks cabinet — and that is one of the most wicked things she can remember — it tasted acidic, a little dangerous at the back of their throats, but otherwise not as surprising as they had hoped, apparently not altering them in any way. They both wanted to be movie stars when they grew up, and practised acting until they were at least ten or eleven when suddenly they felt too old for dressing up and fooling around in that way. Kaye had grown a whole head taller and got tired of Patricia wanting her to play the man every time. It brought about their first quarrel.

One afternoon Patricia persuaded her mother to let them dress up in her wedding dress, which was in a box on the top of the wardrobe. The dress was made of guipere lace over taffeta and had some rust marks on the skirt where the pearl tiara had rested on its little metal head band in the box.

'Well, I suppose so,' Vonnie said doubtfully when Patricia asked her. 'I put it away hoping for you to wear it some day, dear, but you might have to get a new one of your own.'

'I'll wear it today and you can take my picture,' said Patricia. 'That'll be my pretend grown-up. You can be the groom, Kaye.'

Vonnie took a picture of them with the box Brownie. After she had squinted at them for a while and snapped a couple of pictures, she said, 'Now it's Kaye's turn to put the dress on.' She had seen through the viewfinder that Kaye was looking discontented.

Kaye pulled the dress over her head and stood there, her face suddenly illuminated. She stood up straight, the way she did when she was a little thing in the marching team, as Vonnie told Os that evening. She took two steps forward, flicking the train behind her.

'Go on,' Vonnie said to Patricia, 'take her hand.'

'Who am I?' said Patricia.

'My husband.'

'Yes, but what's my name?'

'Lester,' said Kaye.

'Yee-hah,' cried Patricia. 'Kaye loves Lester.'

'No, I do not,' said Kaye, struggling to get out of the dress. 'I do not, I do not.'

2

Ramparts is a town that's off the beaten track, well off State Highway One. It's a place that gets deeply cold in winter. There is a town square and a clock that fell into disrepair but has been restored by a group of enthusiasts. The gardens that edge the square are filled with head-tossing poppies in the spring, a mix of dahlias and snapdragons in late summer. A cenotaph stands by the war memorial hall and beyond that there is a grove of trees that turn deep crimson in autumn. The motto on the war memorial reads, 'Lest We Forget'. There are two hotels in the main street, an antique shop, most of the main banks, a post office, some pavement cafés and the back entrance to the supermarket car park. The population is two and a half thousand. It is much the same now as it was when Patricia and Kaye were children, although some places have closed down. There used to be a car and tractor sales place near the end of the street but people buy cars in the cities now, and the farmers, too, get their farm equipment from bigger centres. It closed down after Selwyn Swanson sold up in a hurry. There was some shaking of heads over that; the Swansons were big noises in Ramparts for a few years.

Wilma Swanson was a bank teller in Wellington when she first met her husband, so from the very beginning she knew exactly how much money he had in each of his accounts. In that early life of hers, she was required to be well groomed every day and she never lost the habit. She always wore eye shadow and a discreet touch of rouge and never missed using moisturising cream at night before she went to bed. Selwyn had been surprised on the first night of their honeymoon at her slightly waxy appearance when they went to bed, she in her apricot peau de soie nightdress, he in his blue shortie pyjamas his mother had bought him for the occasion. She had been concerned that he was marrying a girl with a background in what she called commerce, the retail trade as it were, although he had said that it wasn't quite like working on the front counter of Woolworths. He and his brothers had been left money by their father, a doctor who'd been making money in a city practice for a long time; in a way, it was like one of those fairytale quests where three brothers are each given a sack of gold and told to turn it into ten sacks. Selwyn was already working in the secondhand car dealer business and he could see opportunities. He just had to find the right little town without major competition, and he could live the sweet life forever.

Wilma had been disappointed with her fate when he spelled it out. She had envisaged a house up in Kelburn, somewhere near the cable car, perhaps even Talavera Terrace, where she could invite the girls she went to school with at Wellington East for lunches and cocktail parties. Selwyn said that it would be just for a little while and she could help with the books, and then there would be no end to the things they could do: private schools for their children, and travel to all parts of the globe, and dresses from Paris.

Kaye was the couple's only child, and after her birth, which Wilma described as an unpleasant experience, she gave up on trying. That is, she stopped sex and all that 'funny stuff', pretty soon afterwards, except for once a week because Selwyn said he did have his rights. Tuesday was the night set aside for it. Wilma joined the choral society and took charge of flower arrangements at St Peter's, and pretty soon she was asked to be treasurer, which, as she pointed out to Selwyn, didn't leave much time for working in his airless little office, and they did have a position to maintain in the town. At first, she thought he could do just fine without her. It meant that she didn't have to deal with rough men in singlets who came to pay their monthly hire purchase instalments at the office window. Over time, she believed he had come to recognise she was right about this, that a certain fastidiousness set them apart, brought him more respect.

The showroom was Selwyn's domain. A long white-walled interior with cool concrete floors painted grey, it was shaped like a warehouse, only with big plate glass windows facing the street. A dozen or more tractors stood in gleaming rows, four abreast on the showroom floor, as sleek as new cars and several times as powerful. Selwyn Swanson was a tall suave man with velvet grey skin pinched round the nose, cool eyes that out stared the distance, and a livery pink mouth. He wore made-to-measure suits that he ordered on trips to Wellington. Some thought he was above himself, a man who owned a tractor sales and service, wearing suits like that in a town like Ramparts, but in fact he never got his hands dirty. He had sales reps in hairy tweed jackets, and mechanics in overalls, who could do all of that.

When he walked up and down among the giant machines, he would stop and let his fingers trail lovingly across the rims of tyres, or the bonnets that clad the engines, and for a moment a flicker of happiness would illuminate his face.

The young woman sitting behind the glass reception window kept her head down whenever he glanced her way. She wrote columns of figures in a ledger book, and from time to time opened a cash box and counted out money.

It was at moments like these that Selwyn was most likely to appear at her side, arriving on noiseless soles. 'Didn't they teach you to count at school?' He pointed down the ledger, jabbing at each ink splotched entry. 'There, that should be one thousand two hundred pounds and forty-five pence.'

Ethel Floyd was one of several young women he had employed in the office, and she was the third from a family of sisters he employed successively until each one of them got married. He expected to employ Floyd girls for years to come. They were even-tempered, he told his wife, and good at figures. Until Ethel came along, and things started to fall apart. He thought Ethel had trouble counting to ten; addition and subtraction could cause hours of heavy sighs and rubbing out of figures.

'Yes, Mr Swanson.'

'What should it be?'

'One thousand two hundred pounds and forty-five pence.'

'And what have you got there?'

'One thousand one hundred pounds. And forty-five pence.'

'That's one hundred pounds less than Os Cooper owes me. I don't know why I keep you on. Do you?'

Ethel Floyd raised lazy brown-black eyes towards him. 'Yes,' she said. 'Actually, I do.' She smiled at him. Her teeth were small and neat and very even. She wore a short skirt that just skimmed the hem of her panties when she stood up and knee-high white boots. When she went out to do her shopping at lunchtime she put on a brown leather cap pulled over one eye. In the town of Ramparts, she was a rare sight, the kind who drew wolf whistles from carpenters working on the building of the new supermarket.

'Mr Swanson,' she said, 'you're old enough to be my father.'

The year after Lester left the farm for good was the one when Neil Armstrong and two other astronauts first set foot on the moon. Everyone sat glued to their television sets in the daytime, watching the three men bounce around the barren moonscape, looking like panda bears inside their space suits. Patricia remembers the miracle of it, how the thought of men so far out in space, so beyond the reach of everything earthly, had transformed people, as if their wildest imaginations had new horizons. She can see herself looking out at the night sky and wondering where Lester was, and whether he was as inspired to dream of the impossible, the way she was. The difference between them was that he had succeeded, whereas she would go on doing the same things as others because a sense of order made her happier than most people of her age. Lester had achieved, in that year, a romantic status in her imagination. Her mother had had a couple of letters from which she read out bits, but Patricia noticed she put them away carefully afterwards. The strongest thing she read out was: 'Why didn't anyone tell me about the things that are going on in the world?' And, 'We are mobilising up here, I can tell you. We don't want no shitty war.' She wished she knew what he was making of the moon landing, but she hoped he, too, would be excited and moved.

There had been other changes since Lester's accident and departure, imperceptible at first, but there all the same. Kaye was less keen to come out to the farm. Patricia knew that it was not just because Lester had gone, but something to do with Wilma's sense of propriety, as if she had finally tumbled to the fact that the Coopers and the Swansons were different. Vonnie had hinted at this, because she didn't want Patricia to think this was something she had done. 'She manages to turn other people's misfortune into a scandal,' she said with a touch more acid in her voice than was usual for her. Still, Kaye asked her over from time to time, but the invitations were increasingly spaced out. Patricia didn't mind that side of it so much. She didn't like going to the Swansons much either. There was something about their house that made her uncomfortable. It was hard to describe, but it was a sense of hesitation while meals were eaten in her presence, a silence between the scraping of a fork on a plate and the delivery of food to the mouth. She noticed it most in Mr Swanson, who seemed paralysed by the prospect of chewing, but also in Kaye's mother. Her throat appeared to swell when she swallowed, and sometimes her eyes watered.

All the same, she and Kaye had been friends for such a long time, and she believed it wasn't Kaye's fault, whatever they thought about her and her family. And Kaye was excited as she was about the moon walk. Her own father, though, was not impressed by the space drama that was taking place, right this very minute. He wore the habitual frown he had had since Lester's accident. 'It's rubbish,' he said.

'It's not rubbish,' Patricia cried, 'it's amazing.'

'I tell you, it's not true. They're feeding you a bunch of baloney. There's no little men walking about on the moon.'

'But you can see it, they're taking pictures and sending them back to earth while it's happening.'

He made a noise of disgust. 'Anybody could take pictures like that. I could dress up in funny suits and dance around the paddock in the middle of the night with a flashlight on and it'd look just the same.'

'Dad,' pleaded Patricia, 'you can't say things like that. There *are* men on the moon.'

Word got out that Os Cooper didn't believe in the moon walk. He must have gone to town and sounded off. Most people said it just showed he'd got a bit touched in the head after the trouble he'd had in his family. He probably thought the moon was made of green cheese, too, even though the astronauts had brought samples of the moon's dust back with them. A few said, well, you know, he's always been a down-to-earth kind of man. Perhaps there's something in it.

Patricia said, when asked, that it was her father's idea of a joke. Kaye Swanson told some of her other friends that it was simply hysterical, the things that man said. Poor Pattie, she said. By that time she and Patricia really had drifted apart. These things are hard to stop once they begin, like polar ice cracking under the strain.

'Is that girl pulling her weight?' Wilma asked Selwyn anxiously, now and then. 'You seem to be spending a lot of time over at the shop.'

'There's nothing to worry about,' he would say reassuringly. Wilma had been asking more and more when they would be shifting. He had no answers to this. The drought was a problem in Ramparts, and the farmers were taking a more conservative approach to stocking up with machinery now that Britain was going the way of the Common Market. Even he was beginning to feel the narrowness in his wallet.

There was a particular morning that made him more uneasy than usual.

Wilma had put his breakfast in front of him: grilled tomatoes, one poached egg and two slices of toast with pale milkless tea. She looked ethereal, her blonde hair styled in a perfectly shaped bouffant, her skin translucent even when she wasn't wearing her ivory pancake foundation. She said, 'Selwyn, I've been thinking.'

It was on the tip of his tongue to make the kind of coarse remark that his customers might make, like, take an aspirin for it. Instead, he said carefully, 'What have you been thinking?' Because he knew from the portentous way she spoke that he might not like what was coming.

'I've been thinking, perhaps I should come back and help you in the office. It would be a saving for you.'

'I don't think you need to do that,' he said, after what he hoped was a long enough pause to seem like careful reflection. He scraped a little more butter on his toast with the edge of his knife, and cut it carefully in two. 'I appreciate how busy you are.'

'I don't believe that girl Ethel's doing her job. I think she's pulling the wool over your eyes.'

She looked down at her own plate of sliced oranges so that he could only see two almond-shaped slivers of silver frost covering her eyes. Her eyes were considered her best feature, large, luminous and blue. It was Thursday, and he had forgotten about Tuesday night.

'I'm a bit tired,' he said. 'I think I need a course of vitamins.'

Wilma raised her beautiful eyes, and he saw the glint of tears. She blinked rapidly. 'I'll see to it,' she said.

Their daughter came into the room then. Her mother was always telling Kaye to stand up straight, because it was great to have height — all the best models were tall. She was fourteen now. Often, Kaye didn't seem to be listening, as if he and her mother were irrelevant. She spent a lot of time studying these days.

'What are you up to?' Selwyn asked quickly, which was all he could think of by way of conversation with his daughter.

'Nothing much,' she said. She had new friends now and hardly went near Patricia Cooper. Her mother was pleased in a way, although it had been handy that Kaye had somewhere to visit.

'There's a place come up in the choir,' Wilma said brightly. 'How about you join? You'd like that, wouldn't you?'

Kaye, who could hold a tune, and had started to play the piano, said, yes, all right then, she would like that.

Ethel Floyd had had her twenty-fifth birthday by the time Lester Cooper left town. That was surprising to some who knew the Floyd girls. They were generally snatched up by the time they were twenty. You'd think, her friends said, that Ethel would have found herself someone, with all those young men coming in from the country. You'd think she'd be in clover.

'It's a holiday tomorrow,' Selwyn said, the evening before the Anzac Day parade, when the shops would be shut. 'You can stay in bed all day if you want to.'

'That would be so nice. I love sleeping in,' Ethel said, giving him the full benefit of her white smile and running the tip of her tongue over her top lip. 'Could you possibly give me a lift home?'

'Now?'

'My ride's staying late tonight.' She meant the woman at the bakery who gave her a lift home after work most days. 'They're short staffed, so she's got to stay late and clean up on her own,' she explained.

It was still daylight in Ramparts. The sun had a marshmallow tinge as it dipped towards the hills, a soft centre that was irresistible. In the main street, some bunting and flags had been hung, so that there was slightly festive air about the place. Selwyn wore a red poppy in the buttonhole of his charcoal suit. The clock on the tower struck five, and the men who worked for him filed out, the grease monkeys wiping their hands on rags as they left the building. They called goodnight as they left, their eyes appraising Ethel. A mechanic called Sid winked at her, as if Selwyn wasn't there.

Selwyn glanced across the square, the gardens edged with marigolds and late dahlias. The heads of the flowers swayed very gently in a breeze that was so light he felt as if he could just drift off in it. There were days when Selwyn Swanson felt that he had everything in his life, and not very much. He wanted, as badly as he had wanted anything for some time, to be part of this evening, to not let it slip by, before he went home to vegetable rissoles and cabbage. It was a surprising time of day to take his car out of the yard, when his house was a hundred yards down the main street. He saw his men trooping into the Red Barn Arms for a round of drinks, or two or three, in anticipation of a day off. They didn't look back, not even Sid, a man he kept his eye on.

'It'll only take five minutes,' said Ethel.

'Well, come along then,' said Selwyn. 'I need to call down and see Os Cooper, so it's not out of my way.'

'Are you going to repossess?' She stretched herself against the leather upholstery of his car.

'He's not a very smart farmer these days. His stock numbers are down.' When she didn't say anything, he said, 'Find yourself some music on the radio.' He watched her out of the corner of his eye, steering the car lightly with the fingertips of one hand, his other brushing against hers as he changed gear. Hogsnort Rupert and his band were playing 'Pretty Girl'. Ethel rocked backwards and forwards in her seat clicking her fingers. She chewed gum, open mouthed. Selwyn opened the car window so that the breeze raced through, stronger now, cold on his face, as he pressed the accelerator, picking up speed. He felt suddenly youthful and so joyous.

Anzac Day morning broke with a thin ribbon of light along the eastern skyline, the beginning of a day so clear that the men of Ramparts would say for years afterwards, you could put a ring around that one, 1972. Most of them were used to dawn light, not like those chaps in the cities who give themselves heart attacks just getting out of bed so early for the one day of the year to go to the dawn parade, as if they had never been soldiers. All the same, there was a quality about the air that made it easier to inhale the first gasp of cigarette smoke, as their utes roared into life and headed towards town. You could hear the dogs barking for miles.

Bloody good turnout, the members of the Returned Servicemen's

Association said to each other that morning. Bloody tremendous. The men who had been to the wars were assembling for the march to the cenotaph, three or four old men on sticks who'd been in the Boer campaign shuffling into line in front, followed by the First World War veterans, then what Os Cooper thought of as the young ones, like himself, who'd gone to the second war, in the rear. He had heard young fools say that there was nothing great about any war, but he didn't see it like that. Instead, he saw it as a time when he had gone beyond Ramparts and fought for his country. Blood, sweat and tears, as Churchill had said. Sure, he'd been wounded but he'd seen foreign countries, been to England and seen the King and Queen, and none of it would have happened had it not been for the war. I'll take you to England, Vonnie, he said. I promise you, when we retire that's where we'll go.

The truth was, he couldn't see himself retiring for a long while yet. The farm wasn't doing as well as it should: this spell of fine weather was great for folk in town, but the drought was getting to farmers like himself. He'd had to put on more fertiliser than he could afford, and the grazing he was renting down the road for his herd was costing him an arm and a leg. And the beautiful morning darkened as he thought of what the loss of an arm really had cost his farm, and how there were days when he wondered why he bothered, why he went on at all, now that his boy had gone. But no sooner than the cloud had settled he was being clapped on the shoulder by his old friend Harry Salter, who'd stood alongside him at El Alamein, and he thought about the night they'd crawled back to safety under the stars of the North African sky, that campaign, and others that followed, and how they'd been delivered safely back home.

'How're you doing, old cobber?' Harry was saying. He had tears in his eyes and Os could see that the more time passed the more it meant to you, to have served your country. Harry passed him a tot of rum out of the same hip flask he'd had out there in the desert.

'Bit of trouble brewing,' Harry said.

'What's up?'

'Kids,' said Harry, tapping his nose with his finger.

At that moment, before Harry could explain, the order came to fall in. It was given by a younger man in army uniform who carried the rank of colonel. This man was a teacher, in charge of the school cadets, standing at attention in their shorts and battledress jackets. Os didn't like the way some of them had hair showing under their caps and some of the senior boys had fluffy sideburns jutting down the sides of their cheeks. He wondered if this was the trouble that Harry was referring to.

'It makes me sick,' he muttered, to nobody in particular.

'What's that, mate?' Harry said.

'Nothing.' But he was thinking again about Lester, and how proud he used to be on Anzac mornings when they went into town together and marched down the street to the beat of the same drum. He was sure Vonnie knew where their son was, but she didn't talk about what she knew and he was damned if he was going to ask her.

The parade began to march down the street, past the Red Barn where they'd all gathered on the verandah when they were about to leave town for embarkation all those years ago, and everyone — the old people, and the farmers who were running the place while their sons went to war, and the women and children — had shouted and waved flags and cheered them on, and again, when they came back, and he thought how quiet it was up there this morning, with not a soul on the balcony. They marched down along past the undertaker's and the bakery shop and the tractor and farm machinery shop where that bastard Swanson thought he was God, until they were in front of the monument, and the school teacher colonel made a short speech. Os couldn't help smiling to himself, looking at the bulge where his gun was supposed to be. Lester had once told him that the colonel didn't really have a gun in his holster, because he didn't have a firearms license that covered Anzac Day: it was actually a school staple gun with the end taped over. If there was trouble, the colonel would be sweet Fanny Adams use to them all. But it was still not apparent to him where this trouble might be coming from.

He straightened his neck, wishing he could rub it where it ached. The night before he'd had a peculiar experience at the crossroads near the farm. He'd closed the stock in the rented holding paddock down the road, and was just driving back when Swanson had come towards him doing seventy-five on the straight, not looking where he was going, Willie Floyd's girl sprawled all over the front seat beside him with a silly look on her face as if she was having her twat rubbed, which she probably was; he'd put enough bulls to cows in his time, he knew the look. He'd had to pull up, slam the anchors on. Although he didn't crash with Swanson, he thought his head would go through the windscreen. Swanson had put his arm up over his face, while the girl had slid under the dashboard. As if he wouldn't have known Swanson in his dark-coloured Mercedes.

There had been a brief hiatus, a moment when he contemplated the whisker that stood between the two vehicles, and then Swanson had reversed out of it and taken off, leaving tyre marks on the road. Os could feel where the whiplash had caught him though, a sharp stab of pain that hadn't gone away in the night.

They shall not grow old, as we that are left grow old.

Fine familiar words. Os concentrated on them, turning his eyes away from the school group. Vonnie had told him to stop worrying about Lester. Give him time. You were a hothead too. She meant the way he'd married her when they were eighteen. His mother had been furious. She'll have found someone else when you get back from the war. But of course Vonnie hadn't. She wasn't that kind of woman.

So where the hell was Lester now?

At the going down of the sun and in the morning
We will remember them.

The moment when old men cried, in spite of themselves, tears dribbling down their furrowed cheeks. The service had reached the laying on of wreaths, the town dignitaries coming forward to place circlets of flowers at the foot of the cenotaph and, just then, a commotion began to ripple through the crowd.

It was then that Os could see the trouble.

A group of young people was coming up from behind the parade, holding handfuls of flowers in their hands. The flowers looked as if

Families Like Ours

they had just been picked and he noticed that the last dahlias in the gardens were half-stripped.

Now Os thought about it, he had seen a bunch of kids in the distance a few days back, over at the old motor camp. Hippie kids, girls in caftans and boys with long shaggy hair round their shoulders. They had parked a painted bus by the water, and some of them were swimming in the river. He thought they had moved on, because the next day they were gone and he hadn't seen them again.

There were eight or ten in the group, although afterwards he couldn't have told you how many exactly, because they moved so fast. But he saw that the girls were barefooted and smiling, that their dresses were muslin and flowing, and that they wore garlands in their hair. The young men had peace slogans emblazoned on their jackets and wore beads. Men wearing beads, for Chrissake, with hair down their backs like girls, and soft bushy beards — the only way you could be sure they were men, if that's what they called themselves. And one of these young men had a hook where his hand should have been. Not covered up, or tucked away in his pocket, but out where you could see it, with the sun glinting on it and making it shine.

They didn't say anything and even he had to admit they seemed peaceful enough. One of the young men (not Lester), seeing the crowd advancing, stood up from placing his flowers, and called out. 'We're just remembering the dead in Vietnam,' he said. 'It's the Vietcong's war too.'

Now the group was set upon on all sides, hit and jumped on, and the very old men were waving their sticks and calling out in quavering voices to the younger ones to take them and thrash them, and one of them shouted out to the colonel to open fire. Os locked eyes for just a second with his son and he knew that he, rather than Lester, looked away first. There were sickening thuds, a trail of blood where one of the group ran from the scene. Above the shouting the town bugler was tootling away, playing 'The Last Post' as if nothing had happened. This was the moment Os had been waiting for, the part he liked best; only this morning all he felt was a sick despair, deep in the pit of his stomach.

A red and black mosaic in his head, shot through with pure transparent arrows.

At the blinding of the light.

His boy, Lester.

When it was over, the men who were standing around in knots rather than in line, looked at each other and shrugged. It was like the war. After the moment of exhilaration, when the fight had gone out of them, there was nothing much to be done. They started to drift towards the RSA clubrooms. Nobody came near Os, until he was standing alone in the square; then Harry came back.

'Come on, Os,' he said. 'It's not your fault. Come and have a drink.' He held out his flask, and Os took it, draining the last sweet dregs with gratitude.

'I can't,' he said. 'I haven't got the heart for it.'

'Nobody will hold it against you.'

'I should never have let him have that tap.'

'You've lost me, mate,' said Harry. His eyes strayed restlessly towards the clubrooms.

'It was the tap outside the cowshed. It was stuffed. I thought the thread was done for. He said, "Can I have it, Dad?" I said, "What the hell d'you want a worn out bloody tap for?" He said, "They've got their uses." He didn't say he was going to screw it down over a shitload of explosives.'

'Bang bang,' said Harry.

'Yeah, something like that.'

'I'll have one for you,' said Harry.

'Thanks, mate,' he said. Harry was the sort of person who would come back for you in battle, he'd always known that. Funny that they had to be here, in the town square of Ramparts, before it happened.

Os pulled his keys out of his pocket and walked unsteadily towards the ute. Standing between the line of cars and trucks, he saw Lester waiting for him.

'What do you want?' he said.

'To talk to you, Dad.'

Families Like Ours

'There's nothing for you and me to say to each other.'
'Then a ride out of town. Up the line a bit.'
'Why me? Where are your mates?'
'They've gone. I told them to go.'
'Get in,' said Os wearily. 'For Chrissake, boy, get in.'

Selwyn was so shaken when he got back from taking Ethel home that he told Wilma straight away about giving her a lift. It seemed like the safest course. He tried to tell her in a casual way, as if he was just filling her in on the day's events.

Wilma shouted at him then. She said everyone in town knew what he was up to with that little slut, and what sort of fool did he take her for. What she had had to put up with for years didn't bear thinking about.

He said then that she might have been lucky to get a bungalow in Kilbirnie if she'd stayed in Wellington and what more could he do for her than he had. He'd turned her into someone when actually she was a nobody.

On and on, all night. Kaye put her head under the blankets in her pretty primrose yellow room, trying to shut out the sound of their rowing. She didn't know much about affairs and what happened in them, only what she had heard at school, but there was no mistaking what Wilma said Selwyn was doing with Ethel Floyd.

'Where do you take her in the lunch hours?'
'Nowhere.'
'Yes, you do. I come in and neither of you is there.'
'A coincidence.'
'Go on, tell me where. It's not as if I can't ask someone. Down to the river, isn't that where you go?'
'No,' he said. 'No.' Because, as it happened, it wasn't true, although he wished it was. The discomforts of cramped office sex were beginning to tell on him.

Wilma cried all night and said over and again, between gasps, and small screams, that she and her daughter had had terrible lives and she didn't know what would happen to them next.

Towards dawn, Kaye got up, because she couldn't bear listening to it any more. In the kitchen, she took her father's car keys off the hook, and went out to the garage where he kept his Mercedes, alongside her mother's gleaming Ford sedan. Her father had given her some driving lessons in a paddock one day, on one of the rare times they spent time together. The Mercedes was so easy to drive.

It served him right if she dented his car. Then she thought that it wasn't fair, all the things her mother had said, because her father had never caused her any trouble. He'd never made her feel much of anything one way or another. There were times when she liked being with him, like in the car when he was showing her how to parallel park alongside a fence. She enjoyed his praise.

On the way out to the river, she was alarmed at all the cars streaming towards town. She didn't know where they could be coming from at that hour of the morning, until she remembered it was Anzac Day. Nobody appeared to notice her driving towards them, and she was glad she was tall. In less than a year she would be old enough to hold a licence anyway, which made her almost laugh when she thought of Patricia, who was the same age and would probably need cushions beneath her in order to see over the steering wheel.

Kaye didn't know what she should be looking for when she got to the river. What her mother had said in the night about her father and Ethel Floyd made a weird kind of sense, but she didn't trust Wilma to be right. This was where Lester Cooper had taken her and Patricia to watch something forbidden, whatever it was.

Kaye parked the car at the bend in the river, and set about looking for clues. She found some cigarette butts among trampled grass, but she was fairly sure Ethel Floyd didn't smoke, especially not roll-your-own fags like these, and the remains of a fire, but that didn't make much sense to her. There was a round cloth patch embroidered with a peace sign, which she fingered and slid into the pocket of her jeans. That didn't look like anything that Ethel or her father would have left there either. Kaye sat at the side of the river, suddenly exhausted from her long sleepless night, feeling the enormity of what she had done: taking her father's car out on the road.

It's your fault, she would say — you shouldn't have argued. One or other of them would have to give in, say that it was all right, it was all their fault. Probably her mother, because her father would be incandescent with rage about the absence of the Mercedes. She was in love with this word, incandescent, which struck her as being like white fire.

It was still not far past six in the morning, and she figured that if she went back now, it was just possible they might have gone to sleep, worn out with fighting, and she could take the car home and put it back in the garage. If she could be sure of finding reverse.

While she was studying the car's controls, she was aware of a movement to her left, further upstream, near the bridge that crossed the river to the Coopers' farm.

3

When Patricia was eighteen, her mother died of lung cancer. Patricia nursed her through that final awful illness.

What troubled her about that period in her life was not so much the decay of her mother's body — the bloody sputum and the wracking spasms of coughing — although that was bad enough. Rather, it was the way her mother pleaded with her to find Lester for her, so that she could see him just one last time.

'I know he's out there somewhere,' she said. 'You know your father saw him and talked to him, that Anzac Day. Oh, I was going to go into the service with him that morning, but I just didn't feel like getting out of bed.'

'You had a cough, even then,' Patricia said.

'If your dad hadn't seen him and talked to him, I might have given up on it. But it wasn't that long ago, was it?'

'It was four years ago. And you know what Dad told you. Lester said he was going overseas.'

'That's so sad,' Vonnie had cried then. 'He was clever. Wasn't he clever, your brother?'

'Yes,' said Patricia, 'I reckon he was.'

'He started off to go to university. He sent me his results that first year away. That's what I can't get over — that he never gets in touch at all. I think sometimes something must have happened. You know, something else. If it hadn't been for the accident he might still be here,' Vonnie fretted.

'Well,' said Patricia, sensibly, 'he mightn't have been cut out for farming anyway, so he still might have left.'

'I think it was the shock of the accident. He never got over the shock. Can you imagine what it would be like?'

'No,' Patricia said, as truthfully as she could. It wasn't as if she hadn't thought about it.

'Do you think it was something your dad said? Something Les couldn't forgive?'

'You know what Dad told you. He took him to the turn-off, he gave him a lift. You know he put ads in the paper and how he got in touch with the Salvation Army people. If they can't find him, then I don't know who can.'

'You'll keep looking for him, won't you? You promise me that you will.'

'Yes,' said Patricia, 'I promise. Why don't you get some rest now?' She pushed her mother's hair back off her face and sponged her brow, as the best nurses do in all the movies. The difference was, this was real, and her mother was dying.

It got worse when her mother started to see little dogs with rats' heads crawling over her bed. Os took turns sitting beside her and holding her hand and making soothing hushing sounds, so that Patricia could get some rest. It wasn't fair, he said, not fair that now things were coming up roses on the farm, Vonnie wasn't going to see the benefit of the good times. All the things he had promised her and now that he could give them to her, it was too late. He rocked backwards and forwards, his voice caught between choking sobs. Patricia felt old before her time, having to look after both of them.

The next year she married Dan Matheson, who had been a few years ahead of her at school. His family farmed on the south side of Ramparts. You drove through an avenue of elm trees that his great-grandfather had planted to get to the house. People said she was fortunate to be so well settled. A cousin called Isabel, on her mother's side, was her bridesmaid. She would have liked a second maid so she wrote to Kaye Swanson, who was at teachers' training college in Auckland. Although she hoped Kaye might come back for old times' sake, she wasn't really surprised when she got a note on green deckle-edged notepaper, in a neat composed hand, to say that it was lovely to be remembered with such fondness, and how *honoured* Kaye was, but she couldn't get away from her studies. I wish you all happiness, Kaye wrote.

4

New people have come to Ramparts. Moneyed people from town have bought up farms and subdivided them into lifestyle blocks, and on-sold them to stressed executives and lawyers who in turn have hired architects to build homes that appear in house and garden magazines, or to restore derelict cottages, which they visit once or twice a month. They put stock on their properties that wander off and block the highway, because the fences aren't properly built, or the owners' kids leave gates open when they bring their friends up for parties. The local farmers have to round them up and phone the owners in their legal and accounting firm offices where they are put on hold to listen to symphony orchestras or rock bands until they are put through to voice mail. In a week or so, someone will ring and say, 'Sorry about that, old man. Can you just send the bill if there are any damages?' Then the vineyards were planted and now there are weekend trippers following wine-tasting trails.

On the whole, Patricia has not minded this as much as her

husband Dan. Their own house is something of a decorator's dream, full of wicker chairs and rustic wooden furniture, old pretty china and intensely coloured Turkish rugs, French doors with original bevelled glass leading out on to patios and gardens. The difference is that there is nothing new about this; it has been like this all along. Dan thinks the new people are pretentious. No, he's more specific than this, he says they're a bunch of wankers.

Dan is nearly fifty now, tall, becoming a trifle gaunt and very weathered, with coppery hair that is thinning but not grey. He is perennially attractive to the women in their circle. Patricia believes he is faithful to her, as she is to him. Once she thought about having an affair, just to try someone else. It's not as if she didn't have offers, but when she thought seriously about it, it seemed that it might blow her life apart, and one explosion in a lifetime was enough, as far as she was concerned. In the years when she was having children she watched the way women's lives unfolded all around her as if in a dream, as her father had once viewed the moon landing. 'Of course I'm not a feminist,' she would say with a cheery laugh, when asked. 'I don't know what the word means.'

Special market days are held in the town square when local produce is sold, and arts and crafts and other handmade goods, such as notepaper and lace and pressed floral pictures, are on display. Patricia enjoys these days. It's a chance to meet the people who live here now and she has developed a specialty of her own, a line of fine linen embroidered tablecloths, made from imported materials. She always knew there was a reason for her preferring sewing to science at school. Her linen sells privately but it's fun to be part of the larger gatherings of the town. She is a handsome self-assured woman who wears camel-coloured trousers and cotton blouses tucked in at the waist, and clumps of old gold and diamond rings on her fingers. Her children are called Victoria, Alice, Nicholas and Benjamin. Except for Benjamin, they are away at university and school. The district high school closed long ago, because of falling rolls, and the local high-school students face the choice of a long bus journey each day to the area school, or boarding school, which, mercifully, Dan was able to afford. There was a brief time when Patricia had been really worried about Victoria, who was clever but didn't settle well to study. She ran wild in the holidays when she was home and there was a dreadful summer when she was seventeen and got in tow with one of Ethel Miller's boys, who was already in his twenties. Ethel had been one of the Floyd girls and this boy Adam was her oldest, the one who'd been born before Ethel got married to Dick Miller. Adam was a troublemaker if ever she saw one. And yet, there was something about him that reminded her of her brother Lester, some yearning quality, which almost made her relent and say, oh bring the boy home.

She sees Lester if she lets herself. When she is driving out to the farm to see her muddled old father. Certain places in town, like the local swimming pool, and the old milkbar that still keeps going down a side street. And in dreams, he is a restless force, one she cannot quell, who will never go away even though she wills him to leave when she is on the brink of sleep. He is there in the morning, a school boy still. She listens to him bicker with their father. When she wakes up, it's still happening.

Lester did better at school than Os ever anticipated, but although Vonnie was pleased, he seemed fed up, as if Lester were showing off. Lester, who was both clever at mathematics and imaginative when it came to English, could recite poetry. His teacher commented favourably on this in his reports.

'Poetry, eh?' Os said with a mixture of veiled animosity and curiosity. 'What poem do you know then?'

'The boy stood on the burning bridge, picking his nose and spitting it out,' Lester would say, not looking up. They were hosing down in the cowshed at the time, as Patricia remembers it in her dreams. They have to raise their voices to hear one another. Patricia is sitting on the railing, hearing this exchange. If she had been older she might have worked out that Lester was having her father on. He used to take the piss out of the old man, she will tell her husband. But when she hears Lester say this, she just thinks how weird that he recites this silly poem when she has heard others he knows. Like the one she loves, which he speaks as they walk along the path to the school bus stop. It's called 'The Passing of Arthur'.

And slowly answer'd Arthur from the barge:
'The old order changeth, yielding place to new,
And God fulfils himself in many ways,
Lest one good custom should corrupt the world.'

His voice rises with a sweet melancholy, caressing the words, as if they are filled with special meaning for him.

She has noticed that her children don't seem to be taught this poem at school. Perhaps she was, she can't remember, but then so many things were a blur to her when she went to high school. She knows that she has come to think of it as Lester's anthem, what he believed in.

She remembers the way Lester took her hand and led her to the bus every day when she first started school.

What was it about Adam that reminded her of Lester that summer he was seeing Victoria? Dan would have been so angry with her, with both of them, had he known what was happening. He would have been angry with Victoria for her wilful misbehaviour, and with Patricia for letting it happen and not telling him. Adam was known as a wild child in the town by the time he was fifteen. He drank too much, and fought and drove cars fast before he had a licence. He had a fine slender ascetic quality about his looks, not like his younger brothers and sisters, who were black-eyed and heavy like their mother, though he was supposed to have been Dick Miller's boy.

And yet, when Victoria comes home with flowers in her hair, something silences her objections. One night, Victoria stays up and plays *Under Milkwood* on a scratchy vinyl record, three times all the way through. Somewhere round three o'clock in the morning, Patricia gets out of bed to fetch a glass of water and hears Victoria talking fast and low on the phone, and knows it's Adam. Her midnight cowboy, Patricia thinks, her heart bunched up with fear.

'Adam won't stay in Ramparts,' Victoria tells her. 'He's just getting some money together, and then he'll be out of it.'

'What will he do?' Patricia asks.

'Do? Oh, that's all you think of, isn't it? What people will *do*? As if it matters.'

Then, when Victoria went back for her last year at school, he'd pranged a car up on the bridge across the river. A young architect's son who had started hanging out with him was killed and Adam has a permanent head injury, so that she is grateful Victoria isn't more deeply involved with him, that the time for them to go off together hadn't arrived. Though she thinks Victoria might have given her virginity to Adam (she says given to herself, rather than lost, because she wants to think of her daughter as a woman like herself, who has known only virtue) and what greater involvement does a woman have with a man: he must surely be the one you never forget. It's hard to be certain, because Dan has been the only man in her life, but this is what she imagines.

Victoria is engaged to marry a town planner from Wellington, and Patricia, who has been helping Dan lay new lawns for the wedding, hopes that that particular incident and time in Victoria's life are far behind her. She thinks that it is her role to protect her children from pain and loss and disfigurement. She has saved Victoria from her father's wrath and the knowledge of Adam's stain. The idea of Adam being like Lester hasn't gone away. If anything, his injury has reinforced that view. And yet, when she thinks about Adam, she knows it is more than that, it is about words and about love; she finds herself wondering whether Lester ever knew what it was like to be touched by a lover, whether his clumsy left hand ever stroked a girl's hair.

When Os Cooper gets too strange and wandery in the head to stay on the farm, a lawyer tells Patricia and Dan that it's so run down it's in no fit state to lease to anyone. They would be better to put it on the market. Patricia reminds him that her father still owns the farm and that her brother Lester is entitled to his share.

'Your brother's share is going to cause problems,' says the lawyer, who is called Matthew Templeton. A man with a soft mop of girlish grey curls and a strong Roman nose, he lifts one side of his face when he smiles while the other seems to stay quite still. His voice is laid back and slightly sardonic, his passion, Celtic music. He is the owner of one of the lifestyle blocks but he likes Ramparts so much that he comes there more often than many of the absentee owners. He has set up a two-day-a-week branch in the town that is doing better business than the old established family firm that has been in Ramparts for seventy years. The waiting room of his office has been remodelled to be light and airy and open, with potted palms in the foyer. A stunning Gretchen Albrecht painting hangs in the entrance way, an abstract with a strong sensual curve. Patricia, for perhaps the first time in her life, feels more than curiosity when she looks at this man and compares him with her husband, a stirring of something very like longing. He insists they call him Matthew.

'I can't assume Lester's dead,' Patricia says quickly. She tells him then what Christmas means to her. Among all the shopping and wrapping and cooking and carol concerts and the children coming home with their friends, there is the advertisement in the newspaper that the Sallies put there every year. Anyone knowing the whereabouts of Lester Nelson Cooper, please contact this number. His birth details, his last known place of abode. In Australia, people will be reading the same notice, hungry to make a connection, to become involved in the drama of someone else's family. She doesn't add the bits about collecting Os from the farm, and Dan's mother from the rest home where Os is headed, and how they bicker and argue and the children roll their eyes while they drop food beside their plates. Nor does she say, in front of Dan, that there is a moment when he toasts them all, saying, 'To our family', and she thinks that there are two sides to families: the side you saw, apparently whole and complete, gathered around the Christmas table, and families like hers, lost and disintegrated. A moment of despair.

'I think we can take care of that,' says Matthew smoothly. 'There's an act to cover situations like this. It's called the Protection of Personal and Property Rights Act.' He has thought this through long before they came; already he has negotiated with their old reluctant lawyer, regarding the contents of Os's will. 'You'll need to apply to the court for a property manager to act on your father's behalf and get the court to approve a new will. Presumably, as no one can find Lester, he'll be excluded.'

'Meaning Lester doesn't exist?' Patricia says, in a small voice.

Matthew gives her a keen sad look. 'From what you've told me, it seems he might not. I think you have to proceed on the assumption that he's dead. If you're wrong and he turns up, he can always make a claim which you can settle between you.'

'I see,' says Patricia. 'Yes, I do see what you mean.'

Ethel Miller doesn't guess her life is going to change when she walks up to the Lotto counter one Monday morning. She's called in to the supermarket for some tins of cat food and a loaf of bread and is on her way out when she realises she hadn't checked her weekly Lotto ticket last Saturday night because it was her daughter's twenty-first birthday. There'd been a few drinks and quite a crowd, even her ex-husband Dick had come over and been friendly, or at least about seven on a scale of one to ten, until he'd had one too many, but that was him all over. The ticket is in her handbag so she stops at the counter and has the attendant run it through the machine.

'Mrs Miller, you'd better sit down,' says the young woman.

There isn't anything to sit down on, so Ethel grabs the edge of the counter and feels a prickling sensation all over her body. Just like that, the lighted numbers flashing up on the little screen, she is a millionaire. Nearly twice over. She can have whatever she likes.

Not that it's that simple. There are some things that money can't buy. Like putting her damaged son Adam back together again. At first she considers leaving Ramparts. As other people go there to get away from it all, Ethel thinks that she could leave all the old grief behind her if she leaves. But her sisters are here, and her children have started to settle around the town, and in the end she thinks it would be as well if she did too, for once and for all, with a touch of style. It hasn't taken people long to work out the change in her fortunes, from the day she turned up in a dark green Mercedes, the car of her dreams, and one or two people might put two and two together on that score as well, although perhaps there's not that many who would remember. The old tractor shop has been pulled down and there's a liquor store going in there now.

In the end, Ethel settles on buying the motel on the edge of town when it comes up for sale. It's a bit seedy but she's got some capital left for improvements and it will provide regular work for Adam, whom she can employ and keep an eye on. The motel was called Golden Glow, a remnant of the late seventies when it was built, but she renames it Summer Lodge. Adam says, reasonably enough, that people might think it's only open in the summer, but she says she likes the ring of it. She has turned into a lucky woman and it has a lucky sound.

When Patricia clears the farmhouse out, in the wake of Os's departure, her daughter Victoria offers to help. They leave Lester's room until last. They have never been inside it since he left. It is clear that Patricia's mother must have been in at some stage before she died, because everything is neat and orderly. And yet the room is frozen in time, as if, while tidying up, Vonnie had been loathe to give the impression that she had disturbed his belongings. Patricia realises that the secret side of Lester's life, the part she never knew after he went to Auckland, had actually begun before he left home. There are Rolling Stones and Beatles posters stuck on the walls, a copy of a magazine called *Rip It Up*, a collection of Leonard Cohen's poems lying on the bed with a hen feather marking the place at 'Suzanne Takes You Down'. Some lines have been marked with a red pen squiggle in the margin. They're about Jesus being a sailor, walking on water, watching drowning men from a lonely tower, and thinking that all men will be sailors when they're freed by the sea.

'Morbid,' says Victoria, with a shudder. As well, there are several exercise books with LIFE SUX written inside the covers, like a mantra, and SHIT HAPPENS YEAH MAN on another one. 'Did people really say stuff like this?'

'It was a long time ago.'

'Kind of historic. Did you ever think,' Victoria asks her mother, 'that your brother might have killed himself?'

'Yes,' says Patricia. 'D'you think I'm stupid?'

'No, Mum,' says Victoria. Patricia sees how much, now, her daughter wants her life to be normal and wholesome, how this proximity to her vanished uncle, who seems like a family ghost, is unsettling her. 'I wonder sometimes if you've got much imagination, that's all,' she says finally.

'Probably not,' says Patricia mildly. Her imagination has always been her own business, especially when it comes to thinking about Lester. It's best, perhaps, if Victoria is like her — or, at least, thinks she is.

An elderly man, a retired electrician, and his wife who used to help him in the shop, stay at Ethel's Summer Lodge. The couple, Lou and Shirley Mackintosh, have taken up conservation as an interest. They travel round the countryside staying at inexpensive motels and studying local rivers. They are looking for rubbish, of which there is a great deal. They have read about a young man in America who spends his whole life cleaning out rivers of all the filth and degradation that clog waterways, and though they are past diving and going down beneath the surface themselves, they feel they have a mission in life.

Their method is simple. To begin with, they investigate the banks of rivers, collecting all the rubbish they can find. They stack it in pile number one. Then, armed with rakes and buckets, they patrol the edges of the rivers, as far as they can reach, hooking out their prey and stacking it on the second pile. They find all sort of things, besides condoms and old farm machinery. They find eggbeaters and electrical appliances, lots of old toasters and electric frying pans and hair dryers — naturally, Lou has a very good nose for these — and broken china, just occasionally some rare whole piece that's been abandoned to the waters, and tyre wrenches and complete bicycles and buckets and, of course, lots of plastic, which is the stuff they are passionately seeking and railing against. When all this mess has been piled up, they call in the local newspaper and get them to do a story that will arouse public conscience. It works every time. The great clean-up begins.

They are a little disappointed by Ethel Miller's place. They had thought they would be getting more for less at a lodge, as it's advertised, but it's just an ordinary block-walled unit like most that they stay in, and there is a strange young man who whacks the door with the newspaper when he delivers it, instead of sliding past and leaving it without a whisper, as is the way of most motel proprietors. Still, it's clean and roomy, and the air is fresh and from their room they can see right down to the river that runs through Ramparts.

What they find in the river, among the general debris, is a hook, one of those old-fashioned ones that hand amputees used to wear, before modern prosthetics became available.

It was worth winning Lotto just to see Kaye Swanson walk into her motel, and come face to face with mine hostess, as Ethel describes herself on the swinging sign with her name emblazoned on it.

'What did she say when she rang?' Ethel asks Adam when she sees the reservations book.

'She just asked if she could have a room.'

'For how long?'

'One night. Thursday.'

'So she didn't ask who was in charge, nothing like that? Come on, Adam, think.' It bothers her how she wants to shake the boy sometimes when he gets that vacant look in his eye. Not that she could shake him, he's too big and he's twenty-six years old now.

'She didn't say nothing. Why do you want to know?'

She gives him an odd quizzical look. 'No reason,' she says, finally.

'Do you know her or something?'

'Something,' she agrees. 'She used to live round here when she was a girl.'

It is no surprise then for Ethel when Kaye walks in the door, rattling the bell as she comes. Ethel takes a long look at her, thin as a crisp, beginning to dry up, a briefcase clutched in one hand, an overnight bag in the other. Her hair is like a silver helmet. She wears an olive green silk suit with a matt-finished silver brooch on her lapel. The skirt just skims her knees.

Kaye doesn't know Ethel straight away.

Ethel says, 'It's Ms, is it Kaye? Ms Swanson?'

Kaye glances up then from where she is signing the booking slip, about to make a sharp retort, and stops, her features freezing into an expression of startled recognition. Ethel is a size eighteen these days, but she carries her weight with a hauteur that makes her imposing. Her eyes are still black but they have grown shrewd with time.

'Back for old times' sake, are we?'

'Something like that,' says Kaye, regaining her composure.

'I was sad to hear your parents passed away,' says Ethel. 'Very sad about that.'

'Thank you,' Kaye says.

'Adam here will bring your milk to the unit, it's number seven, up the ramp. You can park the car in the space out the front. Adam will show you. You got any kids, Kaye?'

'No.'

'I didn't think so.' Ethel blows a speck off a manicured pearly pink fingernail.

Kaye is the senior manager in a government department. She expects she will be a CEO, a chief executive officer. She spells out the acronym for Patricia, as if she would be unlikely to know this. They are sitting face to face in the old tearooms. Kaye didn't know that places like this still existed. It has a floral frieze around the walls and a joky sign up above the counter that says 'You Can't Fire Me Dammit, Slaves Have to be Sold.'

'Your job sounds pretty important, Kaye,' she says. 'What's your field?'

'Public administration.'

'But don't you have to specialise in something? I mean, you were a teacher, weren't you? I thought it might be in education.'

'Oh, I left that light years ago,' says Kaye. Patricia sees that her fingers are like threads and the way her glasses perch on the bridge of her spiny nose. She remembers how her hair used to stand out in that light-coloured halo and is surprised at how sleekly it falls now. She touches her own bouncy fair mane of hair and thinks, we are only forty-five. How can it be that Kaye already looks like a woman of sixty?

'I got my degree in policy,' Kaye explains. 'You can manage anything when you've got that behind you. I can't tell what might come up, right now. Transport, education, the arts — who knows?'

'I see,' says Patricia doubtfully. She looks round to see if their tea is coming. When Kaye had rung the night before, she had tried to hide her astonishment. 'Come out to the farm and have a meal,' she had said, immediately. 'Or stay the night. We've got oodles of room.'

'No,' Kaye had said stiffly, explaining that she was booked into a local motel.

And Patricia had said, 'Not Ethel's place?' It was as good as telling Kaye she knew all the Swansons' family secrets. So then Patricia had suggested that if they were going to meet, which seemed to be what Kaye was suggesting, they have a meal in town at one of the cafés on the main street.

But Kaye said no to that too. It was only a brief meeting she was suggesting, so if there was somewhere reasonably private they could have a chat, that would be a help. Patricia guessed that, before Kaye walked in and found Ethel Miller sitting behind the reception desk in the Summer Lodge, she might have asked Patricia to meet her there. Not that she would have gone. She thinks Kaye can see that too, that some territory is being established.

'It's just that it hasn't changed,' she says, her eyes flicking around. Patricia senses she is nervous, but then she feels an unease of her own. She has been tempted to tell Dan about this meeting but something about the way Kaye had spoken to her has cautioned her against this. Being here, buried in the back of the old tearooms feels, if not wicked, certainly challenging. Girls used to have assignments here with boys. Girls like Ethel. Only they would have been girls who met boys their own age, she reminds herself. She imagines that this meeting is about the past.

When their tea arrives, with a plate of brightly coloured cakes, Kaye takes a sip and fiddles with the clasp on her briefcase. Then she opens the lid and peers in. Perhaps she has found an old birth certificate, something like that. But it is a photocopied newspaper clipping she passes over to Patricia, crisp and recent. She clasps her hands in front of her, leans her forehead against them for a moment, before straightening up as Patricia scans the article.

'The piece about the hook in the river,' Patricia says. 'It was in our local paper.'

'It was run in a side bar of the *Evening Post*, the part about the hook. I went to the library and looked up the original story.'

'I don't understand,' says Patricia. She is thinking about the way Kaye's family had left town so suddenly, and put managers into the shop, how someone had told her at the time that Kaye had gone to boarding school. She had hated the way Kaye left without saying goodbye to her, although when she looks back it was clear they had stopped being friends by then. It embarrasses her to recall the way she had kept trying to get in touch with her. After the bridesmaid episode, she had chosen to forget Kaye. And yet, when she rang, it had given her an initial shock of pleasure, as if, after all, there was something between them that might be recaptured.

'Your brother, Lester. He had a hook. Well, someone must have made the connection, surely? You must have.' Kaye's colour is very high and she has trouble keeping her voice down.

'Yes,' says Patricia patiently. 'I thought of my brother, and I thought that it had nothing to do with him, or with me.'

'I can't believe that,' Kaye shoots back, regaining some of her composure.

'And even less with you,' says Patricia, feeling herself overtaken by an active dislike for the woman.

'Then I think you should consider what I have to tell you. I saw your brother the day he went missing.'

'You don't know what day he went missing. None of us know that.'

'All right. The last time he was seen in Ramparts. Oh come on, that was well known. Everyone was talking about it. The whole town was in an uproar over Lester and his mates turning up that Anzac Day. I knew what was going on. You don't have a monopoly on the rustic history of this place. My father ran a tractor sales and service, for God's sake.'

'All right,' says Patricia. 'There was an incident. Something happened.'

'Of course it happened. Now, I've got something to tell you.' She hesitates, choosing her words with care. 'At that time, my own life wasn't great — my parents were going through some bad times. I took off in my father's car early that morning.'

'You did? We were only fourteen at the time.'

'Well, I took it anyway. I drove it down to the river bank. I stayed there for a while and then I thought that what I was doing would only make things worse, and I had no idea why I'd gone there. I was down river from the bend by the bridge and I was trying to put the car into reverse when I looked up and I saw, in the distance, your father and your brother.'

'Yes,' says Patricia, 'my father gave him a ride out of town. He told us.' She feels her flesh creep, wants to stop the other woman talking, force a doughnut into her mouth, anything at all to shut her up.

'Your father got out of his ute and came round and opened the passenger door and then Lester got out. At first I didn't recognise him with all that long hair. I thought he was a girl. They stood there for a moment. Your father was waving his arms around and Lester was shaking his head, and then your father pushed him and he fell into the river below.'

'No,' says Patricia, 'none of this happened.'

'And then,' Kaye goes on relentlessly, 'your father got back in the truck and drove towards me. I couldn't get the car into reverse. He saw me there, and stopped. He asked me what was wrong, what was I doing there, and I said I was in trouble and I didn't know what to do, and so he put the car in reverse for me and backed it on to the road. He said to me, "Girlie, you could get into trouble doing something like this. You could roll down that bank if you weren't careful." He made sure I had my back to the river all the time. I put the accelerator down and drove home very slowly. I was surprised how easy it was. Once I got the hang of it. I drive a lot these days.' She smiles with self-deprecation, as if driving is particularly clever, not that she would want to say so. 'When I got back, I just parked the car in the garage and that was that.'

'And you never told anyone about this?'

'I tried to talk to my father about your father, just in a general sort of way, but he said I should keep well away from the Cooper family. He said you were a mad lot. After what I'd seen, I couldn't help agreeing. Not you, of course, Patricia. We were always friends.'

'I think you're crazy,' Patricia says. 'Why would you come here and tell me this now, after all these years? It's monstrous. You've got no proof.'

Kaye's eyes are watery and shining with sincerity. 'I saw that piece in the paper and I thought you'd want to know what happened to Lester. It's been on my conscience for years. Don't think I'm enjoying this.'

'Somebody would have found him.'

'If they were looking for him.' Kaye closes her eyes briefly, pursing her lips, as if all of this is so obvious it doesn't need saying. 'Of course he could have been found. But he wasn't.'

'So what happens next?' says Patricia, trying to keep her voice level.

'Happens? Nothing happens. I don't want any scandal, believe me, not at this stage of my career.'

'Your career.' Patricia can't stop her lip curling, although at the same time her knees are trembling beneath the table and she has to hold her hands in her lap so that Kaye can't see them shaking.

'I guess it's up to you, really, how you deal with this information.'

'This is not information,' said Patricia. She reaches up and brushes a crumb from the table, steadying herself. 'This is a fabrication. This is something you think you saw, Kaye, but you didn't.'

'Then where did the hook come from? Whose was it?'

'Do you think nobody's asked me since that thing turned up? Of course they have. And then, when you remind them, they remember, after all, that there have been three men in this town with missing limbs, counting Lester. A man who came back from the war, and another old chap who lost his hand felling trees. A long time ago. They're dead and nobody can ask them how many hooks they had or what happened to them.' Patricia stands, reaching for her purse to pay the bill.

'Why would I come here and tell you this if it weren't true?' Kaye is white and swaying on her feet, fumbling with her briefcase.

'I'll tell you why. Because you've got nothing better to do. Because your blood's in this place, and you can't keep away from it, can't stop meddling and poking and looking for absurd clues. Take my advice: keep away or you might find more than you want to know.'

Kaye has crumpled, is turning her head this way and that in distress. 'You always wanted to be the boss of everything.'

Boss. The word has a childish pathetic ring, as if they have moved on to trading insults.

'And you always liked my brother, but he was mine,' Patricia says.

This is a cheap shot for which Patricia will later feel deeply ashamed. She is speaking, after all, to a grown woman who was, as she has said herself, only fourteen when all of this happened, or might have happened.

And yet, in an odd sort of way, it seems to make Kaye happy. Her damp sorrowing eyes blaze with an absurd sudden triumph, as if she has won something. That, Patricia supposes, is how it goes, how victories are won and wrested away in Kaye's world.

The rest home in Ramparts is built on a hill. It looks across a valley full of native bush where birds flit endlessly among the branches of the trees.

In the mornings when he is being given his daily bath, Os Cooper looks around the mirrors with a look of wonder and bafflement. One morning, when he has been dressed in his brown corduroy pants and woollen shirt, with the sleeves rolled up the way he likes them, he stands and straightens himself in front of his reflection and wags his finger at it. 'I'm going straight,' he says, 'What about you?'

Most mornings he shuffles backwards and forwards down the

hallway of the secure unit, with a ceaseless steady tread. In the afternoon his frail body collapses in front of the television in the yellow and blue pretty dayroom and watches television.

Just sometimes, on what the nurses describe as his good days, he can be persuaded to join in an activity. Patricia visits twice a week, on Mondays and Thursdays. Some days he knows her, and others not at all, but he likes her company because she takes him outside the locked wing for walks in the garden, and sometimes for drives. The first thing Patricia asks the staff is whether or not he is having a good day. There are fewer and fewer of these and for this she is grateful. She does not want to see her father dancing around in circles waving scarves. Besides, there was a day when he first went to live in the home that had embarrassed her and the staff.

What happened was this. Someone who described herself as a storyteller had come in for an activity session, to help the patients 'reclaim their lives,' as she put it. Her name was Sadie and she had long black hair that she wove around in her fingers while she chatted and encouraged them to write things down on big blank unruled sheets of paper. The patients were given coloured crayons which Sadie said would be easier for them to hold, and they could make bold headings for the milestone events in their lives: journeys or marriage or the birth of their children.

'It's very important,' she said, 'that you do this work for yourself.'

'What work?' asked Os. 'I thought we were here to have a rest.'

'Well,' Sadie explained, 'I mean that you have to think of these things for yourself, I can't make them up for you.'

'They have to be true?'

'You can make things up if you like, Os, but I'm thinking about stories you might like to leave for your families. This is just a starting out point for perhaps recording some special memories that you can hand on to your children.'

'Mr Cooper. Gunner Cooper, regimental number one two five.' But his memory had left him behind and he could not finish the number. 'Mr Cooper will do.'

'Sure. Fine. Mr Cooper. We can do this another day if you like.'

'You mean we can all stop?'

'No. I mean, everyone else who's interested in doing this can keep going, but you don't have to, not if you don't want to.'

'I'll do what they do. I do what I'm told.' Os searched through the crayons and picked up a purple one. Looking from side to side to check what others were doing, he hesitated and wrote in large letters the word DEATH. He sat back and stared at what he had written.

'Who died, Mr Cooper?' Sadie's voice was soft and insistent at his elbow.

When he didn't answer, she said, 'Your wife? Didn't she die?'

'Not wife.' He chose a black crayon and wrote with angry strokes:

My Son. I killed My Son. I killed him with my little bow and arrow. He got what he deserved.

Sadie said, 'I think we've done enough for today, Mr Cooper.'

'All that bullshit,' he said, beginning to cry. 'All that trouble he caused.'

'It's nearly time for lunch now.' She picked up the paper and folded it so that other people couldn't read it.

When Patricia arrived in the afternoon, she asked, as would become her habit, 'Is he having a good day?' This was when the nurse showed her what Os had written. Sadie had said that she felt she ought to give it to someone: she knew a man in his condition could imagine things, and she thought perhaps her style of working with this group was a bit too intense, that perhaps she wouldn't come back too soon, but there it was, she felt responsible.

Patricia took the piece of paper from her and studied it. 'Poor old boy,' she said finally. 'He's just so deluded, isn't he?'

'It's so sad,' the nurse said. 'It must have really preyed on his mind, losing your brother like that. Young people don't know what they're doing to their families. It sounds as if he'd made up his mind to go missing.'

'Yes,' Patricia said, thinking about what the lawyer had said to her and Dan. 'He's lost, all right. We've given up on him coming home.'

Families Like Ours

When Kaye Swanson drives out of town, Patricia feels as if she has been holding in her breath for a very long time, and that now she can release it.

On her birthday, Dan and Patricia charter a hot air balloon from an out-of-town company to take them for a ride over Ramparts. This is what Patricia has chosen for her gift. Afterwards, the family will join them and they will drink champagne and have breakfast together.

The best time of day for balloon riding is dawn when the air is most still. First the pilot, a short nut-coloured man, releases a black balloon into the air to test the wind. This is the crucial moment, when the decision is made as to whether the flight will proceed.

He tells them it's all go, and as soon as the balloon is inflated they will be away. The slow filling of the giant blue orb makes a monstrous noise, like the Wall of Death. Patricia has not been prepared for this, only for the perfect silence that has been promised her when she is airborne.

The flame that ignites the gas rushes up in huge sighing gusts and then the balloon rises gently into the air and, with only a frail basket between them and the ground far below, they are hovering high above Ramparts, high above the paddocks, and the farms, and the river. Dan exclaims, wants to point things out to her, but Patricia puts her fingers to her lips to hush him, so that she can experience every moment of this, without distraction. She sees where the river is joined by tributaries and how it rushes headlong to the sea. There is silence then, broken only by the waking cries of birds and the first bark of the dogs as they greet the rising sun.

She doesn't speak, doesn't say goodbye, not aloud anyway. From far below she can smell, coming up to meet her, fragrances that she recognises, hadn't expected to detect this far from the ground: the dazzling scent of a honeysuckle hedge which for a moment makes her think she is going to faint; a bank of old Windrush roses that she planted on the Matheson farm soon after she was married and still a teenager. From here, the bank looks like one of the tablecloths she threads and stitches, thrown carelessly across the landscape. She inhales the smell of fresh bread from the bakery in town, then she is hit by the sharp malodorous smell of cowshit in the yards. The flames leap up beside her. A swooning hawk flies alongside them. They seem to be racing its shadow on the ground.

She believes she can see pretty well everything that has happened here.

MISTER BLUE SATIN

The waiting room outside the High Court is not the kind of place anyone should have to sit around in for hours. Tania thinks she could just get up and go, without waiting to hear a verdict. She's only a witness when all's said and done; it's not as if she's on trial. But that's the way it feels. She'd stood up in the witness stand and said, 'That's him, that's the one that did it. He's the man I went off with that night, but he was just supposed to be giving me a lift home.' Twelve pairs of eyes watching her from the jury benches. She couldn't raise her eyes to look at one of those faces. They have all looked at photographs of her body. Perhaps they know her better than she knows herself. Point at him, the lawyer had said, show us the man. And, when she couldn't raise her arm because it felt as if a lead weight was tying it to the edge of the stand, the judge had repeated it: *Point*. Not nastily, but she could tell he was impatient; it had all gone on long enough. Memory is a fine thing, you own yourself if you've got memory, but there were some things she couldn't remember; her whole mind had blanked out now about that night. She'd lifted her arm anyway, her own tired dissociated limb, and said, 'That's him, that's the fella. That's Ruka.'

When she had said it, she'd looked up for him, Mr Blue Satin, the boy man with the shirt that whirled around him like blue cream, but they'd taken him off where she couldn't see him. So now what am I supposed to do, she wondered. Whose big fat stupid idea is it that I've come here?

And now she waits. Among sly little hussies like Dixie who's supposed to be her friend, and her mother, and Gene, Mr Blue Satin himself, in a dirty waiting room, filled with overflowing ashtrays, and scuffed carpet and magazines that are ten years old and have had all the recipes cut out and the women in the celebrity pics have moustaches drawn on their faces, and rude words scrawled on their crotches.

'They'll put the bastard away,' says Gene confidently. But Tania's not that sure. She looked up just as she was finishing her evidence, finally dragging her eyes back to her surroundings, and she'd seen something on the faces of a couple of the jurors: a look of shock, or pity. It wasn't that they didn't like her — she could pretty well tell — it was just that they just didn't believe her.

'They'll be out to get a rapist,' Gene says. Tania sees that he is looking at the jury through different eyes. 'You see if they don't nail this joker.' The week before there had been another story all over the papers. A girl left to rot, the way some men take and use children and then discard them. Disposable kids. There'd been street marches and lynch signs, threatening to castrate rapists. Women who were used to staying at home and peeling potatoes were out on the streets, shouting kill, kill, kill.

'Ah, shut it, Gene,' says Tania's mother. Her thick black hair is tied up in a high pony-tail; her features are sculptured like a bone carving. Except when she's driving her battered Mazda, she's always got her sunglasses pushed up on top of her head, even when she's sitting in a court waiting room at night and the jury's been out for eight hours.

'It couldn't have happened at a better time,' Gene says, smoke curling out of the side of his mouth. It's a little trick of his: you can't see the opening in the corner of his lips where he lets it trickle out. 'They're not going to go soft on a joker who goes round attacking women. They'll bring him down.'

The laundrette is situated down a short side street off the main drag in Newtown, a kind of alleyway, lined nearly all the way down one side with car repair places, quick fix it up and make them go outfits: Automotive Wizards, Rust Repairs, Spray Painting — you can bargain for a price at most of them. There's a row of terrace houses with green pointy roofs, as if they've all been bought by the same landlord. The lawns have been replaced with bark over black polythene that's cracking up and letting the weeds grow through. Round the corner on Constable Street there's a giant block of flats, and at the other end, as you turn left and go on up towards the zoo, there's the biggest block of council flats in the city. At night you hear the lions roar and the monkeys scream, and from the flats themselves, the fighting and swearing, the occasional shout in the night, a dozen languages called from one balcony to another and a trainee opera singer at practice. Howls like blues in the night.

Tania likes living there, or she did when she first moved in from the Hutt. You can feel the joint jumping, not like Taita, where she grew up, and where the streets are wide and empty at night, and the houses are spaced out, so that when you talk after dark you hear your own voice echoing. Its a funny thing about these flats in Newtown — you can take a stroll and find yourself in a sweet pretty neighbourhood with magnolias in front of the fences, or go on up the hill and you're in the town belt with the sea melting beneath you, so it's like you've got everything. But most of all, there's the life of the city, the pubs and the cafs, the juice of the place running through your veins. There's shops, and fruit markets and stalls, and crazy people wandering up and down, wearing hand-me-down caftans and beads and turbans, militant For Christ guys on the corners and addicts and brown and black people, and the smell of herbs and spices and Vietnamese mint mixed with backyard hangis and behind the curtain curries, the whole lot mixed up together.

Tania went to the laundrette the first week after she moved in. You don't have to be rich to be clean. 'You've got the gift of looks,' her mother said, 'just make sure you're always pressed and spotless and you'll make your way in this world.'

Tania's mother feels she's done all right, despite one of her boys being a permanent truant, and her husband being what's generally described as an absent father. She wears denim overalls with three-quarter legs, faded with the constant assault of cleanliness, and overbright slinky skivvies. Tania dresses in much the same way, except when she's going out dancing. Then she puts on her best jeans and a red and black beaded top with a fringed hem that swings when she moves her hips. You could say she shares the same taste as her mother, not that she'd admit it for the world.

Pretty well every Tuesday night two sheets and one pillow slip and her three towels and a face flannel with a picture of a teddy bear, and one pair of jeans go into a plastic bag. She chooses Tuesday because she can only get one channel on television and who wants to watch *Coronation Street*, and there's not much doing in town at the beginning of the week, and anyway she's skint after the weekend, and pay day's not until Thursday. Her work is cleaning offices, six o'clock in the morning start, so she doesn't do too much night life during the week. She's got computer skills: her teacher at college said she shouldn't have much trouble getting an office job, and sure enough she works in an office but they don't seem to be hiring caramel colours on reception at the moment. She did leave some notes out on some desks one night, saying hire me, I'm a nice girl, here's my phone number, and she got fired from that job. It was just lucky that her mother knew somebody who knew somebody else from another firm who was hiring at the time.

The laundrette's got big commercial-sized washing machines and a bank of coin-operated green and yellow-fronted Windsor driers. There's a long formica table with twelve chairs arranged around it where you can sit while you wait for your stuff to go through. She's sitting there chatting to a Samoan girl who's doing really well at

Mister Blue Satin

university, and reckons that's what Tania should be doing too, when Mr Blue Satin comes in. He's a skinny boy, may be one seventy-eight tall, not much more than sixty kilos, with a bit of a swagger, hair oiled like guys in old-fashioned movies — the Fonz or somebody, one of those fifties geeks. She half expects him to start singing or shimmying around the place in his shiny shirt. It's got three buttons undone and, just as you'd expect, a chain hangs among the half dozen hairs that nestle in the hollow beneath his collarbone. It's not a fitting shirt: it rides easy on him, tucked in at the waist with a wide silvery buckled belt. By the unguarded light of the laundrette the shirt has a metallic sheen, melting this way and that like mercury in a bottle, and then turning blue again.

Mr Blue Satin carries a bundle of washing all scrunched up and rolled under one arm, nothing to hold it together, and a box of KFC in the other.

Tania watches him loading his stuff into a machine; she can't help it, he's a guy who's kind of compulsive looking. She could see him as a school boy in a classroom, pulling faces behind the teacher and looking straight-faced while everybody else laughed. An antics kind of boy.

The student girl puts her things together. Her stuff's already dry, but Tania's guessed that she likes it in here, that it's quieter than home.

Tania sees that the guy is holding out another blue satin shirt, taken from his washing bundle, wondering what to do next. 'You shouldn't put that in with your other things,' she says.

'I was wondering about that. The last one I washed came out looking like coloured mince.'

'You should hand-wash it, like underwear. How many blue shirts have you got?'

'Three but now one's not fit to wear. I got Suresh the tailor to do me three all at once to use up his bolt of material. I figured that way I'd always have a clean one.'

He throws his box of fried chicken on the table in front of them. 'Have some.'

'I'm off,' says the student. 'You want to come over to my place?'

'My clothes aren't dry,' says Tania.

'You should still come to my house. You can keep your Kenfucky Tries, you,' she says, addressing Mr Blue Satin. 'You're just trouble.'

'Perhaps I'll come a bit later,' says Tania, picking out a piece of chicken. She hasn't had any dinner, and the hot fatty meat is firing up her tastebuds.

The student lets the door slam shut behind her as she goes out.

'Bit of a cow. Is she a mate of yours?'

'I don't even know her name. She's doing a major in psychology.'

'That explains it. Would you wash this shirt for me? I don't know that I can do it without making a mess of it.'

'You've gotta learn things like that. Two and a bit shirts won't last long if you don't know how to wash them.'

'You could show me how. I've got some good shit at my house.'

'So it's true what she says.' Tania indicates the spot where the student had sat. 'You are trouble?'

'Don't tell me you wouldn't like some good shit. I can tell from the look of you, you're kind of hungry.'

'I could just come and show you how to wash your shirt.'

'Okay, you do that.'

The driers are spinning and humming all around them, while they eat and sit and read a magazine or two, and he presses his knee into hers and she aches at the thought of him, because just lately she's been a bit lonely, and it's shit getting up at the crack of dawn five days a week, and really she wants to know why the hell is she doing this, hanging out just to prove a point and live some place else except with her mother and brothers (although there's the small matter of just a curtain hanging in the bedroom between her and her brother Jason, and the way he pulls his pudding all night long so that she doesn't get that much sleep when she's living at home).

In the morning she wakes up in Mr Blue Satin's bed — she knows now that his name is Gene — and he murmurs in her ear, 'You taste like plums at the end of summer.' Nobody's ever said anything like that to her before, and she feels a wild and dizzying pleasure, as if she's found home at last. It's eight o' clock and too late to go to work. She drinks a swig of red wine out of a bottle he offers her. The bed is actually a mattress on the floor. The room is like a tip, with CD's and ashtrays and dirty socks, which he must have forgotten when he went to the laundrette, empty cigarette packs and a used needle, and wrappers from takeaways, and she thinks that when she gets up she'll tidy up for him.

Around eleven, when she still hasn't started out on this course of good intentions, a woman opens the bedroom door and stands looking at the pair of them holed up there under the purple duvet. The woman, whose name, Gene says, is Dixie, is around thirty, with red and yellow streaks frosted through her black ringlets. She's dressed all in black from head to toe, a black leather bodice trimmed with black fur round the neckline, and a long black skirt. On her hands she wears black lace mittens, the fingers cut away to reveal blood-red fingertips.

She's leaning on the door, looking down at Tania as if she can see her through the bed covers. Gene is on his back, smoking a cigarette not seeming as if he cares. Outside it's started to rain, the noise on the iron roof so deafening you can hardly hear their voices.

'Have one for me,' Dixie says.

'Is she your girlfriend?' Tania asks, thinking she's about to be killed.

'Nah, she's looking for money, aren't you, doll?'

'I've got some for you too,' Dixie says.

'Put it on the table. This here is Tania, my nice skinny new girlfriend. You want to give her a massage?'

'Oh Jesus,' Dixie says, 'I'm dead beat as it is.' But she's started peeling off her gear, throwing her mittens and her skirt into a corner of the room.

'It's all right,' says Tania, rolling over on her stomach. She's embarrassed by Dixie seeing her with nothing on, except the cover.

'No harm,' says Dixie, dropping to her knees beside them. 'C'mon kid, this is my job. Just keep still the way you are.' Before Tania can do a thing about it, Dixie's on top of her, squatting above her buttocks, her fingers digging into her spine, and it's sheer bliss, the way she pushes into the small of her back, finding pressure points she didn't know she had. 'Easy, girl, easy. Now you like that, don't you?'

Which is true, she likes it as much as anything she and Gene have done. Dixie runs her fingers beneath Tania's shoulder blades, then shimmies them down her spine, and it's like a deluge engulfing her, every bit of her body folding out and out, layer upon layer of her, like a big flower showing itself to the sun, even though the rain is torrential, and a trickle of water is seeping into the room around the window frame, and running down the wall near the tip of her nose, and she can tell from the old bleak stains that run side by side with the water that this is no new thing, nothing freshly sprung. When Dixie's got her in a state of such total relaxation that she's drifting out into space, Gene sends her off to make coffee for them all and then he comes down on Tania from behind and it's all right, it really is.

It just seems like Tania and Dixie are meant to be friends. Around ten years separates them in age, but it doesn't matter, there's always a lot to tell each other. Dixie tells her about the two men she'd married and how they abandoned her, and now she has a little boy who was her first husband's but he lives with his stepfather, the second one, and how she'll sort all that out before long. She's had some spiritual experiences in her life which have mapped out a path for her. She takes Tania down Cuba Street to have her palm read, and the woman there tells her that she has a long life ahead of her after a period of indecision. There's a man in her life but he isn't the one for her.

'She has her off days,' Dixie says. 'You and Gene are milk and honey together.'

Tania tells Dixie about the good marks she'd got in school when she was a little kid and how her brothers had taken the mickey over that. And then with some of the kids in the neighbourhood she'd hung around with, it wasn't the thing to be smart, and she didn't believe it anyway. Her mother had got her an apprenticeship in the hairdresser's but, as she tells Dixie, that sucked — all that smarming around old women with little wisps of hair and their grumbles if she shampooed too hard or too soft. All of these things, Dixie appears to understand absolutely. Dixie is there for her, too, when she gets into a mess with money.

Tania didn't quite see how it happened: it was all so gradual you could hardly tell where it started. Except, of course, she lost her cleaning job. It wasn't there for her when she went in on Monday morning and said she'd been sick as a dog, and the boss asked her why she didn't let him know. Too sick, she said, I was too sick.

That was tough, the boss said, because he'd had to get someone else in to take her place, and he wasn't putting off a good worker because she mucked him around. Go to the union, he said, knowing she hadn't joined.

'Don't worry about your job, I'll look after you,' Gene said, when she talked to him about it. She thought it was a bit quick the way it all happened — one night she was sitting in the laundrette, and the next one she was living with him. 'You can stay with me for a while,' he said. 'You don't have to go back to that place.' As if the flats were only fit for dogs. But still, it was nice, just the two of them living together in a little house, and having nice things, because when you cleared away the mess, it wasn't such a bad place, and he wasn't shy about spending money: he bought what he wanted. There was a lounge suite covered with real pale red leather in the sitting room, and a fantastic sound system, and when she said why don't we get a proper bed, he said well, why not. They bought a king-size at Radford's and had it delivered the same day; it just about filled the whole bedroom up.

'I'd better bring my stuff over,' she said, and that's when he dropped the first bombshell.

'I never said anything about bringing your stuff over.'

'Well, what the fuck am I supposed to do with it?' It was the first time they'd quarrelled and she could feel it boiling up so quickly it was like a lightning rod had struck them.

'I didn't say it was permanent.' His voice was sullen.

'You did.'

His voice hooked up a few notches. 'I did not. When the fuck did

I ever say it was permanent? Who told you that goddam lie, goddam bitch, you lying little sow. Did Dixie put you up to this?'

'Gene, I'm sorry, I thought ...'

'Don't think. You hear me? Don't think, bitch.'

'Okay, okay, I just don't have the rent and it's due now.'

'Oh, you don't have the rent. All right, then. Perhaps I can give you a bit of rent.'

'You don't need to do that. I'll go back there tonight. I'll get an emergency benefit.'

'You'd be so lucky. Oh shit, Tania, don't do this to me. You're like my life to me. You're the most fantastic girl I ever met. I'll give you the rent money.'

'So what are you saying? You want me to stay here or go back there?'

'Why do you have to make everything so complicated? Eh? Eh? I said do both. Stay here and I'll pay the rent.'

'So you've got somewhere for me to go when you want to kick me out?'

'Are you trying to provoke me or what?'

At which point, Tania shut up.

She stays at Gene's and makes them dinner some nights: he likes fish fingers with chips, and Sara Lee danish for dessert. They eat up town other nights, and meet Dixie when she isn't working. Dixie gives her some money for tampons and lipstick and a few things like that, because Tania knows somehow she can't ask Gene for any more than he's giving her, and Dixie seems to know this without her mentioning it. Gene has a car, a big old restored Chevrolet with fins, painted green and silver. They drive around town together, Tania as good as sitting in his lap, and one Sunday they go over to Eastbourne and have a coffee in the tearooms in the park by the duck pond. 'This is such shit,' Gene says, looking around at the fathers playing with their children on the green. 'I don't know how people can do crap like this.'

Gene goes out some nights and she understands that this is the time when he works. She thinks he cut a few deals up town but he doesn't talk about that, and she thinks it best not to ask. He tells her one day that he's inherited money. When she asks him who from, he says it's none of her business.

Then he kicks her out, and that was when she's in real trouble, because the rent at the flats hasn't been paid for a month and they say she can't go back unless she can front up with the money.

'Can I stay with you for a bit?' she asks Dixie.

Because she has no bed, no money, no shit, and she feels like hell.

'We're a bit crowded,' Dixie says, which is true. She's sharing with Jane, who has a forty-two-centimetre bust, and Susie, a Goth girl who'd gone to private school. 'Why don't I fix you up with a bit of work?'

'I don't know that I could do that,' says Tania, 'I haven't been trained in massage.'

Dixie sighs. 'Well, you know. It's not a sports medicine degree we're talking about here.'

Which Tania knows, she isn't that silly, but while she has Gene to look after her, she'd thought maybe she could just avoid that.

'I'll have a talk to Gene,' Dixie says.

So Tania, when she's thought for a bit, asks: 'How many girls does he have working for him?'

'Never you mind,' Dixie replies.

Tania has been back in her old flat three nights when Gene comes knocking on the door. She sees him through the spyhole in the door, pacing up and down, his thumbs hooked under his belt, his blue satin shirt spilling out at the back of his pants, his face white.

Opening the door, as far the chain will reach, she tells him, 'Go away, arsehole, you've got what you want.'

'I want you to come back to me,' he says.

Slamming the door shut and turning to lean her back against it. Willing herself not to say anything. Because her mind is made up, she's been through her time of indecision, and she is going back to the Valley on the first train in the morning. She can take things a day at a time out there, the air's fresh and there's room to breathe.

Gene beating the door with his fists. 'Let me in, let me in.' Kicking the door, running against it, so that the place shakes, and people are coming out into the stairwells, shouting to shut up the noise. What did they think they were doing? They'll call the police. Which is a laugh, because people don't call the police in this block of flats unless someone is already dead.

So then she lets him in, shivering and crying and putting his arms around her for warmth, because it's another cold night outside.

'We'll pack up your stuff,' he says. 'You're coming back with me.'

'But why?' she says, as he throws open the wardrobe door and grabs the beaded top and the wind breaker she hasn't worn since she met him.

'Because you're my girl.'

'You mean I don't have to work?'

'Oh c'mon,' he says, as they pull the door to the empty flat closed behind them, 'everybody's gotta work. You're my girl, that's the thing.'

'No,' she says, trying to drag herself free, 'no, I'm not going to work for you. I don't like that sort of work.' Which she doesn't at all. She's been at it three nights, and she's done fifteen or so jobs, all sorts — the working men on their way home, the men in business suits, a bunch of rugby players, and one or two of the grubby old fools people like to think are the only ones who really visit people like her.

'Yes, you are, yes you are, you're going to be my girl, and we'll be sweet.'

'How can I be your girl when there're these other jokers too?' They're in bed, smoking and drinking a smooth red wine, which inches its way down and soothes her, sorts her out, makes her feel unreasonably content.

'That's different,' he says. 'That's work. I'm the one you come home to — nobody else, nobody, you understand. You come straight home every night and I'll be good to you.'

'Okay.'

'Just one thing.'

'What's that?'

'You stay skinny. I like skinny girls. I want to count your ribs every night, okay?'

'Okay, Gene.' Which is fine and what she wanted so why is she crying now, lying here, with the wine working its way down her gullet, and the pink light filtering through the shade beside the bed, and more rain falling on the roof the way she likes to hear it?

Someone says they've seen Gene up town with a blonde called Moira. It must be Dixie who's slipped that into the conversation, she can't think who else would have told her. It's not what she wants to hear. No shit. Perhaps she didn't hear it. It rolls around in her head for a week. She doesn't ask him. He's in a mood she doesn't like — scary, rather cold, not answering her when she speaks to him — which tells her it might be true. One day she talks about taking the train out to the Valley to see her mother.

'No, you just quit it, you just stay at home.'

'Are you frightened I mightn't come back?' she says, which is as daring as she gets. He stubs out his cigarette on the skin beside her navel and because she's stoned and sick in the stomach, there's nothing she can do about it. She has to wear a plaster on it for a week and it's so damn sore she can't lie on it at night, because that's the way she likes to sleep, face down, her natural position.

He doesn't come in until morning for five nights in a row.

Dixie says, 'How come you never come out for a drink? How about you come with us tonight?'

'You know I can't. Gene would kill me.'

'Strikes me, Gene wouldn't know about it. I mean, if you really want to know.'

'No I don't.'

'Yes, you do.'

At the pub she meets Ruka, who Dixie says is her cousin. He's a big man in working clothes, a tree feller with the smell of bark on his skin. An easy friendly voice, an open face that she likes. An untroubled expression, big mouth, big laugh, big white teeth. Big family, Dixie says, at some point in the evening, which should have told her to be careful, but they've drunk so many beers and followed them with so many chasers that one thing's blurred into the next.

Mr Blue Satin stands in the witness box in front of the old dark wood panelling of the courtroom. His shirt is shimmering like one of those auras around aliens in science fiction movies. His hair is slicked up to a point and falls over to one side in a curl. Against the glare of the lights in the room, his face looks dim and pale and pointed.

'Tell us what happened?' the lawyer says.

'I got a phone call about three in the morning.'

'Who phoned you?'

'The witness. Tania.'

'What is the relationship between you and Tania?'

'She's a friend.'

'Your girlfriend?'

'No sir. A friend.'

'Where were you?'

'I was at a friend's place.'

'Another friend's place.'

'Yessir.'

'You seem to have a lot of friends. What time was this?'

'Three o'clock in the morning.'

'What did she say to you?'

'She said some joker had picked up and taken her out to Moa Point and tried to ... well, you know.'

'No, you tell me.'

'Tried to rape her. She was hysterical, crying her eyes out, you know, really sobbing.'

'You say he tried to rape her? That's what she told you?'

'Yeah.'

'But he hadn't succeeded?'

'That's what she said. Well, she said he'd had a go and she'd tried to push him away, and then he went to sleep. When he woke up he drove her home.'

'Did she tell you whether she'd gone with him of her own accord?'

'Objection, your honour. My learned friend is leading the witness into the realms of hearsay.'

'Objection upheld.'

'Very well. What did you do when your friend rang you in distress?'

'I said I'd pick her up.'

'Where from?'

'My house.'

'Oh, so she was at your house?'

'She stays over there. She used to. We shared, you know, some of the facilities.'

'I see, so you hurry from your friend's house back to your house where your other friend, the witness, Miss X, is waiting for you, and then what do you do?'

'She tells me what happens and I say, we'll go out and look for him, you and me. He's not going to get away with this. She says she'll know his car if she sees it.'

'So you think this man might still be driving around town?'

'Well, he might have been.'

'How long did you drive around for?'

'All the next day. Till about three in the afternoon.'

Driving around, not knowing what Gene might do next. Trying to remember exactly what did happen, the night before, because it was like there was a great fog in her mind, a slumbering beast. If she could push it away, get out from under it, she would be able to see. Touring around, cruising from one place to another, places she and Gene'd been to, out to Eastbourne and along the bays, like a farewell trip. Knowing he had the gun under the seat, not knowing who he would decide to use it on, Ruka or her. Wondering, when they stopped for petrol, whether she should run for it, and risk getting gunned down on the spot. Thinking, Ruka will have gone by now, back to wherever it is he comes from, because he has three kids at home. Some time before the blankness took over, when they were still back at the pub having laughs and drinks, and she was feeling the best she'd done in months, he was saying the missus would be after him if he wasn't careful. Gene asking, is that his car, does it look like that, what colour was it, don't tell me you didn't get the registration, what are you? And Tania getting more and more scared that she might actually see Ruka's car, and deciding that if they did, she wouldn't say anything, she'd pretend she hadn't seen him, because next thing there'd be blood and bodies everywhere and it would all be her fault — if she wasn't already dead anyway. And if she could just have one chance to get out of this, she might go home to her mum.

'And all this time, your friend is distressed, and hasn't had any sleep, and she hasn't been to the police?'

'I figured we had to find him before he got away.'

'We figured we had to find him before he got away.' This, echoed very slowly, deliberation after every word.

'Yes. Something like that.'

'Something like that. So then your friend decided to go to the police?'

'I told her go to the police. You can't have people doing that kind of thing.'

Out at Moa Point. Where she'd been the night before. The smell of sewage in the air, because it's the outfall for the city, or it was back then, before they put the treatment plant in. A scummy brown film among the rocks. Bits of toilet paper. The gun in her back. Gene, taking her out across the rocky outfall, underneath the flight path of the planes coming in to land, the roar in her ears coming and going. The surf. The planes. The ringing sound of fear and the total light-headedness she was experiencing.

'Sit down,' he says.

'I've gotta get some sleep, Gene. Please take me home.'

His blue satin shirt, like a kid's dress-up, the violet smudges beneath his eyes, the oily sea behind him.

'What did you do with him?'

'Nothing.'

'He tried it on with you.'

'Yeah, but nothing happened. He was too drunk to get it up.'

'I wanted you to be mine.'

'You can't own me, Gene.'

'I do, but that's not the point.'

'Then what the fuck is the point?'

'I told you, I never had a girl who was mine. Who'd do anything for me. Just for me. I really really liked, really fucking loved you, you dumb cow.'

'I love you too, Gene. Honest.'

'But you went with this joker.'

'I go with lots of jokers.'

'No, you don't, that's different. You wanted to go with him. You stayed out late with him.'

'He just gave me a ride home.'

'Why didn't you try and jump out of the car?'

'I didn't want to get killed. I was scared.'

'You could have run away from him when he went to sleep.'

'He went to sleep on top of me. He was a big fella. Please Gene, this isn't getting us anywhere.'

'Prove it. Prove that he forced you. Make me believe it.'

'What do I have to do?'

'You know. You *know*.'

'You mean go to the police?'

'Yeah, well, he sounds pretty dangerous. You should report an attack.'

'I can't go through with that.'

Gene just looks at her, contempt written on his face, as if she's dirt.

'So now,' says the lawyer, flicking his gown behind him with one practised hand, 'now you're providing the witness with sympathy and support?'

'Objection, your honour. That question is not relevant to the facts of the Crown's case.'

'Objection upheld.'

'Thank you, your honour. I have no further questions for this witness.'

He has another fish to dangle in front of the jury. Dixie. Blinking, awake far too early, still a stunning figure in her black gear. Standing up straight, a small half smile hovering round the corners of her carmine mouth, the matching fingernails peeping out from the black lace mittens, the hair gathered over padding to create a high pompadour, the ringlets flowing from beneath a comb.

'You introduced the first witness to the defendant?'

'Yeah.'

'He is your cousin?'

'Nah.'

'But that's what you told the witness?'

'He was a mate from way back.'

'When she asked you if it was safe to ride home with him, you told her, yes, it's all right. Is that true?'

A toss of her head, 'I didn't know he was a bad fulla then.'

'And now you think he is?'

'Stands to reason, wouldn't you say, mister?'

'I'm asking the questions.'

'Well, we can't all be wise with hindsight, as the saying goes.' A triumphant malice at having got the better of her questioner.

'Well, as you're so full of aphorisms, wouldn't you say that perhaps you're a person who likes two bob each way?'

'Objection, your honour.'

Tania steals a look at Ruka, the first time she has allowed herself a glance. A muscle is working in the thick column of his throat. As if he is swallowing and swallowing. His eyes are very still.

The jury's still out. Tania's mother gets to her feet, restless, knocking a half-empty bottle of soft drink to the floor without noticing what she's done.

Mister Blue Satin

'I'm going out for a breath of fresh air,' she says. She and Tania have been so on edge with each other there's nothing much left for them to say, especially with Gene sitting there preening himself. Tania looks at him, and thinks what a sad person he really is. He thinks he's done all right in that courtroom, that he cut quite a figure. Now that she sees him in this harsh real place, she sees how much of a fantasy world he lives in, and how little she knows about him — what his life was before, where he came from, whether anyone had cared stink for him. She knows he likes Batman comics and George Michael, and that's about it.

Her mother's not hiding her dislike of him, and although Gene doesn't appear to notice or care, it hasn't helped the hours to pass, as the jury sits somewhere and considers all their lives and what's going to happen to them.

When her mother comes back from her walk, she looks indignant. 'That poor woman,' she says.

'What poor woman?' says Tania.

'His wife. She's beside herself out there in the other waiting room.'

'You're not telling me you spoke to Ruka's wife? Tell me this isn't happening.'

'I certainly did speak to her. I've been watching that woman — she's on her own, too ashamed, I expect, to tell her friends what's going on. It must be hard, having to get someone to mind the kiddies, and keep it all to herself. The whole thing's just killing her, you can tell. I said to her, I'm sorry about your trouble, I tried to bring her up right.'

'You said that about me?'

'She's a decent sort of woman. She said, I don't blame the girl, he shouldn't have been where he was, he shouldn't have put himself in that situation. It's just that he's innocent. I said to her, but Tania had all these bruises and things, I've seen the pictures to prove that. She said to me, well, Ruka didn't do it, he wouldn't hurt a fly.'

'You don't know anything. You always think you know better than me.'

'So you tell me what you know, more to the point.'

'You're my mother,' Tania says. 'You're supposed to be on my side.'

'Well, don't tell me you didn't want Ruka,' her mother says. 'Because I can tell you, I would.' She looks at Gene with distaste, as if he's just crawled out from under a stone.

'Oh, I'm out of here,' Tania says, picking up her jacket. But then the court attendant says the jury is coming back and so they file into the back of the court, behind Ruka. She knows exactly what the foreman is going to say, and while they're waiting for him to clear his throat, and steady his voice, she slips noiselessly out again, walks down the corridor and moves into the night.

Waiting for the crash to happen, the earthquake to start toppling things. Feathers of rain touch her skin; soon they turn to bee stings. She thinks if she runs fast enough and far enough away, she will reach open space.

ALL THE WAY TO SUMMER

On the drive home from the hospital Annie Pile stared straight through the windscreen, her baby asleep in her arms. She held him as if he was a snake in a basket. The beaten-up light truck rattled and banged over potholes. All around us, the landscape was steeped in dark yellow sunlight, shining between the leaves of trees, trickling through the dry kikuyu grass at the edge of the road, nearly blinding her husband who was driving the truck.

'I had chloroform when I had my operation,' I said. I was wedged between Annie and the passenger door. My parents had hitched me a lift home from the hospital. I'd had pneumonia, and then, when I got over that, the doctor said, well, she might as well have her tonsils out now and get it over and done with. The hospital was a long way off, more than twenty miles, and because my parents didn't have a car, they hadn't visited me during the three weeks I was in hospital. My mother had started out to walk one day, but the heat got to her. I was seven, going on eight, at the time.

Nobody in the truck responded, although Annie Pile's husband passed his hand over his straight chunky hair, as if this in some way signalled an acknowledgment.

'I read fourteen books while I was in hospital,' I said. 'My teacher at the hospital said I'll probably go up a class when I get back to school.'

'Make her be quiet, Kurt,' Annie said to her husband. Her hair, as plain as his, but fairer, was caught with a pin above her ear, like fencing wire over corn silk. Her mottled cheeks had a raw chapped appearance; beneath her eyes it looked as if someone had made thumb prints on her skin.

'My wife is so tired,' the man said, with a slight foreign inflection in his voice. 'From having the baby.'

I thought about stroking the baby's finger, to see whether that might make the mother happier, but then I decided it wouldn't work. Instead, I looked out at the lush and surprising landscape as we came to the town. In the hedgerows banana passion-fruit hung in ripe yellow clusters. I leaned my head against the cab window, my brown pigtail pressed against the glass. When I shifted I could feel the imprint of my hair on my cheek, as if my face had been tied to a mooring rope.

When we arrived at the gate of the small farm where I lived, my parents were standing side by side, waiting to welcome me home. My mother was dressed in a pair of dungarees buttoned over a checked blouse. She was a tiny woman, barely five feet, but so thin and energetic that she seemed to occupy more space. My father was wearing a tweed jacket and a tie. His English brogues held a reddish tint in their polished surfaces. He was a tall lean man, with hollows in his olive cheeks, eyebrows like inverted tyre tracks and a hawkish nose. He had a suitcase beside him, as if he had just arrived home from a journey of his own.

My mother put her arms around me when I got down from the truck, examining me closely, touching my hair and cheek. 'Mattie. Darling,' she murmured. My father inclined his head towards me, his shoulders stiff.

Kurt climbed down from the truck cab and shook hands with my father. 'A holiday,' he said. 'Nice for some.'

'A few days in Auckland.'

'Oh well. What did you get up to?'

My father was clearly going to say, mind your own damn business, but remembered just in time that he owed Kurt. 'I saw a couple of musicals.' He drew on a cigarette, holding the smoke in his mouth.

'Gilbert and Sullivan? I heard there was some on.' Kurt's lip curled.

My father released a perfect smoke ring into the still air. '*Cox and Box*. At least there's a good laugh or two in it, not all your Mozart and high falutin' stuff. My cobber and I had a good laugh all right.'

'Very good. Good for you. We'll be off then.'

'Better have a look at this young 'un of yours. A boy, well, there's something to smile about.'

Annie continued to stare straight ahead of her as if she couldn't see any of them. Her husband looked at her as at a mystery so large and unfathomable that he was afraid of being caught in it. No, worse than that, that he was inside it but couldn't yet understand what had trapped him. He was a lot older than Annie Pile, but in that moment he looked like a fledgling sparrow, immensely young and vulnerable. My mother approached the truck.

'What have you called the baby, Alice?'

'Jonathan.'

'A sound name. He can shorten it if he likes. Names are important.' She leaned in the truck to peer at the baby, putting out her hand to move the blanket aside a little. Annie snatched the cover back, so that the baby was hidden from view. My mother flushed and straightened. 'Thank you so very much for bringing Mattie home. I hope she was no bother to you, Alice.'

'She needs to hold her tongue more,' Annie said.

'I expect she was excited about coming home.' When Annie didn't reply, she said, 'Let me know if there's anything I can do to help.'

As the truck drove away, clouds of red dust billowing behind it, my father glanced down to check that his shoes were not getting dirty. 'Unfriendly sort of a coot. Pile, my Auntie Fanny. He's a Jerry, you know, name's Pilsener. You know how they change their names, those fellows.'

My mother said, 'Their baby's a Mongol.'

'Oh my Lord,' said my father. 'Well, too bad about that, eh.'

'We're fortunate,' said my mother and, taking my bag in one hand, she led me, with the other, up the path to our two-roomed cottage with the low ceilings. After a moment's hesitation, my father followed her, drew abreast of us.

My mother said, contentedly, 'You're home.' She could have been talking to either of us, but I knew her words were directed towards me. For the moment, we were together again, my mother and my father and me.

We have different ways to describe things now. We would say that that baby had Down's syndrome. We would say that the parents would find joy in their son, regardless. But that was then. Our family was momentarily counting its blessings, on a jewel bright day beneath a Delft blue sky, the gorse pods snapping in the heat. My mother, as you see her in this picture, is so pleased that I am home, and if she is puzzled by my father's absences, she puts it down to the war, that restlessness men get, and she lets the matter lie.

We moved north after the war. My father had served in the army as a signaller. He was an Englishman who couldn't make sense of my mother's relatives, or they didn't understand him — you could take your pick. He dressed differently and spoke 'posh' as my relatives used to say.

'I can't stand it here,' he said, when he came back, meaning the house where my mother and I lived with my grandparents. 'We need a bit of an adventure.'

'I don't want an adventure,' my mother said. 'I've got money saved for a house of our own. Why don't you just settle down and get a job like everyone else?'

My father didn't want that. He'd heard about this place up

north. Some of his cobbers in the army had talked about it, and they couldn't see themselves settling down in the suburbs.

'We'll live off the land,' he told my mother, his voice passionate in its excitement. 'You'll see, this is no nine to five sinecure with nothing to live for except a pension.'

He followed her around for weeks, pleading with her to listen to sense. Then he went away and when he came back, my mother said she'd go. She gave him her Post Office book with all her savings and told him add it to the rehab money from the army. 'Just go ahead,' she said, 'buy a place. I'll manage.'

My father loved Alderton from the beginning. My mother loathed it. A lot of the people there had come out from China, remnants of the imperial army stationed round Shanghai and Tsientin, at the end of the twenties. They'd emigrated to New Zealand rather than going back to England because they had become used to warmer weather, and they hoped their lives might go on much as they had in China, while they planted fruit trees and lived off the land. There were some disappointments in store: the living was not as cheap as they expected and servants were almost impossible to come by. Some of the better-off settlers built big houses; others had to make do with rickety cottages, but they behaved as if they were palaces anyway. You could step through a crooked door frame into a room full of jade treasures; an ornate silk screen would divide the kitchen from the dining room. A bunch of weatherbeaten men and women, getting their hands dirty for the first time, holding parties on the wobbly wooden verandahs of their shacks in the evenings, jitterbugging and drinking gin. They were about as different as you could get anywhere, round then, at the end of the war. Men like my father and Kurt Pile, as unalike as they were, could be as fanciful or neurotic or sad as they wanted to be, and nobody really cared. The settlers had their own world and if you were not part of it you were invisible. My father thought he might be able to join it; my mother thought he was deluding himself.

In the beginning, my parents raised poultry for quick cash but it took them years to get established. They milked a few cows, separating the cream through their hand rotated Alfa Laval, and fed the whey to pigs. Eventually, they planted citrus and tamarillo orchards, and filled their garden with cantaloupes, aubergines (or eggplants as they were called then) and capsicums, whatever was rare and exotic at the time, like pepinos, with smooth marbled skins and smoky flesh, dragon fruit without the seeds. The trouble was, everything had to be done every day. My mother could accept that, but my father didn't always want to be there. He went away down south when he was supposed to be milking cows or weeding in the orchard while she found jobs to keep them going. He often spent days writing letters or just reading. He took to nostalgic books about the English countryside, where, it seemed, it was always May, and the larks never stopped singing.

My mother took a job for a while, cooking for one of the army wives. The woman, who was called Gloria, wore silk scarves like headbands, the knot tied at the back, so the ends drifted down her back, and long beads. She held her tailor-mades in an ivory cigarette holder, or, when rations ran out, smoked fat rolled purple lasiandra buds that smelled like Egyptian tobacco as they burned. My mother reported for duty at seven each morning. The cookhouse was at the bottom of the garden of a big house. Gloria had a rope strung from the house to the cookhouse with a bell on my mother's end. When she pulled once she wanted fresh tea and when the bell rang twice she needed hot toast.

'If I ring three times, it's for an emergency,' Gloria told her friends, with a tinkling laugh. 'I know cook will rescue me.'

My mother left for work right after she and my father milked the cows. It was supposed to be my father's job to get me up and send me to school. He simply forgot some days, except to say *stand up straight, girl*. A part of him seemed to think he was still in the army, although you wouldn't have thought so to look at him. On these mornings, his smart clothes were put away in the wardrobe; he dressed in baggy pants, held up by braces. He was a smoker too, wreaths of smoke curling round his head as he read on, regardless of anything but the book propped in front of him.

He didn't know how I watched this silent life of his. I discovered what a man's body looked like when I spied him taking a bath. A curtained window divided the cottage from the lean-to containing a copper for heating water and washing clothes, and a tin bath. Usually we had baths one after another, using the same grey suds to save hot water. One morning, after he had been away for a time, he heated the copper and took an unexpected bath. I raised the curtain and he was rubbing himself dry in the dark room, lit only by a single bulb and the reflection of the flames from the copper fire. When I was a young woman, I saw Oliver Reed in *Women in Love* and I was reminded of my father, that same pale English flesh, the colour of potato flesh. He was long and spindly, his chest slightly concave, and yet in the flickering light I found him mysterious and oddly beautiful.

I learned that my father had an army friend called Frank whom he often used to ring up after my mother left for work.

'Tolls, please,' he would say nervously after he had rung the exchange. And then, after a pause, 'I want to make a collect call.' He would give the operator a number down south. 'Eight A, Hunterville.' I can still hear him say it. Short long in Morse code. After a period of negotiation with someone at the other end, punctuated by silences, I would hear his voice, joyful and light, 'Frank, my old mate, how *are* you? Just thought I'd ring for a natter.'

At which point, he would suddenly check to see where I was. 'Hold on a tick, old boy,' he'd say, looking at me. 'Shouldn't you have gone to school?' Eventually, I got bored with these mornings of idleness and started getting dressed and walking to school on my own although I was late so often that one of the teachers phoned home and, by chance, caught my mother.

'Why?' she asked my father, when she had put the phone down. 'Why can't you do what you say you will?'

'Why do you nag?' His voice had that pleading sound again.

'How can I live with a man who calls me a nag? Why don't you just say shrew and be done with it?'

'Shrew,' he said, testing the word on his tongue and laughing. She didn't laugh with him.

Then she said, 'Look, I know it's hard coming back from the war.

I know things happened that I can't understand. Why don't we just have a rest today and we'll do the chores together.'

'What about your job?'

'Oh that,' she said airily. 'I pulled the bell off the string yesterday and dropped it in the river.'

'You did what? This is some kind of joke.'

'Not at all.'

'What will they think of us?' He put his hand to his forehead.

'I've got no idea,' she said, and laughed. 'They asked for something special for afternoon tea, the other day, something sweet and light, chocolate but Oriental, something with a little ginger in it. "All of those things in one dish?" I said. "Well, cook, if you could rustle something up we'll leave it to you," said Madam Gloria. So I took everything I could find in the kitchen and mixed it all up together and iced it, and left it to cool, and when it looked right, I cut it into pieces and served it when their guests came. As I was pouring tea, they were all saying things like, isn't this delicious, and where did you find the recipe, and is this the new cook's doing. So then she said, "Oh, the woman's very good at taking instructions, she can follow a recipe, I'll give her that."'

'You're making this up.' My father was horrified and laughing all at once.

'Not at all. So then she said, "I'll get cook to write it down for you", without giving me so much as a look. All right, I thought, all right. And I went back down the path and waited for the bell to ring, and when it did I pulled it so hard it came off in my hand. So I threw it away.'

'In the river?'

'Yes.'

'Then did you go?' I could see he was working out whether the whole situation might still be redeemed.

'No. I waited for her to turn up, trotting down the path in her tatty old silk dress, looking hot and bothered, and she said, "Where's the tea?" and I told her what I thought about her job. I said, "It's much harder to find a cook than to keep one", and I handed her my apron.

All the Way to Summer

"You might need this," I said.'

My father looked at her as if he'd seen her for the first time.

'My God,' he said, 'you're a fine woman.' He was laughing so hard he could hardly stop. 'We can sell a few more eggs.'

'They'll probably think I poisoned them,' my mother said darkly.

She bought nuts and spices and made the recipe for my father and me. She continued to make it every year, at Christmas time and at birthdays, her wicked ginger treat.

One winter, my father's friend Frank came to stay, not exactly with us, although he took all his meals at our house. Frank was a much younger man than my father. He had fresh full cheeks and a raspberry-coloured mouth and thick eyelashes. In later life he would turn plump. You could see the beginning of it now in the softness under his chin. His checked jacket exuded a grassy smell mixed with cigarette smoke, and bananas, his favourite food. He spent his first few nights at the Homestead, a kind of planters' hotel in the village with ramshackle accommodation and the only bar in twenty miles. You had to be a house guest to use it. He bought several rounds of gin and tonics for my father and they sat on the verandah and looked down the shimmering stand of blue gum trees in the valley beyond.

'My cobber bought me a couple of drinks,' my father said the first night after Frank came north. He giggled and sang. My cobber. My mate. These lapses into vernacular, his way of saying he was a bloke's bloke, one of the people, sat uneasily inside his posh English voice, and it irritated my mother. As the ritual at the Homestead persisted over a week or two, it became more than the way he talked that annoyed her, it was something else I didn't understand. She became increasingly silent.

'His money'll run out,' she said.

'He's got a job,' my father said, with triumph.

'Picking oranges?'

'Yes.'

'Maybe you could get one too,' she said.

My father looked alarmed. 'My back would never stand it,' he said.

'Well then, perhaps I could get a job picking,' she said.

'You'd never reach above the bottom branches,' my father said, but he looked at her with interest.

Frank came to dinner one evening soon after this. He'd moved into a packing shed on a neighbouring orchard, sleeping on a camp stretcher my father had found him. The gin and tonics had run out.

The room in which we ate was narrow, not more than six feet across by about fifteen long, a bench at one end and a coal range on one wall, our gate-legged dining table, oval when it was folded out, creating a barrier between our kitchen and the other end of the room, where a wooden-backed sofa stood. Seeing it like this, it is not a beautiful room, ugly in fact, its cream walls stained with smoke, red congoleum on the floor. But consider our table, laid with an Irish linen cloth, heavy silver cutlery, the knives bone-handled, the plates willow pattern. This was my mother's dowry, the remnants of some other life. The men wore their jackets with ties, my mother a short-sleeved satin sheath dress in wide horizontal navy blue and scarlet stripes with a scooped neckline. I wore a cotton print dress sprinkled with mauve flowers, a gift from my grandmother; it had a Peter Pan collar and short puffed sleeves that ended in bands above my elbows. We were eating the last of a broiler chicken, which my mother cooked in a slow casserole. But they drank wine, which Frank had brought, out of crystal glasses. Dally plonk, my father said, grinning. Sly grog, my mother retorted, looking at Frank from the corner of her eye.

'I've come north,' Frank said, obviously for her benefit, because he must have said all this already to my father, 'because I'm thinking about what to do now that the war's over. I don't really want to be a farmer for the rest of my life. My family took it for granted I'd just settle back into Hunterville. But you know, once you've been away and seen a bit of the world, you can't just accept everything the way it was before.'

'So you just up and left?' asked my mother.

He shrugged, opening his hands expressively, a surprising gesture, as if his time in Europe had altered him from the farm boy who had set off for the war. 'The cows are dry. It seemed like a good time to get away and sort things out and make a bit of extra money at the same time.'

'You've got your rehab surely?' This was a sore point with my mother. The rehabilitation money for the men who served in the war had got eaten up in this place when it might have gone into something more to her liking.

'I needed someone to talk to,' said Frank, looking at my father, 'someone who understood. I might go to university, one of the agricultural colleges, something like that.'

'Good idea,' my father said. 'While you're not tied down.' And I thought he looked wistful.

'Perhaps you wouldn't be too tied down to find something for the pot for tomorrow,' my mother said. She was serving up pancakes drizzled with golden syrup for dessert.

'Kill another chook,' said my father.

'We've only got four left. Don't you want eggs for breakfast?'

My father looked alarmed.

'I'll pay some board next week,' said Frank.

'But you're not boarding with us,' said my mother. 'You're a guest.'

'Well, if you don't mind me coming on over in the evenings, perhaps I could pay for my meals, a regular arrangement.'

'Capital,' said my father. It was clear that this conversation had been rehearsed.

My mother was a sensible woman. She knew that if he paid her a little on a regular basis she could make it stretch further than my father imagined. 'Ten shillings a week.'

My father looked taken aback and was clearly going to argue for less when she quelled him with a look so sharp it would have cut glass.

'First instalment next Friday all right then?' said Frank.

When they had finished dinner my father said, 'I'll walk Frank home.'

'Surely he can find his way by now?' she said.

'It's a nice night for a couple of fellas to have a walk and a smoke.' And so it was, one of those starry nights in the north when, even in winter, it's mild and the air holds the tang of citrus leaves and ripe oranges, and there is a great silence over the shallow hills and valleys. I saw their cigarettes glowing in the dark as they walked off down the road.

This arrangement was all very well, but Friday was still some days away, and so the paying guest had to be fed. A time would come when food was abundant, although never meat.

In the morning, my father said to me, 'We're going hunting, Mattie. Get your shoes on, you may need a coat as well.' I think my mother must have had a word because he'd hardly spoken to me in weeks, not since Frank came. It was not, on the whole, an unfriendly silence but he thought I should be a girl who sang and danced around. When he did notice me, he wanted to teach me songs, but I was not a singer and a dancer, I was a watcher.

The invitation to go shooting was really a command. We set off across the paddocks (why did I think of them as fields?), him carrying a shotgun, me tagging along behind. It was still quite early in the morning, the spider webs spotted with dew, light fragmenting and bouncing off them as the sun rose.

'I miss the old Dart,' my father said suddenly, as I trailed along. 'You know there are a lot of people over there, don't you? You wouldn't imagine it, all the people, the streets full of all sorts of people. Merchant bankers, barrow boys, tradesmen, butchers — my goodness, so much meat — and birds in cages hanging in the doorways of houses. We wouldn't have to be up at crack of dawn over there, someone would have done the job for us. Booksellers, artists, writers ... I'm reading a book called *The Purple Plain* right now — its by a man called Bates. Perhaps you're too young to be reading stuff like this, you'll have to ask your mother. Music-hall dancers, poets — *oh my God, oh to be in England now.*'

'What's wrong with here?'

'Nothing dammit, nothing. Don't you listen to a word I say?'

All the Way to Summer

'Well if there's nothing wrong with here, why do you want to be in England now?'

'It's a line of a poem,' he said, almost sullenly. 'And the nothing, that's what's wrong — the nothing of everything. The way people look at you because there's nothing else to look at.'

'Who looks at you?' I mentally scanned my more recent forays into adult territory, trying to work out whether the watcher had been watched.

'Nobody. Here make yourself useful, learn to hold a gun at the very least.' And he put the gun in my hands and showed me how to hold it up to my shoulder, although the weight of it was almost too much for me to support. 'Look, we're out to get a pheasant or two for dinner.'

The sun was rising in the sky and in the golden glow of grass and light I saw something move and my finger squeezed the trigger. A feathered creature rose straight up from the ground and fell back; it was a soft brown hen pheasant. All of a sudden, I was a huntress, a poacher.

Sour fright filled my mouth. I don't have much of a taste for death.

My mother plucked and gutted the two pheasants that we took home (my father shot the second one), her fingers carefully searching for shotgun pellets. She cooked them with rare brilliance, using some of the leftover wine from Frank's visit, and told my father to go out and shoot some more.

Like Frank, my mother got work in the orchards, climbing ladders and picking oranges and lemons with sharp steady snaps of her secateurs. She earned one shilling and sixpence for every case and she filled them at twice the rate that Frank did; my father didn't try again after the first time. She and Frank began to show signs of a camaraderie that hadn't been there before, although the banter was mostly of her making. 'And how many boxes did you fill today?' she would begin. 'Ten, oh my, but then I noticed you picked the lower branches first.' My mother, being small and light and fast, cleaned out the tops of the trees but it was harder work. After a while the orchardists began to pay her a bonus of sixpence a box. By and large it was my mother who paid the bills, while my father worked in a desultory way at home during her absences. His face brightened on the days when she was free to work alongside him.

Sometime round the middle of last century the climate began to change. I suppose it did everywhere but the people in Alderton thought it was a sign that their luck had run out. The summers became drier, and droughts set in: in one year whole orchards wilted and died. At a price, a trucking firm would deliver water, but without natural rainfall, the settlers were at a loss. They ran hoses from taps, but as most of them relied on water stored in tanks from the winter rains, this soon disappeared and then they had only river water to drink. You could see them toiling up and down the banks of the creeks and river tributaries that meandered through their properties, carrying buckets and pots. Sometimes they just sat among the long grass and aromatic pennyroyal near the waterways, looking lost. We didn't come here for this, you could hear them saying, if not aloud, in their hearts. A few packed up and left.

Others installed pumps, or built reservoirs in their backyards which filled with brackish dirty water, unfit for drinking, but temporarily at least, they provided water for the orchards and gardens. My father and Frank built a reservoir behind our house: it needed the two of them to pour the concrete. Frank had thick wide shoulders that he bared to the sun. His fair skin burned easily, so that for days he walked around looking raw and stripped, but he kept steadily trudging backwards and forwards between the mounds of cement and sand. He'd been up north a couple of years by this stage. There didn't seem any pretence that he would go back south now. He was still a big man, but he'd got harder, the edges of his flesh more crisply defined. My father took many breaks, stopping to smoke in the shade of the gum trees, torrents of coughing hurtling out of his lungs. My mother, observing the slow progress of the reservoir, picked up a shovel and carried concrete too, straining against its weight.

All the Way to Summer

This was a summer that held little for me. I had turned ten and my friend Jocelyn had gone away for the summer. Sometimes, in the holidays, I would go south on the train to stay with my grandmother, but my parents had no extra money that year. Water and cement had soaked it all up. My mother was in one of her stubborn frames of mind and wouldn't take charity from her family. One afternoon, I stood under a gum tree with my father, wishing the day would end, because then it would be tomorrow and I could start doing nothing all over again, and it might turn out better than today. Frank saw my father watching him, and came over.

'There must be easier ways than this to find water,' he said.

'Tell me,' my father said, wearily, leaning on his shovel. He hadn't shaved for days and his face looked gaunt and grey, the worse for the cloudy film of cement.

'There was an old codger down Hunterville way used to be able to divine water, you know, find it in the ground so you'd know where to sink a well.' Reaching out, he pulled a slim branch from a young gum tree, choosing one with a forked stem. He took out his pocket knife and started whittling a three-pronged Y-shaped twig.

'See,' Frank explained, 'the old joker turns the stick with the long piece pointing upwards and he holds the sides one in each hand.' He demonstrated how to hold it, curling his fingers right around the two stems, his thumbs pointing away at either side. 'Then he walks along and when he comes to the place where there's water, down where you can't see, the stick begins to turn, pointing out where the water is.'

'Just like that?'

'Well, I saw what he did a couple of times when I was a kid. He's gone now, long dead that old joker.' He threw the stick aside. 'I tried and tried but I never could make it turn. Wood's wood.'

'I have heard of that, now I come to think of it,' my father said. 'A dowser.' He picked up the stick and holding it the way Frank had shown him, began walking through the paddock.

'You have to *think* water. Go on, mate, you've got to concentrate — just think water, water.'

'Jesus, that's all I think of.' My father was going to throw the stick aside in disgust, but my mother had just come down to the paddock, and she asked to try too.

'Go for it,' said Frank, 'you could make money out of a trick like that. Not that the old joker ever seemed to have much — probably spent it all at the boozer. He was a queer old bandicoot.'

My mother was solemnly pacing along, holding the stick upwards. 'How will I know?' she called out.

'They reckon you know, that you can't stop the thing once it starts. Reckon it's got a mind all its own.'

'Ah,' she said, after a while, 'I don't believe in that sort of baloney. It would've been a trick you saw.'

'There mightn't be any water underneath this bit of dirt,' Frank said, not unreasonably. 'Maybe some people who've got the knack can find water, but only if there's water there to start with.' He sounded huffy as if my mother had called him a liar.

Nobody had offered the stick to me. When they started work again, I picked it up, held it in my hands, the way the others had done, and walked slowly down past the hen house and along the hedge line.

At first nothing happened. Then something did begin to stir. Like some live creature struggling to get away out of my hands. I thought *water water* as if I was thirsty and the twig curled down towards the earth. It's almost impossible to tell what something as strong as this feels in your hands: something bucking, like riding horses bareback, stronger than the kick of a gun. I think now that it was more like a sexual tension, not something children are supposed to have. By the time I was grown and married, this ability to locate underground springs had all but vanished. I looked up and saw Frank, gone to take a pee, watching me behind veiled eyes.

I wanted to say, it's a secret, but I could tell that it wasn't going to stay one, and besides, what was I doing, watching him about his private business?

'I can do it,' I said, returning to my parents. 'I can make the twig bend.'

'I reckon she's a little witch,' said Frank, who had rejoined the group.

'You're fibbing, Mattie.' My mother looked furious.

'No, I'm not,' I replied hotly, wanting to prove myself now.

'Show us,' my father said.

'Don't encourage her,' my mother said. But, egged on by my father and Frank, I began to show them how easy it was. My mother watched for a moment, and then turned away, as if I was behaving badly.

When the reservoir was finished, a sudden storm erupted, a timely opening of the skies that caused flash floods and slips on the dry land. The reservoir filled with water almost overnight, and then the summer went back to being the same as before, bone dry, sere heat, blindingly bright. Frogs gathered in dozens at the reservoir, sheltering from the relentless sun. I put on my bathing suit and swam with them, allowing them to cling to my legs with their tiny pulpy hands. I let them use me as a floating log, a dozen or more sitting on my back while I floated on the scummy surface of the water.

'Funny kid,' Frank said to my mother, thinking I couldn't hear him.

'You just leave her alone. Leave my kid out of it,' my mother said.

'Out of what?' Frank said, lazily.

'Just stick to what you're good at, whatever that is,' my mother snapped, turning on him, as if her careful mask had slipped away. I remember that his face was flushed that evening, in a way it often was. He had made other friends in the village and he didn't eat at our place every night, hadn't done for a long time, although he was always there at the weekend, when he couldn't find someone to gain him entrance to the Homestead bar.

There was, if I look at this now, a certain raffish charm about the way we lived. The eccentric settlers. Fruit and produce and self-sustainment. A delicate father with a taste for the good life. The devoted friend. The child, in one sense, abandoned to the natural world. The nurturing but busy mother. But then, in the same breath, there is the question of my mother's life.

There was a day when I went looking for her. I had come in from Jocelyn's place. Jocelyn, the same age as me, was a head taller and confident in everything she did. She always put her hand up in class even when she didn't know the answers, as if by a bright and engaging manner she could convince those around her, and the teachers in particular, that she was clever. I often knew the answers where she failed to provide them, but I preferred to write them down, so that, puzzlingly to her, I often succeeded by examination in those subjects at which she had appeared to shine in class.

There was, between our mothers, a wary kind of friendship. Jocelyn's mother, Viv, who had been a school teacher, prided herself on knowing everyone.

'I'm not going to let all that class nonsense get in the way of things,' she said. She was a meaty woman who wore her hair rolled up at the bottom, pinned at the sides with clips. 'I like making myself useful to people.' Ingratiating, my father said unkindly, but my mother was happy to have another woman to talk to now and then, and pleased there was some place I could visit. The settlers' children kept to themselves. Many went to private schools and only came home in the holidays anyway.

If my mother was careful to keep a slight distance between herself and Viv it was possibly because she detected a willingness to pass on information about others. Or, you could say, Viv was a gossip. I think, on the day I was looking for my mother, Viv had issued an invitation for me to go swimming with Jocelyn, something like that. I called out to my mother several times. I was sure she wasn't far away, because a pot was simmering quietly on the stove. Yet there was something abandoned about the place, that made me panic when she didn't answer. I rushed outside, calling and calling again.

She must have been there all the time because suddenly, as if from nowhere, she said, 'Yes, what is it?'

She was standing among the pale shapes of the blue gum trees, quite still. Absorbed into them, like a branch, or a group of leaves in the motionless air.

When I went towards her she was smiling, pleased, I think, that she had so easily vanished from view. I felt afraid and alone, as if she had been spirited away. But she had been there all the time, and she came towards me, calling cheerfully for me to take a billy of eggs from her, as if nothing had happened. I thought it odd, and began to notice other times when it happened.

This is not to suggest that my mother was other than a vital presence in our household, or that she was wilfully disappearing before our eyes. It was just that she had developed a certain aloofness, especially towards the men in her household. Not towards me, not as a rule. She and I had dialogues of our own, role-playing the characters on the radio serials. 'You can pretend I'm Delia,' she would say, and start vamping among the tamarillos. The fruit had drum smooth red skin, the insides held black seeds and rouge-coloured flesh and, to me, a tainted bitter taste. She clipped and slid the fruit, clipped and slid it, into a bulging pouched apron. 'You can kiss me if you're quick, but nobody must know, least of all your wife,' she'd say in a la-di-da voice.

'My wife no longer cares who I kiss,' I'd say.

'Ah yes, but she does, that's half the pleasure,' my mother would breathe. 'We have our little secrets.'

'How about we sail away in a boat together,' I might say.

She would snort. 'Is that the best you can do?' The question was meant for me, not the character. When we held these sultry improbable conversations you'd swear, catching a glimpse of her hard at work in the orchards, that she was a man, with her overalls and close-cropped hair. I think now that my mother was in despair and that being still, being invisible, was her way of hiding it from me.

One night when Frank wasn't there, after I was supposed to have gone to bed, I got up and found them, my mother and my father, dancing cheek to cheek on the ugly congoleum floor. The radio was playing — *When your heart's on fire / You must realise / Smoke gets in your eyes* — and I saw that my mother was crying.

I crept away without being seen. I could never tell how things would be between them.

Frank came around and said that a military chap, a Wing Commander Thorne, had heard I could divine water and, as he was about to put down a well, could I come round and check it out. My mother was out at the time. I remember my father looking doubtful.

'He'll pay,' said Frank.

'An air force wallah, eh? Must be one of the new lot. You'd better put on some tidy clothes,' my father said, warming to the idea. I could see he was pleased to be asked. He didn't ask me whether I wanted to come or not. Like the shooting expedition.

'Suppose Mattie can't do it?' my father said, as we walked down the broad dusty avenues towards Hubert Thorne's house.

'She will,' Frank said confidently. 'You can tell she's a natural.'

'But we don't know she really found water. We didn't put a well down.' (As it happened, my father had wanted to, and Frank had urged him and my mother to throw caution to the winds and sink a bore, but on this one matter my mother stood absolutely firm. There would be no bore. I think part of her was afraid that I might lose my new-found aura of magic.)

'I can tell you,' Frank said, 'what that girl does wouldn't happen unless there was water at the end of the stick.'

Quite a crowd had gathered round. All the wing commander's family were there, including Maisie who went to St Cuthbert's and her brother Cecil who was at King's in Auckland, and some of the neighbours, along with the well driller and a man who worked for him. Wing Commander Thorne had one lazy languid eye and one that looked at you straight. That lazy eye didn't hide the impatience of his manner.

The well driller had already put down a test bore and not struck water. 'If he puts down another dud, I won't be able to carry on. Too costly. Can she do it or not?' he demanded.

The well driller was looking surly. 'I've got it worked out now,' he said to my father. He could tell by his calculations from the river flow, beyond the rise, which way water would go. You didn't always get it right first time. He looked at me with a mixture of contempt and misgiving. I could tell how I worried him, a kid in a tartan skirt

All the Way to Summer

with straps over the shoulders of her white blouse.

'She can do it,' my father said, in a blithe way.

I felt an urgent sense of excitement, as if I was about to throw off my inhibitions and become a performer after all.

I was offered a twig that someone had pulled from a tree but I turned it down, preferring to choose one of my own. I took my time getting it ready, holding it out and measuring it with my eye, although that wasn't really necessary. I knew when I could get a twig to work. All the same, I was nervous. It was one thing to feel that wild thing in my hand, but I didn't know, any more than my father, whether there would be water below. The twig turning was something that happened to me, in a way, rather than because I made it happen.

I walked around with an earnest expression clasping the twig, and pacing slowly about. At first nothing happened. I heard Maisie and Cecil start to giggle. But I thought *water* and then the twig bent sideways, away from me, so that I had to follow where it was taking me. At a certain point, the twig pulled inexorably down towards the earth.

Someone started to clap, probably Frank, but others joined in. I walked backwards and forwards and the twig pulled only at the one place — five yards from where the well driller had reckoned on putting the well down.

'I don't reckon it's there,' he said. 'You don't know if this kid's a fake.'

'It always turns in the same place,' said Frank.

'Put a blindfold on her,' the man said.

'Excellent idea,' said the wing commander. He spoke to my father. 'How about it, old chap? Will you tie your handkerchief round the lass's eyes?'

A flicker of concern passed over my father's face. I think he realised that things had gone far enough. 'It's all right,' I said. 'You can do it.'

Because by now I knew that whatever force was pulling the twig, it would happen anyway.

And it did.

They sank the bore in the place I showed them. There was water there all right, buckets of beautiful clear water gushing out in a steady stream. Wing Commander Thorne gave my father five pounds for his trouble in bringing me over. 'Buy the little lass a new dress,' he said, which was an expression, more than a reflection on what I was wearing. Cecil and Maisie took up a game of croquet they'd been playing before I came, as if nothing unusual had occurred.

When my mother heard about it, she said, 'You won't be doing that again.' She was in a towering white-lipped rage, and didn't speak to my father for nearly a week. Frank was banned for almost a fortnight.

'She's not a circus kid,' she said, when she'd recovered.

'I know,' my father said, looking embarrassed. 'But for that much money.' Already there had been several offers for my services. He glanced sideways at me. 'She could go away to school.'

'No,' said my mother so fiercely that my father and I jumped. 'No, Mattie stays here. With me.'

Viv visited my mother unexpectedly one day. She said she had a special request. Just as a favour to her, could I look for water down at the Piles' place. Annie and Kurt, the ones that had the strange baby.

My mother said, 'She doesn't do it for anybody.'

'Well,' Viv said, 'Annie is in a bad way. That place is dried right up, and Kurt's so busy looking after her and the baby, I don't know what's going to become of them. My husband bought them a tank of water because things were so dry they couldn't so much as make a cup of tea. But we can't afford to be doing that all the time. Anyway, Annie just takes baths — it's not as if she knows how to save water, or anything, these days. It wouldn't be so bad if she washed a few clothes now and then. The thing is, Kurt got all the pipes and everything a few years back, but they never decided where to put the bore down.'

'We owe them a favour,' my father said.

'Well.' My mother looked undecided. 'If we kept it to ourselves.'

'Of course,' Viv said.

All the Way to Summer

'No money changes hands.'

My father looked disappointed, but seeing he was the one wanting to be helpful, he nodded in agreement.

Things were just as bad at the Piles' house as Viv had described them. She led us into the house before Kurt had time to stop her. Perhaps she really did want my father to understand the situation, thought it best to let him know. Annie was surrounded by an indescribable chaos of unwashed clothing and dirty dishes. The forlorn baby, Jonathan, had grown into an unsteady overgrown toddler, with a filthy napkin falling from his waist. The beds were not just unmade; the mattresses were soiled and full of holes. The only thing of quality was a piano, a rosewood baby grand, that shone with a strange wild lustre among the squalor of the house. Viv told us Kurt played it in the evenings; depending on which way the wind was blowing, she heard the music spilling through the blue gums that divided their boundary lines. (No, this is fanciful; Viv didn't speak like this, but it's how I've come to hear the story, and that music, which was often spoken of in the district.) Annie was expecting another child. She appeared not to recognise me, and although she followed us out when we went to look for water, she wandered back inside almost straight away, looking distracted. Viv and Kurt and my father were my only audience.

Not that I found anything. I don't know whether there was water there or not but while I walked around the place, the twig felt dead in my hands, as still and lifeless as if it were all a stupid game. Like Delia and Dr Paul. I wasn't a miracle child after all.

Word got around, of course. My self-importance ebbed away. At school, people fell silent in my presence, as if I was some sort of charlatan, to be avoided at all costs. After I'd moved away from a group, I'd hear them starting to talk again. I stopped being Jocelyn's friend and she had a birthday party to which I was not invited. I stayed home and watched the settlers' daughters walking to the party carrying gifts. After the birthday, Jocelyn started talking to me again, and I was invited over as if nothing had happened, but I didn't go.

Frank said I needed a manager and he could have told my parents the conditions weren't right at that place. If he'd been there, he'd have advised against me going on a fool errand like that.

Annie Pile's health got worse. Her sister, Petal, came from down south to stay for a while. Early one morning, Viv arrived at our house, and introduced Petal.

'I was the baby of the family,' Petal said, self-deprecatingly. 'They'd kind of run out of names.' There were eleven siblings: Annie was number eight, three above Petal, who was a bright-eyed woman in her late twenties. Short, not unshapely in a heavy-breasted, big-beamed way, she was so different from Annie that it was hard to think of them as related. She had lovely neat ankles beneath her cotton-flowered skirt. It was Viv, of course, who had sent for Petal, because somebody had to do something about Alice. Viv knew that Petal was a nurse. She was a single woman, good at her work; the hospital had agreed to take her back when she'd finished looking after her sister.

The purpose of this second visit soon emerged. Petal needed someone to help her clean up the Piles' place — it was beyond her on her own, what with having to look after Annie and Jonathan at the same time. With the new baby due any day, she was working against the clock. Naturally, she would pay my mother.

'I don't do cleaning work,' my mother said. I could see her glaring at Viv, as if to say, why can't you do it? Surely this was charity again, of the worst kind.

'I told Petal you'd done some housekeeping,' Viv said apologetically.

My mother began to shape her refusal, then changed her mind. I guess she was thinking, as my father had before, that the Piles had helped out once. And there was the matter of the well that I had failed to deliver. Perhaps there was something, too, about Petal's open friendly smile that my mother liked. She said she'd be right over.

Here is another dinner party. My mother and my father and me and Frank and Petal. My mother has cooked chicken in cider, with green capsicum and apples. She has made the cider herself. There is a dessert to follow, light sponge floating on lemon cream.

Kurt has been invited to the meal but has chosen to stay home and play his lonely broken chords of Mozart, spilling them on the fragrant night air of Alderton City. Annie has gone away, probably for good. Their children, Jonathan and a new and wholesome baby called Derek, are being taken care of by another of the sisters, who will end up keeping them. Soon Kurt will move to Auckland where he and his wife and children will live under different roofs, but at least they will see each other from time to time, and then, slowly, less and less. My mother will know about all this, because Petal will tell her when they meet, which will be often in the years ahead.

Something has been decided before this meal takes place. I don't know who, exactly, decided but an event is all set to happen. Frank and Petal are going away to be married. This dinner is their farewell. At the end of it, my father proposes a toast.

'To Frank and Petal, good health.' His voice quavers and, this time, it is he who has the burnish of tears in his eyes.

After Frank and Petal had gone, my mother fell ill for many months. She'd had boils, a sign of overwork and distress and perhaps something lacking in her diet. One erupted on the back of her head and turned into a carbuncle, a boil with several heads. She walked up and down all night, taking my father's cigarettes and smoking incessantly. Sometimes she tried to lie down but that was worse than standing, keeping her swollen poisoned head upright. My father called the doctor, a man known for strong drink and occasional incoherence. He wiped his eyes with the back of his hand as if he didn't believe what he saw, then reached inside his bag and took out a scalpel. Hold still, he told her, and lanced the thing open.

It got worse instead of better. By the time Viv came round and arranged for her to go to hospital the thing had thirteen heads, each like living putrid creatures with existences of their own. My mother nearly died in the hospital. I went south to live with my grandmother for a while. It was not unlike Annie Pile's situation, only my mother did recover. In time, I went back home, changed and less wayward.

Frank and Petal visited as often as they could. They had four children in quick succession, and there were times when they couldn't get away from the farm. Frank bought out the farm next door, and developed a big herd. Later, my parents shifted away from the north and lived closer to them, although that was a matter of chance rather than design. Sometimes they all went away for holidays together.

There was a particular day I remember, not long before I met my husband. I was working as an advertising copywriter for the radio station in the town where we lived. There was a lake near our house. My father had a row boat that I used to mess around in some weekends. I had gone on liking the outdoors, even though my head was absorbed with men. I had long since stopped divining water, as if a certain energy in me had been subverted.

I didn't know that Frank and Petal had come for a visit. I had worked overtime at the station and, afterwards, I cycled straight to the lake, thinking that I would row out a little way, or perhaps along the shoreline. But when I got to the lake I found that the boat was already in use. My father was rowing Frank vigorously out away from the shore.

It was a calm golden afternoon, willows trailing in the lake, small fish leaping. There was a tart smell of autumn in the air. I watched the boat, and saw my father rest on the oars, in a patch of sunlight. He and Frank exchanged some banter. My father's face wore a look of such sweet peace that it has stayed with me forever.

Later that afternoon, when everyone had returned to the house, they got me to take their photograph together on Frank's camera. My mother doesn't look like her old farm self; she has changed and become suburban, in a way she had wanted to be, all those years before. She wears a knee-length tweed skirt, a cream Viyella blouse, a jumper and scarf fixed with a brooch my father gave her one birthday, a little pearl on a spiralling gold wire, and sensible comfortable shoes.

Her hair is grown longer, to cover an appalling scar. Petal wears an acrylic powder blue pantsuit with beige ankle socks and black slip-ons. The men wear jackets but their shirts are open at the neck. This is more or less how they will go on looking, for another thirty years, all of them growing stouter, except for my father, who will grow thinner, and fade away first.

There they are, the four of them: my mother and my father and Frank and Petal.

SOUP

A woman from Liese's past calls her unexpectedly at the newspaper office where she works. Liese is a theatre critic, rumpled with tiredness after another late night. She wears a navy crewcut jumper with jeans, and her face isn't made up. Later in the day she will change into something simple and black and put on subdued expensive lipstick, the sort that doesn't come off when you eat and drink. For the moment, she's struggling her way into a review of the new play at Circa, *The Blue Room*. Hare's play has disturbed in a way she can't explain to herself, and hasn't had time to analyse. It's based on the old idea of *La Ronde*, Schnitzler's circle of characters who have sex with each other and work their way back through a dozen partners until they end up where they began, the connection of the first and the last. People take off their clothes in the play, one man representing all men who fuck around, his penis hanging in the strobe light in front of the audience, and it's funny how the youngest women in the audience can't take it, leave at half time. What is it they are afraid of? she has written in the first draft of her review. That it's too like their own lives? Or are they afraid he might become aroused, and they will have to witness this in front of old men and women in the audience? On reflection, she thinks she won't put that in — that it will say more about her, than it should. Liese has been a theatre critic for more than twenty years; she is used to interpreting what people see on stage, of articulating opinions. Let them ask the questions.

Its weariness, she tells herself, three late nights in a row. She's going to let the phone ring, then picks it up because it might be her husband Ned. Ned, her second husband. Only it's not, it's a woman called Prue, who lives in a dark part of her life.

Prue's voice sends a shock down her spine. 'Fraser's gone,' Prue says. 'He went sometime in the night.' Liese understands that she means Fraser's dead. 'It wasn't unexpected. He'd been sick for a little while. I thought you'd like to know.'

Once, a long time ago, Liese and Prue were friends. They lived in a small port town up north, on a sweeping coastline, where their husbands were both scientists. Prue was a beautiful woman then, with large eyes, and cheekbones like carving blades. A famous portrait painter had painted her before he was well known. Not that this seemed important when they first knew each other, although later it would seem more significant. Prue ran her household much as other women Liese knew. She had more money than most, and probably more than her husband, Fraser, but that was because she came from wealth. 'I brought the money and the breeding to this marriage, he brought the brains,' she'd been heard to say, after a few drinks. She was older, and belonged to the wives' club that arranged social functions for the staff at the Science Centre, and, in the beginning, she had been kind to Liese, appearing to like her and her husband, David.

After a pause, Liese says how sorry she is. She knows something more is expected of her, but she is unable to fill the silence, as she sits there, tucking a strand of frothy greying hair behind her ear.

'He'd have wanted you to come,' Prue says.

'Can I get back to you on this?'

'Oh. Of course, I hear you're a busy person these days.'

'I'm sorry,' Liese says yet again, and puts the receiver down. Instantly she regrets this, but really, perhaps, that's all she can do.

She sits, absorbing the news she's just heard. At this time of her life, just past fifty, she feels sometimes that she's in a state of grace, even of redemption, although perhaps that's extravagant. Some women she knows don't look back, still leave their lipsticks under other women's pillows when they sleep with their husbands, but Liese has gone beyond that, not asking to be forgiven but at least to be allowed to forget.

'It's such a staid town,' Fraser and Liese say to each other, as if they are the first people in the history of the town to fall out of love with the people they are married to, and in love with each other. They are contemptuous, these two, of those who live here, because they don't believe others experience love the way they do. They do silly things, advertising the remarkable quality of their love, like pulling leaves off citrus trees and rubbing them on each other's skins. Oranges and lemons. They go home with sharp citrus scents on their bodies that are as telling as sex. Liese takes that home with her as well, intentionally careless, because if she is found out, she won't have to be the first to tell, to get them all in trouble; she won't need to tell lies any more. She thinks they have discovered something nobody else knows, the piquancy of an affair.

They walk where it seems they are less likely to be recognised — near the seafront, along the Marine Parade, away from town, towards railway houses that crouch by the cutting. When she looks back on those years, she thinks of the white wings of gannets and the languorous taste of wine, and of art deco houses and shops and the feeling that the shivery earth might open up again and consume its inhabitants, and of Fraser and his wife Prue. On this day, when they walk together, both afraid and defiant, Fraser is talking about poetry, something she knows very little about, but she's eager to soak it up. He knew the poet Jim Baxter, the one who died young, after founding a commune. Liese's fair flyaway hair blows around her collar. She is going to leave the town soon. Her husband David has a new job down south.

'I sometimes wonder,' she says, 'if he does know. If maybe he's taking me away to punish me.'

'No, I don't think so,' Fraser says. 'Your husband's no actor. I'd know.'

'Why don't we tell him? Tell both of them?'

'You know that's not what we decided,' he says.

Of course, she is waiting for him to say to her, don't go away. Stay here and it will be all right. She has a plan worked out in her head, if he will only say this to her. 'Go on ahead,' she will say to David. 'I'll follow with the children in a little while, when you've got a new house for us, then we'll come down.'

But she won't go; she'll stay on in her L-shaped house angled towards the sun, with ranchsliders opening to the verandah, and the magnolia tree on the front lawn. She will start burning incense and leave books of poetry lying open around the house, and Fraser will come and stay with her, and say never leave me, never abandon me, I can't live without you. He will have to be brave and tell Prue. She will send a short regretful note to David. In the holidays, David will take care of their children, their three boys. He will meet someone else and get married and be happy.

Instead, as she walks along the seafront with Fraser, and practises saying goodbye, a hearse travels past, loaded with a coffin and flowers. She puts her hand in his duffel coat pocket, pinching the rough woollen seam with her fingers, and after a few minutes, with a quick backward glance, he puts his hand inside the pocket with hers, and they talk about death.

'I don't think I'd want a funeral as such,' he says. 'Just you and Prue there, just the two of you.' Fraser has had his second wind, he has had the time to panic. As men often do. He is afraid but he can't give her up. Perhaps he does feel like dying right there and then.

'What about your children? They'd have to be there,' Liese says, taken aback, as if he were planning something that might happen quite soon. Besides which, he is talking as if he loves her and Prue equally. Equally, but not the same, perhaps.

'They'll be grown up and off,' he says. 'On the other side of the world. That's what children do.' Reassuring her that they will be in each other's futures, somehow, for ever, if not together. What he has said, will turn out not to be true. One of his children will die before him.

Were Liese and David so unhappy? Odd to consider this now, but things that seemed awful at the time have receded almost to vanishing point. Some of it was excellent, so damn fine, as her sons would say.

When they first meet David has a sea-washed blondness. This is partly the way he looks, but it is intensified by his long hours of research in the open, around rock pools, in the salt air. He's such a catch, her girlfriends say. Their wedding picture is posted on the front of the local newspaper, not just in the bride of the week column. The caption reads: *Local belle weds her sweetheart. Mr and Mrs David Sheehan made such a striking couple last weekend, we think they're news. Mr Sheehan is a research scientist, specialising in marine biology. He hails from Auckland.* Nothing about her job as a sales clerk at Toomey's, the stationery and office supplies shop where she works.

It's the year of Woodstock, but you wouldn't tell it from looking at that picture. True, David has sideburns that look almost white and his suit trousers are flared, but Liese's dress is hand sewn with seed pearls and about as pretty and traditional as wedding dresses get. She glows, a taller than average girl who is happy on her wedding day, with a very good looking man. She thinks she has never entirely forgiven David that — those astonishing even features, eyes the colour of African violets. Later, she will accuse him of being a Nazi. Not true at all, not even remotely. His mother was a Dutch woman with plain hair and even peg-shaped teeth that shone when she smiled. She had been more reserved about the picture than Liese's mother who, on seeing it, said, 'Oh I'm so proud of you, you're both just gorgeous.'

David had snatched it out of her hands and torn it in half.

It's such bullshit, he'd said, which at the time made Liese furious and sad, although now she thinks much the same way. Of their two sons who are married, one has had an open air ceremony in his and his wife's pocket-sized garden in Newtown — that's Robbie, the youngest — while James, the eldest, has married without telling either of them, in a registry office. Their middle son, Simon, lives with a man and says they'll marry in time, by which he means, when it's legal for gay men to marry. Liese is fine about this, in principle, but she wishes she liked her son's lover better, as a *person*, she emphasises, and that her son didn't break so many things when he was in a rage. But then, where had he got that from? For when all was said and done, Liese and David were just a couple who had mortgages and three sons, each roughly a year or a little more apart, and at some point, she began breaking things.

Fraser is much older than David, or so it seems when they first meet. He's heading for forty, which seems a great age. (It seems less when Liese falls in love with him, and he has passed this milestone some years before.) Like David, he works at the Science Centre, part of a group of local scientists with varying disciplines. There is much to be studied in the area: earthquakes that have devastated the town in the past and soil and water cultures, which are important because the region is well known for its orchards and wine growing. David and Fraser, the two marine scientists, are something of a minority, part of a small group who work with the fisheries department. David doesn't hold Fraser in great respect, although they get on well enough. In his view, his research is lackadaisical. There are changes in atmospheric conditions that are affecting sea life, and with it the livelihoods of fishermen. David complains to Liese that Fraser lives in scientific isolation.

'He thinks it's enough to study the life cycle of a starfish because he likes the look of it,' he says, one Saturday afternoon. 'He doesn't consider its place in the scheme of things.'

'Well, what is the place of a starfish?' she asks him lazily.

'You don't understand, Liese. There are bigger issues here.'

'But a starfish is still a starfish. Like Myrtle is a turtle.'

Myrtle lives in a terrarium in their sunroom, a rumpus room, as they call it then, with a desk in the corner where David works in the evenings. The children have to stay out of the room then. David expects them to be in bed early. 'No rumping when Daddy's busy,' she tells them.

'Rumping's not a verb,' David says.

'No, but rumple is,' she says. 'It's what you get when you try to work in the rumpus room.' He looks at her then in a puzzled manner, as if she is someone he can never hope to understand.

No, that's not the way it is, either. Rather, he is coming to the view that she will never understand him. When she sees him looking at her like that, she thinks it is to do with her being the uneducated one in the family, that perhaps he wishes he had married someone cleverer than she thinks she is, who had stayed at school longer, one of those bright Baradene girls back in Auckland who went to university. (David was brought up a Roman Catholic and renounced the church for his twenty-first birthday, before he met her.) She doesn't say any of this to him. If she voices these thoughts aloud, he might some day agree with her.

There are pets Liese would have preferred to a turtle, but David is allergic to cats and she doesn't see how she can fit in the time to walk a dog. In the afternoons, after their naps, she and the boys take Myrtle for a walk in the garden. The turtle is patterned brown and pale caramel on its shell, with a frilly yellow underside, and light stripes down her head and legs. Liese doesn't like the feel of the dry fleshy belly as she lifts her out for her walk, but the boys don't seem to mind. They want to pick her up and nurse her.

'You can't do that with turtles,' David explains to them. 'It's bad for turtles to be cuddled.'

She buys the children extra fluffy toys and James, the eldest, sleeps with his panda bear until he starts school. During the winter months, when the sun goes off the house in the afternoons, a thermostatically controlled heater switches on in Myrtle's terrarium.

David is away on a field trip in a fishing boat when the heater breaks. Myrtle has been lying across it, and the glass suddenly shatters. Simon, the second boy, comes racing into the kitchen where Liese is making meat loaf. She hears his howls before he reaches her.

Soup

'Myr'le's upside down,' he yells. He is having speech therapy to help him learn to say his t's.

'She'll be all right,' Liese says. 'I expect she's just having a sleep.' The way mothers do, when they are distracted and their heads are away in some fairy tale of their own.

'No,' wails Simon, 'Something big hi' her, and me too.'

She sees he is as pale as milk, and suddenly understands. Robbie, the baby, is making his way to the terrarium when she catches him. Myrtle really is upside down. The miracle is that Simon isn't dead like Myrtle, and Robbie too. If James had been there, not playing outside with the children from next door, he would have wanted to rescue Myrtle, would certainly have been electrocuted. He is the bossiest and most self-contained of the boys. She sees each of her children, as if in some slow-motion horror movie, dying, one by one, in front of her, the expression snuffed out of their bright faces.

Liese gathers Simon and Robbie around her, and turns off the electricity at the mains. She rings the doctor to see whether she should bring Simon in, after the shock, although his pulse is steady and his colour has returned. It's Saturday afternoon, and she gets the doctor's wife. 'Just keep an eye on him,' the woman says, because the doctor is out watching rugby and she is just taking calls and passing them on to the duty doctor.

She thinks she should get an electrician, but doesn't know where she will find one at the weekend. Does she imagine it or is there a crackle and pop about the thermostat? Myrtle seems to be hissing, as if the air is being released out of her. The heater is a sealed unit, with a wire leading through the wall behind it, connecting it to something else. Something David has done, perhaps an illegal connection.

First, she rings Brenda, who she worked with in the office supplies shop. Brenda is a booming competent woman, who says 'And how are we today?' when she sees you and 'toodle pip' when she's saying goodbye. She has answers for most things, but she isn't home when Liese phones. That is when she thinks of ringing Prue, who has been so kind. Prue's tongue is said to be sharp, but so far Liese hasn't experienced this.

Prue gives a theatrical sigh when Liese calls. Liese has a feeling that Prue will tell her friends she's the kind of woman who can't change a light bulb.

Prue says, after a pause, 'I'll put you on to Fraser. He's not doing anything, as usual.'

Fraser was supposed to have gone on the fishing boat expedition with David, but he's told David he's had enough weekend work to last him a lifetime. He comes on the line, and says, in a comforting, chortling way, 'Don't touch anything. I'll be over in ten minutes or so to disconnect the heater.'

'I don't want to put you out,' Liese says. Prue and Fraser live on the hill, the smart part of town where better off people have houses that overlook the sea. Their house, at the end of a cul de sac, has a whitewashed Mediterranean look, and vines around courtyard walls.

'No trouble. Leave the mains off. See you soon.'

'Thank you,' says Liese faintly.

When she hangs up, she thinks that Prue's annoyance is not with her, but something between her and Fraser. She and the children huddle in the kitchen as if some large natural disaster has overtaken them.

He arrives, wearing a thick plaid jacket and a black woollen hat pulled down over his ears, his horn-rimmed spectacles pushed up on his nose. He's a sandy-complexioned man, his head coated with crinkly receding hair that's brushed back, so that his brow looks high and domed. He has freckles sprinkled over his eyelids and even his broad flat lips, and a small neat mole on his left cheek.

'By Jove,' he says. 'What have we got here?'

Liese is on the verge of tears. She explains how casual the doctor's wife seemed. He nods his head and inspects Simon in a way that reassures her, as if he knows what he's doing. 'He's all right, Liese,' he says. 'That heater's about the same as an electric fence, nasty but not deadly.' He expresses his surprise that Myrtle has 'turned turtle'. He laughs at his own joke and disconnects the heater in the terrarium, making sure the socket is safe.

'Perhaps you could put the jug on,' he says. 'That's if you've nothing stronger.'

'I have,' she says. 'There's been some brandy in the cupboard ever since Christmas.' She and David have started drinking wine because spirits make her dizzy and David thinks beer is common, although it's what everyone drank when she was young and going to her first parties.

'Get it,' he says firmly, opening her kitchen cupboard as if he's in charge, and taking out two tumblers. He takes the bottle from her and splashes in the brandy. They stand there, she leaning against the table, and he against the bench, alongside the sausage meat and mince for the abandoned meat loaf, and drink brandy on a Saturday afternoon, talking about what to do with upside-down Myrtle.

'We should have a funeral for her,' Fraser says. 'That's what we did for our kids when their pets died. Where does David keep his spade?'

'You mean now? We're going to bury Myrtle now?'

'Well, you can't keep a dead animal in the house for very long. Suit yourself.'

Simon has become tearful, perhaps in the aftermath of his shock, but he is patting Myrtle. 'Make her live, Mummy,' he says.

'I can't,' Liese tells him. 'We'll do it,' she says to Fraser.

She calls the neighbour and asks her to send James home, and then she explains to him what has happened, and lets him pat the dead turtle. James is blond, like his father, and, also like his father, restrained in his manner. Sometimes, when Liese looks at him, she thinks a time is coming when she will not know him as well as she would want, as if all the wiping up and feeding him and reading his favourite stories at bedtime will count for nothing.

'Shall we sing a hymn?' James asks. He has been to his grandfather's funeral, David's father, the year before. He knows what ought to be done.

Fraser collects the spade from the garden shed and digs a hole in the ground, beneath the peach tree. A weak sun struggles through the clouds where he works, casting a pattern of shadows through the branches. 'I'm not sure about a hymn,' she says, and finds herself wondering what Fraser would think appropriate. Did he sing hymns with the children when the cat died?

'I think Myrt would have just liked you to sing a song we all know,' she suggests. She has found an old pillow slip to wrap the turtle in.

'How about "Row, row, row your boat?"' says James.

'That would be perfect.'

So that's what they do, the sun filtering through, and the clouds flicking shadows across the sky. The children sing:

Row row row your boat
Gently down the stream
Merrily merrily merrily
Life is but a dream.

Fraser picks up the children's melody and starts the rondo again while he heaps dirt over Myrtle. He whacks it down with the back of the spade and invites the two bigger boys to jump on it and flatten it down further. They jump up and down and say loudly, 'Goodbye, goodbye, Myrt.'

'Do you think she can hear us, Mummy?' says Simon.

'Probably,' says Liese, her head spinning with the brandy, and the sight of Fraser standing there among her children, chuckling and singing. It's late August and she sees that the lilacs are coming, the faint flushed spears of buds pointing skywards. Maybe she could get up a petition to get the trees across the road trimmed so that they could all get more sunlight. At least, spring is just around the corner. Something will change, something will happen, of that she is certain.

'You could have put her in the shed and waited for me,' David shouts, the next night, when he comes home.

'Why?' says Liese. 'The children were upset.'

'She was my turtle.'

'I thought she was the children's,' she says.

'I bought her for the children. But she was my pet too.'

'This is ridiculous,' says Liese icily. 'What am I supposed to do when you're not here?'

He shrugs and goes on eating his dinner. She's made the mince into spaghetti instead. Spaghetti bolognaise à la Burbville. Mince again. A strand of pasta trickles down his chin. It isn't bad, as mince goes, but perhaps she's in a rut.

'I'm sorry,' Liese says.

'Me too,' he says, his eyes watering. They cling to each other when they go to bed. She cradles his head on her shoulder as he dissolves into sleep, exhausted from his weekend at sea. When she is sure he's sleeping deeply, she gets up and looks out the window. The trees outside look like a dark mountain range. She walks around the house barefooted, looking at her children and pulling the covers up over them.

'Liese.' He calls out to her in his sleep. She hurries back and climbs back into bed, curling her cold feet close to the heat of his body.

Fraser just turns up the next time David is away at sea.

'Shouldn't you be at work?'

He says he's come to pick up a reference book from David that he'd meant to collect on Friday. He runs his hand over his head, and smiles disarmingly. 'Working at home this weekend — I've got a paper to write. Anyway,' he says, 'I'm the boss, remember?'

'I'm surprised you didn't know he was away.'

'I could use a cup of tea,' he says, as if she hasn't been rude.

She bites her lip. 'Of course.' Her period is due: her breasts are swollen and heavy and her head has ached all day. 'Thank you for helping out with the turtle. David really appreciated you coming over,' she says, as she fills the kettle.

He sits down at the kitchen table and waits for her to bring him tea in mugs. Simon and Robbie are having a nap and James has gone to the neighbour's place again, where they're allowed to watch television in the afternoon. Sometimes she lets them switch it on in the middle of the day, but always with a feeling of guilt, because she and David have talked about it years ago, when they got their first set. We won't let it rule our lives, they swore at the time.

She tells Fraser this, for something to say, and he laughs. 'We've got a second set in the bedroom,' he says. 'There are some good plays on television.'

'I saw a play on television last week,' she admits. 'I think it was a repeat. With Judi Dench. It was one of a quartet about a family. *Gladly My Cross-Eyed Bear*. But it wasn't about a bear.'

'Of course not. It's a line about Jesus carrying the cross. Those are called mondogreens, running words together like that.' He shifts the subject sideways. 'Do you go to the theatre at all?'

'My friend and I won some tickets to the Little Theatre last year,' she says. '*The Killing of Sister George*, all about a woman in broadcasting who had a girlfriend. It was pretty weird.'

'But so interesting,' he enthuses, 'such challenging ideas.'

'Brenda said she didn't really want to go again.' Brenda had actually wanted her to walk out at half-time, and there's been a coolness between them since then, because Liese wanted to stay. She doesn't tell Fraser how disgusted Brenda was; she decides she won't even tell him who her friend is.

'Perhaps you and David could go. I'm sure Ivan would babysit.'

'Oh, perhaps,' she says, without enthusiasm. She can't see David going to plays.

'Or, why don't you come to a play with me?'

'Me? Go out with you?' Her voice is scandalised.

'I didn't mean go out,' he says, as if she's a preposterous child. 'What a virtuous woman you are, Mrs Sheehan. Look, I'm going to see a play the local Repertory's doing down in Havelock North on Friday night. Prue's cousin's been sick, so she's going down to see her, and I'm sloping off to the play. You'd be coming with us.'

So that is where it starts, her interest in theatre, and her understanding, too. Just a peek under the curtain, but it turns out to lead her somewhere different, somewhere unexpected, even if it's a long way ahead. While they have been talking she feels something hot and sticky uncurling itself from her body. Her period has started. She touches the faux leather seat of her chair furtively; drawing it away, she sees blood on her fingertips. She keeps on talking to Fraser because she feels the flood spreading in a pool between her legs. She thinks that if she just sits there and talks he will get fed up and go away. If it wasn't for the blood, she would have stood up before this, so that he would know it was time to go.

Only he keeps on sitting there and talking to her, until James bursts in through the back door. He's come up the path from next door. 'Mum,' he says, 'Myrt's come alive, she's crawling out of the ground.'

'Don't be silly,' Liese says, her voice sharp with disbelief, and embarrassment at her predicament.

'But she is.' And then Fraser gets up, and she has to, too, although she keeps her back away from him, hoping he won't see the blood-soaked back of her dress. He walks on ahead of her.

'She says, 'I'll be out in a moment.' She thinks he hasn't seen the blood but of course he has. One night, when they've been making love and she hasn't quite finished her period, she asks him if he noticed anything that day, and he says yes. 'I smelled you,' he tells her. 'Then why didn't you go?' she asks him. They are in a motel room together, in a town beside a river, years afterwards.

'Because it was when I got to know you,' he will tell her. 'You had to talk to me, you couldn't get up and leave, and I thought, here we are at the beginning of things, and I can smell her blood.'

'That's sick,' she tells him. Their affair will be as good as over then. He will be desolated and half dead with an incalculable grief. They won't realise that they are talking of their past, but they are, sooner than they think.

Liese hastily cleans herself and puts on a fresh skirt, and follows Fraser and James out into the garden. Myrt's head and front paw are sticking above the earth, as she heaves and pulls to free herself.

'The resurrection,' says Fraser. 'It looks as if we were a bit quick off the mark.'

One of Myrt's legs is infected and has to be amputated on Monday. Apart from that, she is fine. Liese doesn't mention to David that Fraser had been there when she re-emerged, and the children are so excited they forget to tell him. What is there to tell him, except that Myrt had come back from the grave?

Liese and Fraser and Prue travel to Havelock North, while David stays home and minds the children. Liese and Fraser go to see Pinter's *The Homecoming,* while Prue goes visiting. Prue is talkative and sharp during the drive. A new woman has moved into her neighbourhood on the hill. She is renting a little house at the end of their street, which Prue had thought due for demolition. The woman has billowy black hair and a dead pale face, and two children.

'Cheap white trash,' says Prue.

'Why do you say that?' asks Liese.

'You can tell,' Prue says, dismissing the subject, and ready to move on to something else.

'That seems a bit rough, old girl,' says Fraser. His voice is mild, but Liese realises he is taking up the cudgels on her behalf, even though she hasn't meant to create an argument.

'Your trouble is, you can't see some things for looking,' says Prue. She lights a cigarette and smoke fills up the car. Liese sees the way she sucks her lungs full and blows it out of the corner of her mouth, so that it trickles between the seats, surrounding her in the back. The rest of the journey passes more or less in silence. Liese wishes she hadn't come.

She doesn't understand much of the play, but she understands Fraser's hand holding hers in the dark. At first she tries to pull away but then she thinks how much she likes his hand, which is large and warm, with a certain dryness about the skin. He pushes back the cuticle of one of her fingernails absently with his thumb. If she were asked to describe the play now, she would express a certain feeling of nihilism (she's seen this and other Pinter plays since and has learnt how to express her thoughts about them). She was not sure then if she could see where things were going or why. She finds herself leaning slightly towards him, so that their shoulders touch.

On the way home, Prue is animated and talkative again. Her cousin has given her a present, her silver-backed dressing table set, embossed with her initials, which she has had since she was a girl. Prue rubs the back of it with her sleeve and holds it up for them to admire, even though they can't see it in the dark interior of the car, and Fraser has his eyes on the road ahead of them anyway. This time it is he and Liese who have little to say.

Awful things will happen to Liese and Fraser. Already she knows this, and is determining that nothing will prevent them from happening. He knows it too and believes he can avert them with reason and persuasion. The best of both worlds. Eating his cake and having it too. The whole old ragbag of clichés that Prue will employ before it is all said and done. He might think he knows a lot, but he has no idea how strong Liese's hunger for him will be, how unlimited her capacity for desire. She has the first warnings, the beginning of a catastrophe, and she is doing nothing to avert it.

There are days when he should be at work, but he comes to visit her instead. In the morning the house is often empty, the children off at school or kindergarten. They have become adept at meeting in the evenings, under cover of dark, leaving their houses under one pretext or another, trips to the library, visits to Brenda (whom she sees only fleetingly), committee meetings — all the ways and means that lovers employ. They have made swift rough love in a locked bathroom at a party. When he visits her at home, they just talk; even she can see it's still her and David's house. When he talks, she thinks he should never have taken up the line of work he's in; he's more interested in poetry and books. Or was he just wooing her, she wonders when she is older. Perhaps he saw something that had been overlooked in her life, a capacity to think and learn, a mind worth flattering with information.

    On these days, when he visits her at the house, she asks David idly, while serving him dinner, 'How was Fraser today?'

    'I didn't see him,' David says, reading the newspaper, as if she isn't there.

    'Goodness, wasn't he at work?' She can't stop herself.

'I don't know. I suppose he was. I don't see him every day.'

'Okay, I was just interested. I thought you took coffee breaks together.'

'Well, we didn't today,' he says one evening, with particular irritability.

Which she knows, because that morning Fraser had helped her to pick peaches off the tree in their garden.

The tree is laden with oozing ripe fruit that must be dealt with. When he arrives she is arming herself with a bucket. Months have passed, and David has announced the move south. She phones him, to ask if he has remembered to take the antibiotic he's been prescribed for a virus. It's her way of checking he's at work, isn't likely to duck home. He hesitates and says, yes, he has taken it, is there anything wrong?

'Nothing, nothing at all,' she says. 'I love you,' she adds, and hangs up.

Fraser has already gone down the garden to the tree. He climbs up on to the lower branch and picks peaches, throwing them down for her. His face appears between the leaves, sticky with juice.

'Catch,' he says, tossing her the fruit. When she bends over he aims one at her back. After that, he comes down and helps her fill the clothes basket with fruit like hot balls of fur.

'You should make jam,' he says.

'I don't want to.' The whole neighbourhood is full of women bending over huge pans of preserves at this time of year, boasting about how many bottles they've put down. She thinks it will be different when she moves away, and for the first time, the idea of the shift seems almost a relief. If she can't stay, perhaps she can change herself in the new place, have a career, ignore women who do bottling.

'Prue will use them,' he says.

'Oh for God's sake, if you want to pick peaches for Prue, that's fine. I thought you were helping me.'

He puts his arms around her and licks juice off her face. She pushes him away. 'Stop it.' She thinks the neighbours will see her standing in the yellow morning light in the circle of his embrace.

'Please.'

Inside the house, he pulls her against him, his hands lifting her skirt as he flattens her against the wall of the hallway. He cups the washing board ripple of stretch marks between her navel and pubic hair in his hand. She opens herself up to him, her ragged breath panting, lets herself be carried to the bedroom. 'I love you,' she says, for the second time in half an hour.

In the afternoon, when Robbie and Simon are home from crèche, she puts them in the car, and they drive over to Prue and Fraser's place, the boys holding the bucket of bruised peaches between them in the back seat.

'I wondered if you might like some fruit to make jam,' Liese says artlessly, when Prue opens the door.

'Well, look at that,' says Prue. 'I'll bet you've been having a busy time.'

'I haven't done many bottles,' Liese says.

'Come in,' Prue says, 'that's really thoughtful of you.'

So Liese sits on a high stool at the divider between the kitchen and the breakfast room in Prue's house, which is painted several shades of pretty blue in each room — water blue, sky blue, and one shocking room the colour of cinnerarias — and talks to Prue, who is surrounded by glowing red jars of bottled tomato soup. The children have gone out to play on an abandoned swing in the garden. Prue smokes a cigarette while they drink some coffee and seems to have forgotten the night when she and Liese and Fraser went to the play. While they are talking, the phone rings. Prue picks it up — too quickly, Liese thinks, on reflection.

After a pause, Prue says, 'I've got someone with me, I'll call you back later. Will you be at home or the office?'

It's the 'at home' that Liese remembers, as she constructs and reconstructs that conversation, on and off over the years. It isn't Fraser at his office. Not a woman, because Prue would have told her. Someone she knows well enough to phone at home or work. For a moment, she almost wonders if it's David.

'I'd better be getting along,' Prue says, although it is Liese who is visiting. Liese understands that this is an invitation for her to leave. She puts her cup down slowly, as if to say she's in no hurry.

'I'll give you my tomato soup recipe,' says Prue. 'You really should try it.' She has recovered herself, is no longer trying to hurry Liese out.

'Thanks, I'd really like that.' She remembers Prue sending over jars of the delicious soup when Robbie was born. She waits, as if that's what's expected of her.

'Right,' says Prue, with startling fierce coldness. She pulls a recipe book off the shelf above the stove with odd jerky movements. Grabbing a shopping pad, she hurriedly jots down a list of ingredients and instructions. The recipe on the curling page will survive long after the letters her husband writes to Liese:

Tomato Soup

12 lbs tomatoes
7 onions
1 oz celery salt
7 cloves
1 cup sugar
2 tblsp salt
2 tsps pepper
1 tblsp parsley
1 lb butter
8 tblsp flour

Quarter tomatoes and onions. Add the celery salt, cloves, sugar, salt, pepper & parsley and boil a half hour. Strain through a mouli. Melt butter, stir in the flour carefully. Add the sieved pulp & boil 5 mins. Bottle & seal at once.

Prue's flourishing hurried scrawl, her abbreviations.

'I'll get some tomatoes on the way home,' says Liese. 'I'll make it.'

'You do that,' Prue says.

'I will.'

'I was talking to my lawyer,' says Prue, as if to frighten her, and then seeming to regret it straight away. She bites her lip and fiddles with her cigarette packet.

'Oh. Well, I'll leave you to it,' Liese says, knowing she can't outstay her welcome any longer.

'Do you know any good lawyers?' she asks Fraser, a few days later.

'Not really,' he says, but she notices a change in his voice, something alert and wary. 'Why do you want a lawyer?'

'Idle curiosity. We really ought to have one, David and I should make a will.' (This is misleading, of course they have made wills and appointed guardians to their children in the event of their deaths; David is far too careful not to have taken all the necessary precautions to make them safe in the future. At least, as safe as he knows how.)

'You can get someone when you go south. Not much point in having one here when you're leaving.'

'What if David should change his mind and stay?'

'You know he won't do that. His transfer's already gone through.' Yet again, later, she will catch herself thinking that this is what he's known all along: the certainty that she and David will be gone, the safety of having begun an affair with her.

'I might stay for a while.' Voicing this thought aloud, at last.

'No you won't,' he says.

'So who is your lawyer, anyway?'

Fraser shrugs. 'Prue does all of that. There's a lawyer up north we used to know when I was at university.'

'A friend?'

'Prue's friend. He talks a lot.'

'You don't like him?' Some chime is ringing in her head, a surprising yet familiar ring.

'Look, what is this?'

'Nothing,' she says.

Not Prue, she thinks. Prue is not a woman who dallies. Prue is a woman of virtue who starts her housework at seven o'clock sharp and washes her long silky hair at nine, after she's finished the chores, and everyone's gone off to school or work. Between nine and midday she prepares the evening meal, her hair flowing around her shoulders as it dries. At noon she winds it up into its customary loop on top of her head and spears it in place with invisible pins. Prue plays tennis with her women friends and they have lunches. She serves on a school committee. Her children bring home glowing report cards.

All of that will change. Ivan, her and Fraser's first born, will die of meningitis in a student flat in Auckland one Sunday afternoon when his friends think he is suffering from a hangover. Prue will become a woman who, for a long time afterwards, sits listlessly through one day after another, while things come undone around her.

But not yet. That is still to come.

Liese wants to get home to Ned, to start dinner so that he has something to eat before the concert. He is a musician, a man with infinite patience and sinewy beautiful hands, used to drawing a bow. He surprises her how careless he seems about these hands of his; he likes doing woodwork in his spare time. 'I was considered good with my hands,' he says mockingly of himself. 'I was expected to be a carpenter.'

'Like Jesus,' she says, kissing his fingers where they touch her. He is the kind of man who will do for her the things she most hates — like cleaning the oven — as well as what she loves. He's playing some Handel in a new series with the Sinfonia. Ned reminds her of a blackbird, or Tom Conti. She met him when she was in the last year of her degree in English, and he was a music student. They ate their sandwiches together on the Mount Street cemetery at the edge of the campus, huddled against the wind, on the edge of tombstones. Both of them were desperate for money, but at least she had a place to live. She offered him a room in her little house in Aro Valley, and he's never left. She is ten years older than him, and it still surprises her that he loves her, has not wanted children of his own, was prepared to put up with the rudeness of her own while they were growing up.

Liese has become a woman who plans and organises to good purpose. Although she gets tired some days, she doesn't seem to need as much sleep as she did when she was young. In the early mornings, while the sweet notes of Ned's practising fill the house, she rises and prepares her days. She makes lists. She believes she loves Ned, but sometimes feels herself retreating to a place where he can't follow. There is a stillness in her centre that sometimes frightens her. She calls it her critical self, but that's an excuse. He says, in rare moments of exasperation, I don't get it, because sometimes she holds back, doesn't always understand the music. You would think, he says, that a woman so acutely aware of the theatre and all its nuances, would hear music with greater sensibility. I like it all around me, she tells him, isn't that enough?

David. Fraser. Ned. Three men in her entire life. It doesn't seem like too many. Some women are taken up by a lot more. About a dozen, says one of her friends when they have been drinking wine. I don't know, who counts? Her friend is an ordinary outgoing woman who specialises in lighting design, a woman strong from hefting equipment, the mother of daughters. The idea of so many men between her muscular legs shocks Liese. About average, says another woman, agreeing with the first. You remember your best.

Fraser had not said stay.

After the move, she writes to him every day. He writes twice a week and she collects his letters from a post office address. Like a poste restante. She knows which days to expect his letters but she goes every day, just in case. His letters are addressed to her under a different name, so that she feels as if she has begun a different life, living under the alias of Mrs Black. She lives in fear that she will be asked for identification but it never happens. Probably there are hundreds of Mrs Blacks like her, haunting post office counters.

She and David find it hard making ends meet in the city. They buy a huge rambling house in Khandallah with a spiralling staircase which has sold them the house, but is rotten at its core. There are breathtaking views of the harbour, and big rooms with high studs. The mortgage is colossal. Liese takes a part-time job in a bookshop, which interests her, but doesn't pay very well, and she's on her feet for hours on end. In the weekends, they spend their time stripping down varnish and staining floors, restoring leadlights. She's not sure why she's doing this — it's not what she wants to be doing — but the fact is, they've got three children and the habit of marriage. Often they quarrel as they go about their self-imposed tasks. David likes his new job down near the waterfront, but the business of working and raising the boys and fixing up the house leaves them exhausted. Liese throws things at David, heavy objects, like hammers and spirit levels, that miss, but one afternoon, she catches him on the ear with a potted cyclamen. The pot, glancing off him, shatters on the wall behind, spilling earth and plant and red clay shards.

He takes the children out to the movies, away from the carnage. One night his mother rings, and he carries the telephone, trailing its cord, into their bedroom and closes the door. Liese presses her head against the door. She stops when she smells a damp jersey and knows James is standing near. James is growing big, and doesn't like her much. She hears David say, 'I know I was brought up a Catholic, Mum. Can't you just leave it?' She walks away from the door. These are old arguments between him and his mother. What brings them on again? Perhaps they are talking about her. David might be thinking of leaving her.

Fraser comes to town and she takes time off work. He is energetic and high-spirited. He is on his way south for a conference, the first he's been to in years; he's planning research that will take him south now and then. Liese worries about him and David running into each other, but their careers seem to have gone in different directions.

They go to a hotel room, under the name of Mr and Mrs Black, and order room service, and watch the clock so that Liese will get back in time to pick up the children from school. This is the first of several meetings. They meet in coffee shops and art galleries. One day he kisses her for a long time behind a Toss Woollaston painting in Peter McLeavey's gallery. 'It's funny,' he tells her, 'but you've kind of pushed me up the promotion ladder.'

'Prue'll be pleased.'

'Oh yes, and she likes time to herself. Mind you,' he adds, a gloomy note in his voice, 'she doesn't like sex much these days.' Liese doesn't know why this makes her so angry. She still sleeps with David. Somehow, though, she doesn't expect Fraser to need this from Prue, now that he has her. Even though they live far apart and see each other only now and then, months apart, not weeks. Even though years are starting to pass since all this began between them.

Her friend Brenda sends her the notice of Ivan's death. She has remembered that Liese and David knew the family. Liese steels herself, and tells David, because it would be strange not to tell him, although, as a rule, she never mentions Fraser's name to him, as if it's tempting fate. But David already knows. 'We should send flowers,' she says, and he agrees, even though the funeral is over.

Liese waits to hear from Fraser, but there is nothing but silence. Eventually, a printed card edged with black and bearing a small printed picture of Ivan arrives in the mail. *Thank you folks* is scrawled across the bottom. Prue's handwriting, the same as Liese keeps pressed in the pages of her recipe book.

In time, she thinks, she may have been delivered a gift: her freedom from Fraser. She supposes that he will see what has happened as a punishment. This is what happens when children die, no matter how: the parents don't just grieve for the child, they grieve over their own lives, and how they might have shown the missing son or daughter a brief life that was better. They either settle down for the long haul or, quite soon, they go their separate ways.

There are no letters at the post office and Liese stops going there, finds herself too busy to go out of her way, sees that it won't do to get in the way of such pain, that it is nothing to do with her. This equilibrium will pass for a kind of happiness.

She and David break fewer things. They start to save money. It seems to Liese that they are gaining a measure of control over their lives, a control she understands, even if David appears simply to accept it, without knowing why. She goes to the theatre, with new friends she's made at the shop, including a couple of the customers who seem to think she'll know all about the books she's sold them. One of them suggests she take an English paper at university, and she enrols. It's the eighties, and it's nothing to be a mature student, studying Marvell and Donne and Katherine Mansfield. She loves the dusty smell of chalk in Von Zedlitz, the building that houses the English Department. Before she knows it, she's hovering in the stairwells, exchanging marks with fellow students, a sort of delayed adolescence, while the world beyond the red brick walls is into aerobics and power dressing, and Ronald Reagan rules the world, but not her.

And then he rings. A year or perhaps two have passed. Liese is rushing to catch a lecture, and she picks the phone up on the run. 'No,' she says, when she hears his voice. 'No.'

'I wanted to know how you were,' he says. 'I'm sorry I never got in touch with you, didn't tell you at the time.' His voice is slower and older than she remembers it.

'I know,' she says. 'It's all right, I'm all right.'

'How are those boys of yours?'

'You don't want to know.'

'I do, though. We're lucky, we still have the girls,' he says.

She tells him then how the boys are doing. How big they're getting. Jamie is at intermediate school. Simon's interested in art, Robbie likes cricket. She thinks they will be all right, they're good kids. Barring accidents. She has begun to cry, whether for him and his loss or for herself, she isn't sure. She worries about the boys. And yet, here she is on the end of the phone, betraying them, full of the old sharp longing, wanting to console him.

He seems to know, choosing this moment to put his proposition. 'I've got some work to do in Wanganui next week,' he says. 'Could you get there?'

'No.' She hesitates and hears him fill the silence with a sigh. 'I don't know.' And then in a faint voice she finds herself saying yes.

She is out of practice at telling lies. 'I need a break,' she says. 'I've got this essay to finish. I thought I'd go away for a few days.' This is not all untrue: lots of women she knows take some time out from their lives, and go away to secret locations to sort themselves out. One woman goes to a health resort, another to a spiritual retreat, and she's met several writers who pitch their tents, as they say, away from distractions, in other people's houses, in motels, in cottages rented far away in the country.

'It's okay,' David says. 'We'll manage.' He passes his hand through his hair and sighs.

'Just this once,' she says. 'I need to catch my breath, Term will be over soon and I can focus on home again.'

'That's good,' he says. And he grins at her, gives her a playful slap. She is wearing a flowing crinkly pink skirt scattered with green leaves that look like marijuana at first glance, and a tight green blouse. She is growing her hair longer, down round her shoulders.

'I love you,' David says. 'I love the way you look.'

'Do you?' she says, surprised.

'I always have.'

'Right from the beginning?'

'Of course. That's generally what men see first, the way a girl looks. The rest comes later.'

'Yes. Yes, I suppose so,' Liese says restlessly, anxious to be on her way.

'You just remember that,' David says.

'Even when I make it hard?' She wishes she hadn't said that, as soon as it's out.

'Even then,' he says. 'But it takes two. I know that.'

A river town. Small, provincial, quaint, with historic old buildings lining the main street. Dickensian. That's how she would describe it to friends in late-night café sessions when they tell each other all about their lives. A paddle steamer takes tourists sightseeing up river. Beyond the reach of the tour boats is the village of Jerusalem, where Baxter founded his commune, and Mother Aubert tended the sick. Since Fraser's call she has been reading Baxter again. *The river bent like a bright sabre.* A different river, she thinks, but it doesn't matter. It was Fraser who got her started, along with the theatre, though she's gone long beyond those random beginnings. There are poems she thinks she will never understand, some make her weep uncontrollably. She supposes that that's why she is here, because there's something that's not finished, that still makes her cry at unexpected moments. She remembers pictures she's seen of Baxter, just before he died, a crumpled heap of tattered clothes and untidy beard, an old man in his forties. Perhaps that is the toll of a passionate life.

She stays in the town for three days before Fraser comes, and finishes her essay; in a way this makes her feel better, as if Fraser is secondary to her presence in the town. As if she really does have a purpose of her own.

When he arrives, she finds him much changed. She has expected this, but the reality is hard to manage and makes it difficult for her to be herself. Making allowances. Talking about Prue. They can't avoid that. 'We had to do it right, all the ceremony, you know. I'd have liked something more informal. The girls wanted to speak but Prue thought that wasn't right, them speaking at their brother's funeral.'

'I don't know what I'd do,' she says, because thinking about it is intolerable, and she doesn't want to appear to be taking sides with Fraser against Prue. This, in itself, seems odd.

'Some day we'll be able to sort it all out,' he says. 'I have to stay with her for now.'

'Yes, of course. I don't expect you to leave Prue. Anyway, I couldn't come away with you, you do know that.' In the dark, she silently acknowledges what a terrifying thought that's become. It feels unfair that he is saying these things to her now, when it has all become so impossible. For both of them.

'I thought that that's what you wanted,' he says, his voice tetchy.

'I don't know. I truly don't know any more. I'm here, aren't I?'

'But is that enough?' he persists.

'Hush,' she says, 'go to sleep.' Later, she gets up to the toilet. Very quietly, so as not to disturb him, she lifts a slat of the venetian blind and looks outside. Dark shapes of trees roll away towards the river. It reminds her of the past. The air is very still and there appears to be a bank of mist over the town. *A rose of flame in a room in a house by the rivermouth.* Liese shivers, overtaken by a strong sense of things going horribly wrong. In the morning she will turn her back on this, for once and for all. She has no business in this room. No flames, nothing; she's had a death of her own, here in this room.

She lies down beside Fraser again, but the bed is very hot. He snores against her ear. She moves to the other bed in the unit. Sometime, in the middle of the night, she wakes up and sees that the room is illuminated by an outside light, a dismal fluorescent glow. There are footsteps. A voice at the door. An imperious rapping.

'You come out of there, Fraser. I know you're in there.'

He sits up, startled and wide awake. 'Prue,' he says.

'Don't go out there,' says Liese. 'Please, Fraser. I'll call reception, tell them there's an intruder.'

He says, 'I think we're in the soup, old thing.'

Prue has called David before her raid. David has told her that he knew all along, there's nothing new he couldn't have told her, nothing he hadn't known for years. Prue says his wife is a cunt and a whore and he is no better, letting her carry on the way she did.

'I'll leave you to it,' David has said, when Prue asks him to go on the raid to Wanganui with her.

All of which Liese learns before she drives back to Wellington.

Over the next few months, Liese stays at home. She gives up her studies and has dinner on the table every evening at six. On the weekends, she watches the boys and takes an interest in David's work. When the house is empty, she plays tracks of some records over and again. 'Don't Hang Up' drives her insane, won't stop running through her head. *Surprise surprise/There's a hell of a well in your eyes.*

'I think you should go back to university,' David says. 'We need to be constructive about this.' This has become one of his favourite lines. Ever since he has been in charge of their emotional lives. No scenes. No tears. He knows she loves him. It was a mistake. They can work it out.

'You don't care about this,' she says childishly.

'Only as much as you make me,' he says. 'Really, you should get back to your work, get over it.'

'D'you mean, get over him?'

'There wasn't much to get over, was there?' he says, which as near as he gets to being nasty. She hates him for this niceness, this unfailing kindness about all the silly ruinous things she's done. *When the barman said, 'What're you drinking?' /I said marriage on the rocks.* Damn song. Over and over.

She does what he says, goes back to study, but she's slow. It feels as if she'll never finish her degree. She does some work at the bookshop, and reconnects, as they all say.

Surprise, surprise. One day she comes home and there's an atmosphere in the house she can't make out straight away. It's as if the place has been burgled, but everything is orderly and in place. She opens the wardrobe to put away her coat and all his clothes have gone. The boys have got home from school ahead of her.

'Have you seen your father?' she asks.

None of them have. She doesn't tell them immediately that he's removed all trace of himself from the bedroom and the bathroom. This happens two years after the night she and Fraser were caught. David is in love with a woman called Marina. She is a thin tanned woman with electric frizzy hair and startling blue eyes, that make her and David look more like siblings than lovers.

'You bitch,' James says. 'It's your fault.' He is fourteen at the time. That is the hardest part, the very worst moment. Why James? she has wondered aloud to her friends. It's the old thing of the first born, they say, offering comfort. You know, the one who is there in the beginning, the one who knows everything and never lets you go. But he was always outside, playing in the garden, she will say.

Liese's pad is scribbled with hieroglyphics from her note-taking at the play. Coincidences are not a great way to resolve a play, or anything in literature for that matter, but perhaps, she thinks, it's the way life often resolves itself. Here she is, wondering how to review Hare's play, and here she is, trapped in the circle of her own past. Her deadline is upon her. The young are afraid of the dark, she writes. They know what's out there waiting for them, more than we did when we were young. You could say *The Blue Room* is a touchingly moral play, or a very scary one, depending on whether you've touched bottom yet, or are still treading water.

When Liese and Ned were still students, eking out and making do, up there at the university, he'd asked her a question she's never answered. It was one night when there was a party at the end of term (no, not a party — come round for drinks, was what they said now), at one of her lecturer's houses. She'd just finished her degree and was thinking about going on to a masters. 'You write so well,' the lecturer said, a woman she liked, about her own age, with a lean face and owlish spectacles. Later, her lecturer is less impressed with her career as a journo, thinks she could have tried something more literary, but Liese tells her she's not given to haiku or sonnets. She remembers being a bit tipsy, and not wanting it to show, thinking her transformation complete.

She was standing outside on a balcony, overlooking the harbour, and Ned had come out and stood beside her. 'Did your marriage break up because of anyone else?' he'd asked, as if it was something he must know.

She could have brought up the obvious matter of Marina, but this seemed like a lie she didn't want to tell. Sometimes, to this day, she looks up at family occasions, and sees David looking across at her with a startled puzzled look, as if reaching for something just beyond his grasp, before he sighs and settles back into his new life, the one he took up after he left her, with his new wife and their daughters. She could have told Ned, David left me for Marina; instead, she said nothing, kissed him on the mouth, and found herself being kissed in return. Somewhere, in that still space, she has held on to the truth which so far she hasn't shared with anyone.

If she hurries, she'll just make the supermarket, plus a task that she's set herself at home, before she goes to the concert. She checks her list, making sure it's current. All these lists drive her crazy, sometimes she finds she's shopping from last week's, and she doesn't need what she finds herself buying. What would anyone make of her list for the weekend, she wonders. How would one be judged by such a list? That she keeps stocked up, stays prepared? That she nests, perhaps, and is content. That she will come home at the end of the day. She and Ned have given each other constancy.

This is her list:

toothpaste	*olive oil*	*mushrooms*
tom. paste	*chicken stock(Tetrapak)*	*3 tins whole tomatoes*
limes	*wine*	*2 coconut milk*
spinach	*basil*	*eggs*
Mex. chili powder	*new potatoes*	

chicken thigh cutlets (check whether Si and Keith are coming for dinner 6 or 8?)

| *cereal* | *granny smiths* | *cheese* |
| *6 pack yoghurt* | *jar pasta sauce* | *macaroni* |

Not much to be gleaned except, perhaps, a particular culinary domestic trail of a working woman somewhere early in the 21st century. She adds *12 lbs tomatoes, 7 onions* to the list. It's not the best time of year to lay hands on a case of beefsteaks but she thinks the tomatoes she buys will do. She has the rest of the makings for soup at home. Liese makes Prue's soup every year, choosing a weekend late in summer. This weekend has chosen itself. The warm homeliness of the finished jars is her annual bow to domesticity.

'I don't see why,' Ned says, shaking his head, as she toils away at churning the pulp through a mouli, 'you can buy stuff that's as good these days.'

But it's not true. This is the best soup, with its rich unparalleled flavour. He knows this; when he eats it he agrees. Just sometimes when she's making it, she blinks away a thought about how her life might have been. She thinks she had a lucky escape.

Not that she didn't see Fraser again.

She went back again, even then, after everything that had happened, and saw him once more. She sees herself, sitting in a battered Prefect, waiting for Fraser to walk down the street to meet her. In the afternoon she has rung him at work and said she would be driving up. She will be there at nine o'clock. She has something she must tell him. His voice, when he registers this, is cool and unfriendly.

'That's not a good idea,' he says. 'I'd rather you didn't come.'

'I'm already on my way,' she tells him, and hangs up.

It's cold in the car, a hint of frost, though it's supposed to be spring. Her limbs feel weighted down. The neighbours wouldn't recognise the car, but if they see a woman sitting alone as the hours pass, they will come and look, thinking either that she is up to no good, or that she's in trouble and will have to be helped. Around her, the lights begin to go off. The day before she had sat in the office of a lawyer specialising in divorce. He took snuff, carefully holding one nostril while he listened to her talk, inhaling with noisy snorts while she wept and helped herself to the box of tissues he kept on his desk. A line of peppery mucus dribbled down to his lip. 'Your husband's taking you for a ride, woman. What's the matter with you? I can get you a better settlement than this.'

But she isn't prepared to argue. In her heart, she believes she's being served her own rough justice.

It is eleven o' clock when at last she sees a figure outlined against the street light at the end of the cul de sac. She sees how his head turns, as if listening for something, perhaps the sound of her voice, the way his shoulders hunch as he heads towards her.

'Why are you here?' he asks, when he comes alongside her, and the rolled down window of the car. 'What do you want?'

She wishes she knew. It was just that when she walked out of the lawyer's office, she wondered if she might have been mistaken.

'I'm divorced,' she says.

'I don't want to hear this.'

'I didn't think you would.'

'Then why come? What's the point?'

'I needed to be sure. Something you said. It's been quite a high price.'

'Oh, come on,' he says, his voice rough, 'you're not telling me it was my fault. That was years ago.'

'You asked me to go away with you,' she says. They are both whispering but their voices seem loud.

'You can't imagine what it's like to lose a son,' he says. 'I thought you'd understand that.'

'Of course, we talked about that,' she says, distractedly. 'No, I don't really know. But it's not what you said.' Their voices, hers anyway, have risen. People will start appearing, looking for strangers in the street. They will see, instead, that it is Liese who is supposed to be hundreds of kilometres away, and that it is Fraser whose had trouble in his home and should be there, comforting his wife. They have known all along, they will say to each other. Although, really, you can tell that Prue is the strong one; she went to pieces for a while but then she snapped out of it, got herself sorted. (Liese has heard this from Brenda who insists on annual visits on the way to the South Island for her holidays. She had been noncommittal when Brenda told her, although she did say, 'Have you any idea when it was she came right?' Brenda had looked at her quizzically. 'It was her faith,' Brenda said, 'she's strong in that, you know.' Liese didn't, but she accepts that it might be so.)

'Unfinished business,' she says to Fraser. 'Never mind. I always knew it was Prue you really loved.' This isn't true, but as soon as the words are out, she feels as if it is. How could she not have known that Fraser loved beautiful wicked Prue, with her dallying ways, the way she drove him to his crazy acts of defiance. Like being with her.

'I don't want to set eyes on you again.' He turns to walk away, but suddenly she's angrier than she's ever been in her life. As he begins to walk down the street, Liese presses the horn. Once. Twice. He stops and comes back.

'I can't,' he says. 'Don't you see, I can't. Besides,' he says, 'Prue's not well.'

For years she lives with the cleanness of her anger. Her life, she thinks, is an old-fashioned morality play: a woman laid low by bad behaviour. Then she meets Ned, and eventually it matters less. Not a well-structured play, but there it is — a bunch of flawed characters, lurching from one thing to another, and it hasn't turned out so badly.

And now Fraser is dead, and Prue seems remarkably alive, and she is making soup. While she blinks away real and onion tears, she imagines the conversations Prue and Fraser must have had about her, how their own bad times together will have become tragic and romantic and full of nostalgia. He will have told her, it is clear that he must, about the day when they walked on the seafront and talked about dying.

'I thought you were coming to the concert?' Ned says, when he comes in.

'I am,' she says. The soup is a sexy brilliant red, softly plopping away in the pot. The jars are lined up, hot and gleaming, on the bench, waiting to be filled. 'This won't take long.'

'I don't get it,' he says shaking his head.

'You're not supposed to,' she says.

He puts his hand out and touches her arm. 'Liese. What is it?'

She turns the heat down beneath the soup, turns round and folds her arms, leaning against the bench. The thing is, she tells herself, it's songs and a poem or two, a box of photographs, recipes and lists, stories and fictions, especially the ones that leave out the worst bits (for there is more to this story, but that's enough) that get them all through. After all, Prue has listened and remembered. She has asked Liese to come. 'Once, a long time ago, I had an affair with a married man,' she says. 'I was still married to David.'

'Oh. This is the secret?'

'Yes,' she says, 'this is the secret.'

'It's not an unusual story.'

'But it's one I haven't told you.

'And now you're going to tell me all about it?'

'Not really,' she says. 'He's died and his wife wants me to go to the funeral, that's all.'

'Ah, now that's less usual. That's masochism. So are you going?'

'No,' she says, after a moment, because she's only just decided. 'I'm not going.'

'If it's important to you, you should,' he says.

'I think it's better left. I'll write her a note.'

'What will you say?' he asks.

Liese looks at the soup she's made; there's something about its rich dark saucy centre that reminds her of herself, her old self, carefully put away for so long, wearing its disguise. A gift from Prue. She's not glad Fraser is dead; she's not anything, at last, not even regretful, and that's the best part of all.

'I'll tell her I made it,' she says. 'Soup.' She is thinking about Ned's music and how she can start listening to it properly, the high notes and the low notes, and savour the still pauses between movements. Like the split second before applause at the end of the play.